ART OF LOVE

VICKI THARP

ART OF LOVE

ACKNOWLEDGMENTS

Thank you to author Renita Bradley for her sensitivity read. I value your kindness and insight, but most of all I value your friendship.

Original Cover Design by Book Designs EE

Photo by: CJC Photography

Model: Jered Youngblood

ISBN 979-948798-34-1

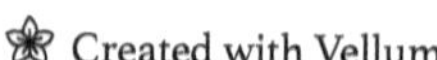 Created with Vellum

1

A GUST OF WIND CAUGHT ROMAN REED'S DOOR AS HE GOT OUT OF his car in front of the Cory Center. If he were of the mind, he might consider it the *winds of change* blowing his way, but the practical side of him knew the Santa Ana winds had come early.

On his calf, he brushed the scuff mark off his newly polished shoes and walked through the Center's door, his résumé tucked neatly in a clear protective sleeve.

He glanced at his watch. Early. But he needed to make a good impression if he wanted to work at the Center for the last semester of his senior work-study program.

"In here," a voice called out, over laughter, shouts, and the hollow bounce of a basketball.

A kid in shorts and a tank top bounced into him. "Whoa," Roman said with a laugh, "you're coming in like a freight train."

The kid spun on his heel but kept going. "Sorry, mister."

A man appeared in a doorway down the hall, his hands in the pockets of his basketball shorts. If this man were his interviewer, then Roman had overdressed, but that was fine with him. Far better to be overdressed than underdressed.

"Sorry about that," the man said as Roman approached. "Jonathan only has one speed."

"It's all good." Roman extended his hand. "Roman Reed."

"Grant Hardy." Grant stood back and ushered Roman into the office ahead of him.

It was a basic, no-frills space. A desk, a couple of chairs. The required filing cabinet against the back wall.

"I figure if I get the job, that comes standard with the kid package."

"And then some." Grant settled into the chair behind his desk, *The Cory Center* stamped across the chest of the sweaty T-shirt he wore, the hair on his forehead damp from exertion. He pointed to himself. "Please excuse the way I look. The kids put together a mini five-on-one basketball game."

"We could do this another time if—"

"No. Now's fine. It was a good excuse to quit. I was getting my ass kicked."

"Mr. Grant." The kid with only one speed ran into the office. "Dominique says that—"

"Jonathan, come back and play." An athletic Black woman walked in, equally as sweaty as Grant. "Mr. Grant has a meeting."

"You must be Roman. Oh, wow, beautiful eyes. I've bet those beauties have gotten you la—"

Vondra cut herself off and snuck a glance at Jonathan. "It's nice to meet you."

Roman got that kind of reaction all the time. And yes, his green eyes had gotten him laid more than once. "Thank you. Nice to meet you, too."

The woman caught herself staring and offered her hand. "I'm Vondra Mumbee, by the way. Official wrangler of kids. Sorry one escaped."

"*Hey.*" The blond, skinny kid gave Vondra an annoyed glance.

"Hey, kid." When Roman got Jonathan's attention, he said, "You give us a few minutes, and I'll take you and your friends on. You think you all can beat me?"

Roman hoped he hadn't spoken out of turn. For all he knew, Grant wouldn't want him interacting with the kids until he'd passed a background check, but the short nod Grant gave Roman told him his instincts were dead on.

"Dunno," the kid said, "but anyone's going to be better than this dude."

Grant gave the kid a playful punch in the bicep. "Watch it, buddy."

"I don't know," Roman said. "Just because I'm Black doesn't mean I'm any good at basketball. Maybe I played music as a kid, or was into computers, or—"

Jonathan squeezed Roman's biceps through his suit coat. "Naw. Computer nerds don't have muscles like this."

Grant laughed. "I'm positive you can be Bill Gates and be buff, too. Now go on and finish the game. We'll be out in a bit."

"*Fine,*" Jonathan said with a roll of his eyes. "You've got five minutes."

Vondra gave them an apologetic smile as she ushered the kid out. "Sorry about that." She closed the door behind her, then popped her head back in. "Take your time, but also hurry. Volleyball's my jam, not basketball. I'm sucking wind out here."

She didn't wait for a reply before shutting the door again.

Grant apologized again. "It can be crazy around here in the summer, and we're a little short on staff."

"Hopefully, we'll be able to help each other out." Roman handed across his résumé and leaned back, waiting as Grant read through it.

"Utah, huh?" Grant asked.

"Born and raised. And had enough." Roman mostly managed to keep any bitterness out of his voice.

"I bet California is a bit of a culture shock."

"Only in a good way, so far. But then again, I've only been here a week."

"Good? How so?"

Any other time or place, Roman would have made something up, but he was talking not only to the man who'd founded The Cory Center to help support local LGBTQ youth in the San Fernando Valley, but a man who was a semi-famous or *infamous* gay man, depending on your point of view.

Roman's view had been from the front side of a computer screen in his dorm room in Utah, watching Grant Hardy's gay porn.

How often do people go into a job interview not only knowing what their boss's junk looked like, but had jerked off to him on many occasions?

Roman managed to tamp down his blushing. "Here, two men or two women can walk down the street holding hands and not turn any heads. I can't imagine what that feels like not to have to look over my shoulder every second and wonder if someone is going to drag me into an alley and beat the shit out of me for holding hands or kissing another man."

Fuck. Roman hadn't meant to go there. He should have said the weather was nice, or he liked the beaches.

Grant took in what Roman had said, his face serious for the first time since Roman sat down. "It's better here. I'm not going to lie. But this isn't a Utopia. We have our own problems here. There wouldn't be a need for a center like this if it were one. There are still LGBTQ kids around here getting bullied and getting kicked out of their homes."

"I know. And I want to help those kids. If there had been a

place like this for me when I was growing up, it probably would have changed my life."

Grant rubbed his chin, his gaze assessing. There were more personal questions in his eyes, but Roman appreciated that Grant didn't press. None of those answers would determine how good of a fit he'd be for the Center.

Grant picked up Roman's résumé again. "Transferring to a new college when you only have a semester left, that's a little unusual."

"I needed a change of scenery." Roman didn't elaborate, and his tone didn't invite any more conversation on the matter.

You're fucking this up.

Roman quickly sidestepped that line of inquiry. "And there wasn't an organization like yours anywhere near my college. Working with these kids is what I want to do. It's why I'm studying social work in the first place."

"On the phone, you mentioned that you had another job. Will it interfere with your work here?"

"It's a part-time gig with a catering company my friend helped me get. Most of their events are in the evenings after I'd be done here. Plus, it's easy to get people to cover shifts. Besides, once classes start and I have to start studying more, I'm probably going to have to drop that job if I want to make my grades."

Roman couldn't tell how that answer landed because Grant didn't waste any time launching into the next one. So much for being done in five minutes.

"You're kind of old to still be in college, yeah?"

"I'm an untraditional student."

"Ex-military?"

"Ex-getting my life back together." He couldn't be more honest than that. After all, if the kind of man he'd turned out to be wasn't what Grant wanted, then the Center wasn't the place for him.

Don't go where you're not wanted.

He'd learned that lesson while trying to get his life straight.

"I'm not a stranger to that myself," Grant said with a self-deprecating smile.

Grant slid the résumé back toward Roman. Fuck. Was this when Roman was supposed to stand and thank Grant for his time? If Grant didn't want him, Roman would have preferred Grant waited and tossed the résumé in the trash after he'd left.

"I like what I see," Grant said.

Wait? He does?

"More importantly, I like the way you handled Jonathan."

Something loosened in Roman's belly. He hadn't even realized how tight his nerves had wound it up. "Thank you. He seems like a cool kid."

"If your background check pans out, I'd like to offer you the job. But I can't do that without you knowing what you're getting yourself into."

His stomach knotted again at Grant's tone. Grant leaned forward, his elbows on the desk, the corners of his mouth twisted down. Roman didn't know Grant well enough to read the man's emotions, but he would have said *concerned* if he'd had to guess.

"What's up?"

"It's about the community project that you'd be helping with."

"Besides the work with the kids, the project is another one of the reasons I'm interested in this job. It dovetails nicely with my minor in art. I thought the project had been approved. Are there problems?"

"The deal with the land went through. A donation from a local benefactor's estate, but..."

"I know these revitalization projects take a lot of hard work," Roman said, filling the silence. He didn't want Grant to think he minded getting his hands dirty. "But I'm up for the challenge. I've got the muscles for it." Roman bent his arm and raised it for Grant to see his bicep. Not that Grant would be able to tell much through his suit. "Ask Jonathan, if you don't believe me."

"I'll take your word for it." Grant laughed but sobered quickly. "It's not the amount of work. It's the vacant lot's neighbor. The lot sits between a strip of shops and a church. The pastor at the church is... I guess the best way to say it is he's not my biggest fan.

"He tried to block us from receiving the land, and he's not afraid to let anyone who will listen know how the Center is a haven for depravity and godlessness. Frankly, the way he makes it sound, the project is going to wreak destruction on the whole valley. Plagues. Locusts. The whole biblical nine yards."

"Wow. Um... It's going to be a playground and garden benefiting the whole community. Now that pot is legal in this state, the good man should maybe take a few puffs and chill."

"Christ, you're not kidding. If I thought it would help, I'd be happy to pony up some of the grant money the Center received and buy him a stash."

"Maybe it won't be as bad as you think."

"Maybe not. I'm hoping that after the city heard and rejected the pastor's objections that he'll back off. But I'm not placing any bets. Bottom line, whoever is working out there could conceivably have a lot of contact with him, and I can't have someone out there who can't take a little heat."

"Got it," Roman said. If there was anyone used to taking crap from homophobes, it was him. "Kill 'em with kindness."

***

"DAMN IT!" THE SHOUT CAME FROM DEMETRI STAVROS'S GUEST bathroom. "I thought you said the water was shut off."

Demetri glanced up from the easel in front of him and met Collin's eyes. His nude model was a twenty-something local kid who, from the looks of his social media account, made it a habit of getting naked in front of people, whether it was from behind the camera, or in this case, real life.

"Oops." Collin giggled. "That can't be good."

The perfect light for drawing streamed through the floor-to-ceiling windows in Demetri's mid-century modern home, but he set his charcoals down and stood. "Why don't we call it a day. I have a feeling it's going to take me all afternoon to mop up."

Joss Kincaid came rushing out of the bathroom, his T-shirt soaking wet as he hustled by on his way to the front yard to turn off the water main.

"Mmmm." Collin stood, his eyes locked on Joss's retreating form until the man disappeared out the front door. "You, know, I'm not usually into the ultra masc lumberjack type, but holy shit *gurl*, I might have to rethink that."

Demetri laughed and handed Collin his clothes. "Same time next week?"

Collin balled up his clothes and wrapped one arm around them, not even bothering to cover his half-hard cock. He leaned in, his eyes ablaze with mischief. "Or... you could give me a call before that. For some *off the clock* time."

There had been a time when Demetri wouldn't have hesitated to take the guy up on the offer. The model had a swimmer's body, all that long and lean muscle that Demetri had a thing for, but Demetri wasn't the same man that he was a year ago. Besides, it was past time he started seeing guys his own age. Maybe someone who might better understand the enormous pothole in the middle of his life's path.

"I'll keep that in mind."

Joss returned and must have overheard because he chuckled and shook his head as he passed them by again. Water had soaked the whole front side of Joss from his *Cessna* T-shirt down to his athletic shorts.

Then came the splash of water. Joss hadn't even made it back to the bathroom. Demetri closed his eyes, not even wanting to see how far the mini flood had traveled.

He bumped his chin toward the bathroom and gave Collin a *sorry, but I've got to go* kind of smile and started backing away, leaving Collin's invitation open. He wouldn't take him up on it, but there were more important things at the moment than trying to find a kind way to let the guy down easy. After all, Collin did a great job as a model and, as hard as was to find someone who'd sit for him while he worked, he didn't want to fracture their working relationship.

"I'll see myself out," Collin said as he stepped into his bright pink jockstrap and pulled on his shorts.

Demetri headed toward the hall. "Thanks."

Splat. Splat.

Demetri's bare feet slapped through the half-inch of water flooding his tile. He'd bought the home for a steal—by California standards—the year before. He'd thought he'd fix it up himself. But between teaching at the college and his art projects, the house hadn't received more than a lick of paint. Confronting the rusted and slowly leaking water valve on the toilet convinced him he wasn't the handyman he'd imagined himself to be.

Which brought Demetri to the now shirtless man kneeling in a puddle of water in his guest bath, wrenching on the stubborn valve.

"Sorry about that," Demetri said as he retrieved the bucket and mop from the hall closet and started sopping up the mess. It could have been worse. Instead of clean water, he could be mopping up sewage. "I turned it on this morning to take a shower and forgot to turn it off again."

Joss grunted as the rusty valve finally broke free. "Don't worry about it. It comes with the territory on remodels."

"I appreciate you helping me out. I needed to start the remodel process somewhere. The leaky valve pushed me to stop putting it off."

"Yeah, well, it's you I should be thanking." A flush of crimson rolled up the back of Joss's neck, and he glanced over his shoulder at Demetri but couldn't or wouldn't make eye contact. "When the Santa Anas kick up, and I'm grounded, I need a distraction, something to keep me from reliving Dan's accident over and over again. The supplemental income doesn't hurt either."

Demetri didn't know Joss well, and only knew the basics about how Joss's partner, Dan, had died some years before in a skydiving accident.

"I'm sorry."

Joss shrugged but didn't turn around. "I'm pretty much over it now. It was a long time ago."

If Joss was so *over it*, why did he need a distraction every time the wind kicked up? "That's not what Vin says."

"I love the guy, but Vin needs to learn to keep his mouth shut."

"*Love?*" Demetri poked, mostly teasing.

Joss pivoted, the replacement valve in his hand with some sort of white tape wrapped around the threads. This time, Joss met his eyes, and Demetri stopped mopping. "It's not like that. Vin had his eyes on your cousin for a long damn time, way before the two of us ever got together. We were never meant to last. I'm glad he finally got the man he wanted. It's good to see him happy."

Demetri couldn't argue with that, so he started mopping again, trying to get as much water as he could out of the bathroom so Joss would have a dry space to work.

Joss picked up his wrench and started tightening the valve. "You going to take that guy up on his offer?"

"Who? Collin?"

"You have another naked guy out there propositioning you? Because if you do, maybe I need to move closer to town. That never happens to me out there in the foothills."

"To answer your question. No. And no." Demetri wrung out the mop for what seemed like the hundredth time, feeling like he was trying to sop up the overflow of the Hoover Dam with a kitchen sponge. "You on the dating apps?"

Demetri wanted the question back as soon as he'd asked it because the natural follow up to that was, *are you?*

"Occasionally." Joss shrugged as he stood and wiped his hands on a red shop towel. "The apps fill a need. But I'm not expecting anything more out of those one-and-done encounters."

Then came the question Demetri had dreaded.

"How about you?"

"It's complicated."

"Isn't it always?"

Demetri hated being so vague, especially when Joss had opened up a bit to him as they negotiated the corners and boundaries of their budding friendship. Demetri's diagnosis wasn't a strict secret, but it also wasn't something he disclosed to just anybody.

Hence the *it's complicated* answer to Joss's question.

And while Demetri applauded the way some men on the apps didn't shy away from putting their similar diagnoses on their profiles, Demetri had reasons to conduct his life with a little more caution and care.

Besides, as difficult and heart-pounding as it was, he preferred to deliver that kind of personal information face to face.

If his truth became general knowledge, he worried it would affect his bid at tenure at Winston College. And he wasn't at a point in his life where he wanted to find out.

"Well, maybe someone completely unexpected will drop into your life," Demetri said, pivoting the attention away from himself. "App or no app. All I'm saying is maybe you should be open to it."

"Good advice." Joss planted his hands on his hips. He was a big guy, and there was hardly enough room in the bathroom for two grown men. "Maybe you should take it."

"Fuck that," Demetri said with a grin.

"Yeah, that's what I thought."

Demetri's front door closed, and at first, he thought Collin had left something behind, but then his cousin, Niko Stavros, called out. "You ready?"

Niko came around the corner of the den. The water had seeped out of the hall. Before Demetri could call out a warning, Niko stepped into the puddle in a pair of Louboutins that probably would have cost Demetri a month's pay. But then again, when you owned Black Stallion Studios, one of the premier producers of gay porn, you could afford a lot of the finer things in life.

"Why are you so dressed up?" Demetri took his cousin in from his water-splashed dress shoes to his custom-tailored suit in a light charcoal gray. The thin material probably worked well with the summer heat.

"Why aren't you?" Niko stuffed his hands into the front pockets of his suit pants and lifted that dark brow that always seemed to have too much to say.

Because... "Oh, shit." The answer hit him. He dug his phone out of his pocket and checked the time. "The art exhibit is tonight."

"Bingo."

A noise came from the bathroom down the hall. From where Niko stood, he wouldn't be able to see who was inside.

"You're not alone?" It came out more as a statement than a question because unless his house had suddenly become haunted, the answer to that was obvious. And the way Niko said *alone*, with that upward tilt to one side of his mouth, it had a conspiratory *spill the deets* kind of tone to it. As if Niko had walked in on Demetri sucking a guy off in his bathroom.

Wouldn't have been beyond the realm of possibility.

Before.

Joss must have stepped out of the bathroom because Niko's brows knitted together, and a deep line formed between them. "What the hell is he doing here?"

2

ROMAN DRESSED IN HIS BLACK SLACKS AND WHITE DRESS SHIRT FOR his shift with the catering company. His experience as a bartender was one of the things that helped him land the job with the company his roommate, and best friend from high school, worked for.

Work being the operative word. Moses Padillo did as little work as he could get away with. But then again, he could afford to. Roman wasn't as lucky to have a parent sliding him money for rent every month. He had to hustle for every dollar. Sometimes that meant making sacrifices, but he was determined to do what it took to graduate and get on with his life.

He grabbed his keys from the kitchen counter on his way to the front door. In the den, Moses sat on the couch playing video games.

Over the back of the couch, Roman lifted one of the earpieces of Moses' headset. "I'm out of here."

"Wait. What?" Moses scrambled to pause his game and twisted on the couch to give Roman his full attention. Moses was a small guy with big eyes, black hair, and sweetly dark sense of humor. "I thought we were going to Exeter tonight."

"Chris needed me to take his shift. My wallet is running on empty. I need all the shifts I can get before school starts up."

"But—"

"But nothing. You don't need me to help you pick up guys. You can get laid without my help."

Moses rolled his guyliner-enhanced eyes. "I know that. I wanted you there in case I picked up more than one. We haven't had a foursome in—"

"That was *one* time."

"One *fun* time." Moses pouted. "Besides, I worry about you. You haven't gotten laid since you've been here and—"

"I get laid plenty."

Moses laughed. "Since when did *plenty* become synonymous with *hardly any*? Do you think anyone told Merriam-Webster? Or do you think it's an Urban Dictionary kind of thing?"

"Remind me again why I thought it was a good idea to room with you?"

"Because you love me?"

"Like a diabetic loves chocolate, maybe. Besides, not everyone can be as slutty as you. And I mean *slutty* in the best, most sex-positive way. Go get you some. Don't wait on me."

"I won't." Moses grinned. He had the best grin. All teeth that always added a shine to his eyes. It was one of the first things Roman had noticed about him on his first day of algebra class back in middle school. They'd bonded over the fact that they both couldn't get enough of Mr. Levitt's ass as he wrote on the whiteboard.

"Besides," Moses continued, "you like that old, dried up dick. You won't find those guys at Exeter. They're all up in Palm Springs with—"

"Just because sometimes I dig guys who are a bit older—"

"Don't look now, Roman, but I think your daddy issues are showing."

Roman swatted him up the backside of his head, but Moses only laughed. What did Moses know about daddy issues anyway?

And liking older men, that didn't mean Roman had daddy issues.

Probably.

WHAT THE HELL IS HE DOING HERE?

Niko's words echoed in Demetri's head, and he wondered if he was going to have to break up a fight. "Back off, Niko."

Joss pulled his still-damp shirt on over his head, the wet patches clinging to his broad chest. He had a good four or five inches on Niko, but when you were as big as Joss, you towered over most people. Sometimes Demetri wondered how Joss ever fit behind the yoke of his plane. Did they make cockpits in jumbo sizes?

"You're not still cross with me, are you?" Joss didn't seem annoyed with Niko's open hostility. If anything, Joss seemed amused. "You won. You got Vin. I'm not a threat here. And honestly, hindsight and all, I never really was."

Niko took a step back, making a move as if he were about to run his hand through his hair, but he must have thought better of it since he'd gone through the trouble of gelling his dark hair. Instead, he raised his hands in surrender. "You're right."

Those two words... it sounded as if someone had reached deep down into Niko's throat and pulled them out with a barbed hook. It looked painful.

"Look," Joss said to Demetri, "I'm going to get out of here. I replaced the valve and can turn the water back on for now."

"Yeah. Thanks."

Joss bumped his chin toward the front of the house. "You hiding Vin in the car?"

"No. He's working on some film edits. He's meeting us there."

"Be sure to tell him I said hello."

"I'll do that." Niko sounded sincere enough, but Demetri knew better. Despite the fact Joss wasn't a threat to Niko and Vin's new relationship, Demetri figured Niko had zero intention of passing on the greeting.

Demetri walked Joss to his Jeep and returned to find Niko with his suit coat off, his sleeves rolled up, and the mop in his hand.

"Go get a shower. We're running late."

Which was Niko's sly way of changing the subject from his blatant jealousy to Demetri's inconvenient forgetfulness.

"Can't you give Grant, Bass, and Tavi my excuses and—"

"No. I can't. You promised you'd be there. It's not every day Grant and Sebastian's foster kid has his first art exhibit. You need to be there to support them. And if you don't want Bass on your ass at every family dinner from now until eternity, you'll keep that promise."

"Look, the kid's got talent, but today's not a good day. I don't see why—"

Niko took Demetri by the shoulders and turned him down the hall and gave him a light shove. "Grant and Tavi are family now. That's why."

Fuuuck.

Demetri loved his big extended family, but that didn't mean he liked it when Niko was right.

After a quick shower, Demetri stood at his sink, a towel wrapped around his waist as he lathered his face with shaving cream.

Niko came into his bedroom and leaned a shoulder against the door jamb of the bathroom. "Oh, and by the way, I volunteered you to help Grant with his community project. You know, the one with the vacant lot and—"

Their eyes locked in the mirror, Demetri's hand stilling, mid-stroke. "You've got to be fucking kidding me, right?"

"Do I look like I'm kidding?"

This was why Demetri was sometimes glad he didn't have an older brother. Niko could be overbearing enough.

"Well, I told them you would, so..."

Demetri rinsed his razor and continued shaving. At this point, the event would be over before they got there. He stretched his neck out to shave underneath his jaw. "Then I guess you'll have to *un*-volunteer me. I've got classes starting up next week. I don't have the time."

"They'd only need you on the weekends. Besides, it's not like you've got anything else going on in your life."

"You're such an asshole."

"Yeah, but that doesn't change the situation any. If I could draw something more than a stick figure, I'd have volunteered myself, but you're the artist of the family, and you know how important it is for this project of Grant's to make a good impression on the city council. If he can get the council behind him, it will be that much easier for him to bring additional services to his Center."

With a final swipe, Demetri rinsed his razor and wiped the remaining shaving cream off with a hand towel. He turned to Niko. "If I'm volunteering my time, then you're ponying up the money for the supplies."

"That'll run into the thousands."

Demetri looked his cousin up and down. "Or the price of one tailored suit."

Niko barked out a laugh. "Fuck, you're grumpy today. But it's a deal."

They didn't shake on it. Niko was as good as his word.

Demetri disappeared into his closet to get dressed. Through the open door, he said, "And I'm not grumpy. I would appreciate a heads up before I'm being volun*told* to do something."

Niko sat on the bench at the foot of Demetri's bed. He had a direct line of sight into Demetri's closet. Being a porn director, Niko didn't think twice about privacy, and Demetri had gotten so used to Niko's lack of boundaries that he didn't even turn around as he dressed.

"Maybe you just need to get laid."

Demetri sifted through the clothes in his closet. He located a summer weight, light gray suit he usually saved for spring graduations. "You know damn well why I haven't."

"You're more than your diagnosis, Dem." Niko's voice dropped, and the compassion in his words made Demetri's throat tight.

Niko had been there when Demetri had received the news and had metaphorically held his hand the entire way through the early, uncertain days and the start of treatment. Demetri couldn't have asked for him to be more supportive.

He wished Niko would now mind his damn business and stay out of his sex life. Or the shredded remains of it.

"I know that." Demetri didn't know if he said it loud enough for Niko to hear. Didn't matter. Maybe *he* was the one who needed to hear it most.

Demetri slipped into a light pink dress shirt and knotted a dark purple silk tie around his throat and called it good. "Let's go already."

They drove in Niko's car. Now that Niko had a captive audience, he wouldn't let Demetri's sex life drop. "There are plenty of guys out there living full lives with HIV. You're no different."

Easy to say when you weren't *poz*.

"I tried getting back into dating after I became undetectable."

Niko took his eyes off the road, and Demetri had to tell him to go when the light changed. "You never told me that."

"That's because my sex life isn't your business. I keep trying to tell you that, but you don't listen."

"Well?"

"Well, what?"

"How did it go?"

"Let's just say that people are less forgiving and less willing to educate themselves that *undetectable equals untransmittable* than I'd given them credit for."

"You disclosed?"

Demetri stared at Niko as if he'd lost every last one of his marbles. "Of course, I disclosed."

"On the first date?"

"Well, yeah, I don't want—"

"Maybe you shouldn't. You take your meds religiously. You're undetectable. You are a safer guy to have sex with than someone who doesn't get tested and know their status. Maybe you don't need to disclose anything."

"I know some guys who don't. And I get it. I've been tempted so many damn times. But I can't. I don't have a problem kissing or jacking a guy off or giving him a blowjob. He wouldn't contract it through that kind of contact even if I were detectable, but I'm not going to have penetrative sex or let someone suck me off without disclosing. I think my sex partners have a right to know, so that's a personal hard line I've drawn."

"Okay," Niko said, drawing the word out as he thought. He pulled into the parking lot of the art gallery and shoved the gearshift into park. "Have you thought about maybe waiting to disclose until a guy gets to know you first? Maybe once he's a little invested in you, he won't be so quick to run."

"I don't want to be dishonest."

"It's not dishonest. There's nothing wrong with not hooking up on a first date. It might be boring, but—"

"Fuck you," Demetri said with a laugh.

"Give it a try, will you?"

Demetri hated to admit that Niko might be right twice in one night. A wide grin spread across Niko's face. He knew it, too.

"Fine. I'll give it a try. But if this blows up in my face—"

"You can blame me."

Damn right, he would.

3

Demetri and Niko stepped into Premier, the most prestigious art gallery in the San Fernando Valley.

As the prize for winning a local art contest put on by the Cory Center, Tavi—Sebastian and Grant's foster kid—won a showcase of his artwork at the gallery.

From what Demetri had heard, the kid was some kind of an art protégé. Now that Demetri was at the gallery, he was glad Niko had made him come. In his world, art always made things better. And he needed to get it through his sometimes-thick skull that life goes on. Even when you're poz.

"Hey, you made it," Vin said as he greeted them at the door.

Niko leaned in and gave Vin a lingering kiss. Niko's smile was more genuine than Demetri had seen in a long time. And it had everything to do with Vin.

Demetri was happy for them. And if he had to force a smile onto his face, he'd do it. He could go home and feel sorry for the sad estate of his own love life later.

Maybe over a glass of single malt scotch.

Demetri pulled Vin in for a hug and said, "You look good."

Vin chuckled and straightened his turquoise tie. "Niko says I clean up well."

"It's not the suit. It's the grin. I'm glad you two found each other. I really am."

"But?"

"No buts."

"You're going to find someone." Fuck if Vin didn't know exactly what Demetri was thinking. Vin leaned in. "Hey, with the new semester starting up soon, I'm sure you'll have a whole crop of hot college guys to choose from."

Demetri cut him a look that would have left a lesser man abraded and bloody. "I don't date my students."

Vin laughed. "Yeah, Niko had that rule about dating employees, and we all saw what happened there."

A waiter wandered by with a tray of champagne flutes. Vin grabbed two and passed one to Niko. He took another and held it out for Demetri. "Want one?"

When you're feeling sorry for yourself, a little bubbly is not the classic drink of choice. Only something stronger would do. Demetri bobbed his chin in the direction the waiter had come. "I'm heading to the bar. I'll catch up with you guys later."

But before Demetri could make it to the bar, the crowd shifted and parted, and he had a direct line of sight to Tavi standing next to his art hung on one of the walls. The kid looked stiff in his rented tux and tugged at his too-short cuffs.

Demetri detoured. The whiskey could wait.

One of the gallery's patrons finished up their conversation with Tavi as Demetri stepped up. Tavi tugged at the collar of his shirt, a fresh razor cut on the edge of his jaw. He was a lean fifteen-year-old with a messy mop of hair who would have looked much more comfortable behind the counter of the tattoo shop he apprenticed at than gracing the halls of a gallery.

"You hanging in there?" Demetri asked.

"I think." It came out more like a question as if Tavi weren't sure how he was doing. "When I won the art contest, I figured when the exhibit came, I'd be pacing an empty gallery counting the minutes until it ended. I never expected people to come *and* want to talk to me about my art."

Tavi raised his hands out to the side. "I mean, I'm a kid and—"

"And naturally gifted and talented," Demetri added. "Seriously."

He glanced at one of the drawings on the wall—an enlargement of Tavi's winning illustration. The emotion in each line, each stroke, couldn't be taught. It had to come from within. Demetri would love to get this kid into one of his classes when he was old enough. "You've got the stuff."

Tavi's eyes dropped to the floor, and the color rose to his cheeks, looking nothing like the defensive, hard-knock kid Grant and Sebastian had pulled off the streets not so long ago. "Thanks."

An older couple approached, and Demetri knew they would have questions for Tavi. He took a step away. "Enjoy your night. You deserve this."

Demetri backed up and leaned against a pillar, taking in the drawing from afar. He couldn't take his eyes off it. The contest prompt had been 'family,' and Tavi had nailed it in the scene of him, his boyfriend, Grant, Sebastian, and his Nana in a booth at a local pizza joint.

The way Tavi had captured the love in Sebastian's eyes as he glanced over at Grant brought a lump to Demetri's throat that only whiskey would be able to wash down.

Demetri turned and started a determined walk toward the cash bar set up at the back of the gallery. He pointedly avoided Grant and Sebastian as they stood hand-in-hand beside Grant's grandmother, talking to a couple Demetri didn't know. He'd swing back through the gallery and speak to them later, but not before he had a drink.

Demetri waited in the short line, watching the twenty-something bartender work. He watched the play of the man's biceps as he mixed and poured drinks, appreciating how the white shirt hugged the man's chest.

He belonged naked under the lights on the dais in Demetri's live drawing class, not behind a bar.

The line shifted, and Demetri found himself at the front of the line, staring into the greenest eyes he'd ever seen.

"What can I get for you?"

'An EKG,' Demetri wanted to say because he thought his heart had just stopped. The bartender's emerald green eyes had the depth and clarity of a triple-A-rated gemstone, and Demetri got lost in their natural beauty. "Um... I..." He couldn't spit the word 'whiskey' out. Instead, he said, "Surprise me."

The man grinned, and Demetri's heart jolted, thumping against his sternum. *Guess you haven't died and gone to heaven after all.*

"Enjoying your night?" the man asked as he pulled out a stainless-steel shaker and poured in different liquors, and a mixer Demetri didn't immediately recognize. He added a few cubes of ice and gave it all a good shake.

"It's improving." Demetri held in the eye roll at the cheesiness of the line. He'd take his drink and find Sebastian. The bartender was here to work. Not flirt.

The man poured the colorful drink, put a wedge of lime on the rim of the glass, and set it on the narrow bar top, his smile impossibly wide. "Funny, I was going to say the same thing."

Demetri handed over his cash along with a healthy tip and took a sip of his drink. It had a bite and a tang, and the alcohol slid down smoothly. If he weren't careful, he could quickly get drunk and never see it coming. "What do you call this?"

"Why don't we call it The Spice of Life."

"Never heard of it."

"That's because it's a one-off I made only for you."

The bartender probably said that to all the guys he served drinks, even if he'd made Demetri feel as if he'd been the only one.

Demetri held up his glass and started to leave. "Thanks for this."

"Come back and see me," the man said. The flirtatious tone had Demetri thinking he might be interested in more than another generous tip. Or maybe that was dickful thinking on Demetri's part.

Demetri returned to the main gallery, nursing his drink as he circulated among his family and his colleagues from the art department, his attention divided between the conversation, the drink in his hand, and the captivating man who'd made it.

As the evening wore on and the crowd thinned, Demetri found his way back to the bar. The bartender was stacking dirty glassware into bins to return with the caterers.

Green Eyes glanced up and smiled as Demetri approached. "If it isn't Mr. Spice of Life. I thought you'd forgotten about me."

Forgotten about him? Demetri hadn't stopped thinking about him all night, and he sported a semi behind the flat front of his suit pants to prove it. "What was in that drink, anyway?"

"My little secret. Everyone needs a little mystery in their lives, don't you think?"

"Maybe." Was the bartender flirting with him?

The man leaned his arms on the bar top and gave Demetri a glance up and down. "Want more?"

They weren't talking about drinks anymore.

Definitely flirting.

"Does anyone tell you no when you ask that?"

"I've never asked anyone that before." The bartender's voice dropped low, an intimate growl meant only for Demetri's ears. "At least not while I'm working."

From somewhere behind him, Demetri heard Niko laugh, reminding him he hadn't come to the gallery tonight looking to hook up. But then again... "What time do you get off?"

What time do you get off?

Looked like Roman might *get off* sooner than he'd thought. Roman smiled, and Mr. Spice of Life smiled back, the fine lines at the corner of his eyes crinkling. He pegged the man to be in his late thirties, maybe. A ten-ish year age difference wasn't such a big deal. Especially in Gayland.

Which was a lot like Disneyland, only more colorful and gayer and a hell of a lot sexier.

"I should have been off the clock ten minutes ago." He glanced around the gallery. The crowd had thinned to a few stragglers. Those who were left were hugging and shaking hands and telling their friends goodbye. He bumped his chin at the glass Spicy set on the bar. "I can make you another one if you like."

"No. I'm good."

"Dude," Sherry, Roman's supervisor, swept by on her way to the gallery's small kitchen in the back. "The van's waiting on those dirty glasses."

"I was just taking them out," Roman said to her retreating back. To his potential hookup, he said, "Sorry, I've got to—"

"You want some help with those?" Spicy took off his suit coat and laid it across the bar.

He had a stack of plastic crates full of dirty glasses. He would need multiple trips if he were going to get them all into the waiting van. If he said *yes*, he could finish the job quicker and spend a little more time with a man he'd like to get to know a little bit better.

"Sure." Roman picked up the top crate and handed it to him. "Follow me."

On their last trip back to the bar to get the remaining two crates, Roman's eyes stayed glued to Spicy's ass. The man had left his suit coat back by the bar, and Roman appreciated the view. What would it take for him to get his hands on that ass?

Just your hands?

Well, he'd start there and see where things went.

They loaded the last of the crates into the catering van. Roman slid the door closed and thumped his hand on the side, telling the driver it was safe to leave.

As the van pulled out, Roman turned to Spicy and said, "Thank you."

"You bet."

"Hold up." Roman caught his arm before the man could disappear back inside the gallery. Just because they were done loading the van didn't mean he was finished with him.

The man stopped. "What is it?"

"I didn't get to thank you properly."

The man's brows went up, and he smiled, stepping into Roman's personal space. "Oh, yeah?"

"Yeah." Roman kicked the doorstop out from beneath the door and let it close. He didn't know if he'd locked them out, but right then, he didn't care.

He put his hands in the middle of Spicy's chest and stepped him back until the brick wall brought him to a halt.

"You mean here?" The man looked equally cautious and tantalized.

Roman glanced both ways down the alley. For an alley, it could have been worse. No dumpsters were overflowing with stinky garbage and cats screeching and clawing over the contents. There was a weak security light above a door a couple of units down, but now that the gallery door was closed, they were in relative darkness.

"Here's good for me." He leaned in and pressed his lips to Spicy's. Spicy's hands immediately fisted in Roman's shirt and pulled him closer. *Fucking hell.*

Roman broke the kiss. "What's your name? In my head, I keep calling you Spicy."

The man laughed, and it made Roman's heart stutter and trip. "Spicy will do. After all, it was you who said we all need a little mystery in our lives."

Roman couldn't help the grin from spreading across his face. "All right, if that's the way you want to play it. No names then."

He angled his head as he stepped closer, straddling one of Spicy's thighs and pressing his semi against the man's hip.

"Mmm," Spicy groaned, his hands going to Roman's hips and hitching him up against him. "Fuck, you're hard."

Roman took advantage of the open mouth and slipped his tongue inside. He liked a man who gave as good as he got, and the man he had plastered against the wall in a back alley proved no exception. He deepened the kiss, goosebumps skittering down his arms despite the warmth of Southern California in August.

Reaching down, Roman cupped and stroked Spicy's hard dick through the soft, thin wool of his pants. Spicy's head lulled back, his eyes rolling closed as Roman kissed his way across the freshly shaven jaw and down over the Adam's apple that bobbed up and down.

Earlier, the man's intoxicating cologne almost had Roman pulling him over the top of the bar for a kiss and something more, but beneath that scent, Roman thought he caught a hint of paint thinner in his hair.

As a part-time artist, the scent was some kind of a crazy turn-on.

Spicy ground against Roman's hand, looking for that friction, chasing that slow burn. But fuck slow. He promised Spicy a thank you, and he damn well wanted to give him one.

With steady hands, he unfastened Spicy's belt and had the pants undone and the zipper down in one fluid motion. Spicy's thick cock stuck up through the waistband of his underwear, and Roman ran his thumb through the slick precum gathering there.

Spicy groaned, but his hand came down over Roman's, stopping him before Roman could slide his hand inside the man's underwear.

"Is there a problem?"

Spicy huffed out a breath, his glazed eyes coming back into focus. "I want to suck you off."

Roman's dick flexed in his slacks. His dick didn't seem to have an issue with the proposition. "I'm the one who's supposed to be thanking you."

"Is that a 'no,' then?"

Bracing his hands on the brick on either side of Spicy's head, he ducked his head and kissed him again. Roman tasted the lime on Spicy's tongue from the custom drink he'd made. Roman couldn't keep his lips off him, and he was having a damn hard time keeping his hands off too. But if the man preferred to blow Roman instead of the other way around, he wasn't stupid enough to argue.

"No." Leaning in, he whispered in Spicy's ear. "I'd love to have those lips wrapped around my cock."

In seemingly one motion, Spicy spun Roman around. His back hit hard against the bricks, the rough edges digging into his back, but that only made it hotter. Spicy wasted no time stripping Roman's pants down low on his hips, his rock-hard cock springing free.

"*Jesus Christ*," he thought he heard Spicy mutter, but a motorcycle zipped by on the side street, and Roman couldn't be certain.

A warm hand slid beneath Roman's shirt and up his abs as Roman fisted a hand in Spicy's hair. It was soft and thick as it slipped through his fingers. Then that hot, sexy mouth came down on him. And oh, sweet baby *jeezus*...

Spicy's tongue grazed the underside of Roman's shaft, tracing a warm, wet line up to his sensitive tip. His balls drew up, as a couple walked by the alley, shoulder to shoulder, holding hands and glancing their way as they passed.

Had they been seen?

Roman didn't panic. The chance of getting caught only made the blowjob more thrilling. It wasn't often that he'd had sex in an alley, but the times he had were fucking hot.

And the guy on his knees in front of him knew what the hell he was doing.

Score one for the older guys.

Roman pressed harder on the back of Spicy's head, encouraging him to take him deep. Spicy didn't disappoint. In one long, languid slide, he took Roman to the back of his throat.

"*Umph.*" Roman's brain went offline for a flash, the words in his head disappearing before flickering back. "Fuck, don't stop."

Spicy chuckled as he stroked Roman's cock, using his hands and his mouth, his tongue working the tip, the suction enough to shift Roman's soul. He'd never had head this good, and he knew it had nothing to do with the heightened sense of danger and everything to do with the man himself.

Things shifted. Now he wanted, *needed*, a name. The base of his spine tingled as the first inklings of his orgasm built. With his oxygen-depleted, coherent thought became a precious commodity. The building held him up as his knees grew weak and indecipherable groans clawed their way up the back of his throat.

"I'm coming," Roman warned as the first pulses of his orgasm hit. Somewhere in his mind-melting pleasure, he became vaguely aware that his phone vibrated against his thigh. He ignored it.

Instead of pulling off, Spicy took him deep one last time. His climax slammed into him, and he shot his load. Spicy's throat worked as he swallowed and swallowed again. The man didn't pull off until Roman sank against the wall, aware of little besides Spicy's satisfied hum and the lazy stroke of his hand down Roman's quickly softening cock.

Spicy stood and pulled Roman's pants up over his hips. Roman had never seen a man with such a smug, pleased look on his face. Now it was Spicy's turn to box Roman in with his hands on the wall, going in for a kiss. Roman opened immediately, tasting the saltiness of himself on another man's tongue. As soon as he could stand without support, Roman planned on returning the favor because as hard as he'd come, he wasn't done with this man yet. And by the erection pressed up against him, Spicy was far from done either.

Roman thought about inviting him back to his place. Moses would be gone most of the night, and even if he came back at some point, it wouldn't be a big deal. They had rooms on opposite ends of the apartment. Not that he cared who heard. Not when he had a man like Spicy in his bed.

Roman's phone buzzed, then buzzed again with an incoming text. *Fuck.* Spicy broke the kiss, a softer, sweeter smile on his face. "Maybe you should get that."

"If it's important, they'll call." Roman cupped the back of Spicy's neck, bringing him in for another kiss. His phone rang in his pocket.

Spicy reached into Roman's pocket and handed him the phone. This better be good. Roman answered and held the phone to his ear. "*What?*"

"It's me." Moses sounded breathless.

"Wha—"

"I have an emergency. Where are you?"

Roman stilled, and Spicy must have either overheard or sensed something was wrong because he stopped nibbling and kissing his way down the length of Roman's throat. "I'm at Premier, it's—"

"I know where it is. I'm close."

"Meet me by the alley."

"Why?"

"Just... just meet me there."

Moses hung up before Roman could ask anything else. He leaned his forehead against Spicy's. He smelled the fresh sweat on their skin and the faintest hint of musk. If it were anyone else who had called, Roman might have told them to call someone else, but this was Moses.

"I'm sorry. I have to go," Roman said.

"It's okay." For a guy about to be denied a back-alley blowjob, Spicy took the news exceptionally well. "Maybe it's better that it ended this way."

A sadness had crept into Spicy's voice that didn't quite jibe with what had transpired. But before he could ask about it, Moses pulled up at the head of the alley and honked his horn.

"I guess that's your ride," Spicy said.

Roman stuffed himself back into his underwear and fastened his pants. "What's your na—"

Moses honked again and, through his open window, called out for Roman to hurry. Then the Premier's back door opened, and a man in a light charcoal gray suit stepped out.

"There you are," the man said to Spicy. "I've been looking all over for you."

Was this a boyfriend?

A husband?

That would be Roman's luck, the one guy who'd turned his crank in a while might be taken.

Moses honked again, and Roman didn't have time to stick around to find out.

4

DEMETRI TURNED TOWARD NIKO AS HE ADJUSTED HIMSELF. "Don't look at me like that."

Niko chuckled. "Like what?"

"Like you're a proud papa after finding out his son has gotten laid for the first time."

"I'm just standing here." He handed Demetri his suit coat. "You ready? Everyone else has gone. They've even locked the front door on us."

"I'm ready."

Niko fell into step beside Demetri as they walked down the alley and made their way back to Niko's Jaguar.

"That was..." Niko started, but it didn't seem like he knew how to finish the sentence.

"Unexpected?" Demetri filled in for him.

The mild night made it ideal for walking, even with the winds. Demetri hooked his suit coat on his finger and hitched it over his shoulder, his balls and semi-hard cock heavy between his legs. He'd have to jack himself off later if he wanted to get any sleep.

But what he wanted most was the bartender's sexy lips on

his dick, but the relief of not having to come up with an excuse as to why that wasn't going to happen almost made up for the fact that he'd probably missed out on some fantastic head.

That late at night, even for the valley, traffic came in spits and spurts, especially on the side streets. He glanced up at the sky, but the light pollution blotted out all but the brightest stars.

"You going to see him again?" Niko asked, bringing Demetri back to himself.

"I didn't get his number."

He should have. But in Demetri's experience, alley sex had never amounted to anything more than scratching an itch.

"I'm sure you could look him up on social media. He's bound to be—"

"I didn't get his name, either," Demetri muttered.

Probably a good thing. In a very short time, Green Eyes had made Demetri question all of his morals and values and almost had him consenting to things he damn well promised himself he wouldn't.

A man who could move Demetri's moral line that easily was far too dangerous.

They drove back to Demetri's place in near silence, guilt starting to nibble at his edges. What if they hadn't been interrupted? Would Demetri have let the man go down on him?

Would he have been tempted to do more?

In Demetri's driveway, Niko parked. "You didn't tell him, did you?"

"Why do you say that? Because he didn't run?"

"No, because the self-recrimination is wafting off of you like something foul a dog rolled in."

"I didn't do anything unsafe." Demetri brushed the dirt off the knees of his pants, where the threads had been scuffed and scraped. He'd probably ruined the pants. Then he glanced up at

Niko, his cousin's features in harsh relief in the blue glow of the dash lights. "But I fucking wanted to."

"He scared you."

"*I* scared me."

Niko stared out the windshield. Demetri had left the lights on when he'd left, and through the front plate-glass windows, you could see through to the backyard.

Niko looked at Demetri, not speaking until Demetri held his gaze. "You didn't put him at any kind of risk. You know that. Go easy on yourself."

Easier said than done.

Especially when Demetri knew exactly what else he'd wanted to do in that alley.

"You are one of the most compassionate people I know," Niko said. "Try saving a little of that for yourself, yeah?"

Demetri gave him a curt nod, more because it was expected than because he agreed.

Back in his house, he stripped off his tie and unbuttoned the top buttons on his shirt. He poured himself cheap box wine. It had been sitting in the fridge since God knew when.

He dropped onto the couch in the darkness and stared out the floor-to-ceiling windows overlooking his pool.

Demetri couldn't get the bartender out of his head.

And being half hard didn't help.

After two glasses of wine, the stupid thought that he might be able to find Green Eyes on one of the hookup apps popped into his brain. It took another glass while arguing back and forth with himself before he called himself an idiot and pulled his phone out of his pocket anyway.

You would have thought that the minutes it took for him to re-download several of the more popular hookup apps would have given him enough time to come to his senses.

You'd be wrong.

On the first app, he set the location radius to two miles, having no idea where the man lived. He scrolled through grids of faces and bare chests, one after the other. He recognized a few. Some were friends, and some were people he'd hooked up with in the past. But none of them were the man he'd sucked off in the alley.

For all Demetri knew, the man could have driven up from Los Angeles or somewhere else.

Demetri tossed his phone onto the cushion beside him. He got up for another glass of wine and drained the dregs from the bottom of the box. Probably a good thing the box hadn't been full.

Flopping back down on the couch, he picked up his phone. Finding the bartender would be like finding a needle in a gay haystack.

But the man's friend called and was there within minutes.

Demetri widened the search area to five miles but still came up blank.

Maybe this was the universe's way of saving him from himself.

He rinsed his empty glass in the sink and shuffled his way into his bedroom, kicking off his shoes and stripping to his briefs on the way, leaving a trail of alley-scuffed clothes on the floor behind him.

Dropping onto his back on the bed, he closed his eyes. All he saw were those mesmerizing eyes, that heart-stopping smile, and a hard cock that went on for a mile.

Okay, maybe not a mile, but it had been impressive. Demetri still felt the tightness in his jaw from the strain. And thinking about the feel of that thick dick in his mouth turned the semi he'd had since he'd left the gallery into a full-blown hard-on.

He shoved his underwear down his legs and kicked them out of the way, having zero shame as he took hold of himself. He'd never see the guy again, and there was nothing wrong with some harmless jacking off.

Precum quickly slicked his tip. Even after all the wine, Demetri imagined he could still taste the man on his tongue. Could still feel the pulse of the bartender's orgasm slamming into him, and the cum shooting into the back of his throat.

His balls grew heavy and tight as Demetri continued stroking himself, his shaft now slick with his precum. He teased the ridge and the head, wishing it were a tongue or the bartender's hand.

He came quickly, and with little of his usual warning, his load landing on his chest and abdomen. As he lay there, with his spilled cum drying on his skin, he knew the universe had been looking out for him.

His kryptonite wasn't an alien mineral from another world...

It was a sinfully sexy bartender.

ROMAN JUMPED INTO MOSES' CAR, TRYING TO BUCKLE IN AS MOSES sped away from the curb. He looked his friend up and down, searching for blood or something, he didn't know what. But besides looking a little frazzled even for Moses, nothing seemed out of the ordinary.

"What's wrong? What's happening? Where are we going?" Roman couldn't get the questions out fast enough. His heart still raced from the mind-altering blowjob and the fresh dump of adrenaline.

Moses glanced over at Roman, his eyes sweeping down Roman's body until they landed on his unfastened belt. "Did I interrupt something?"

"Are you fucking kidding me? What's the emergency? Why did you call me?"

Moses grinned, his usual mischievous grin, but this time a little *oops, my bad* lurked around the edges. "Did you just get sucked off?"

"Would you forget about my dick for a minute and answer the fucking question?"

Moses stared straight ahead as he accelerated to avoid the red light, in a rush to get wherever they were going. Roman's first thought when Moses had called was that Moses or one of his friends had gotten jumped and beat up leaving one of the clubs. It didn't happen often, but it still happened.

"Look, if I'd known—"

Something in the way Moses glanced back at him, his smile wider and devilment powering the spark in his eyes, Roman clicked onto the reality that the reason Moses had called hadn't been life or death.

Roman should have been relieved, but he was too pissed to feel anything but lied to.

Moses should have known better.

At the corner, Moses slowed and pulled into Exeter's back parking lot. The heavy beat of the bass escaping the club vibrated throughout Moses' piece of shit car.

"There they are." Moses pointed.

Two guys were lip locked and leaning against one of the cars, completely oblivious to anything going on around them.

"Who are they?"

"Our tricks for the night."

Roman already had perfectly satisfying anonymous sex that night. He didn't need these guys.

"You've got to be fucking kidding me." Roman shoved the door open with his foot and headed down the sidewalk in the opposite direction.

"Wait!" Leaving his car running, Moses scrambled around the trunk and caught Roman's arm at the street corner. A metallic purple lowrider drove by, the windows down, the bass from the music at a bone-vibrating, ear-numbing volume that put Exeter to shame.

Roman shook Moses off and stepped into him. Roman's vision narrowed, and the bass from the music vanished as he stared down at his friend, his fists shaking at his sides.

"What's your problem?" Moses said. "How the hell was I to know you were getting yourself some? I thought I was doing you a favor."

"I thought someone was dying, I thought—"

Moses laughed. "Yeah, dying to get into their pants."

Roman spun away from his friend, stalking to the curb before turning around again. "You said it was an emergency."

"I didn't think you'd come otherwise." Moses raised his hands, having the decency to look the tiniest bit chagrined.

"Is this your friend?" The two guys walked over. They scanned Roman up and down like a side of prime beef. "You weren't kidding."

The taller one, the one with his shirt unbuttoned and his hair all sweaty from dancing in the club, grabbed the end of Roman's unfastened belt and tugged Roman against him. "I call dibs."

Roman shoved him away. "Not tonight, guys."

"Hey, man." The shorter one had a harness holding up his unfastened pants, his fly open, his jockstrap exposed. "We're just looking for some fun."

The two guys in front of him were young and muscled and easy on the eyes.

But they aren't Spicy.

Roman poked Moses in the chest with his finger. "Don't ever pull crap like that again. You got me?

He didn't wait for an answer. He turned on his heel and started walking the few miles back to his car. Even if he'd had the money to spare for an Uber, he needed every step of that walk to soften the edges of his rage.

Are you mad because Moses lied about an emergency? Or are you mad because you had to leave before getting the guy's number?

The emergency. You don't lie about—

Bullshit. Any other day you would have laughed it off with him. And probably hooked up with one or both guys.

It still didn't make the lie right.

Annoyance trailed Roman back to his car and followed him home. He slapped together a sandwich as Moses came through the front door, towing the two guys from the parking lot behind him.

They guys kissed and giggled and tore at each other's clothes as they stumbled their drunken way down the hallway and into Moses' bedroom, hardly noticing that Roman was there. Just as well, considering the dark mood cloaking him.

He hid in his room, closing his door and stuffing a towel underneath, but he still heard every thump and laugh and 'oh fuck' and 'I'm coming.'

So much for having rooms on opposite ends of the apartment.

And the whole time, all he could think about was Spicy's mouth and lips on his face, neck, cock. He lay on his back on the bed, hard again.

He thought about joining Moses and the other guys, but while he had nothing against it, they weren't what, or rather *who*, he wanted.

You're never going to see Spicy again, so you might as well take advantage of your opportunity while you can.

Which was legit.

But felt... *wrong* somehow.

Later, after the guys had left, a knock came at his door.

Roman had kept his work clothes on because sometimes,

when he moved, he caught whiffs of Spicy on the fabric and his skin. "Come in."

With the towel stuffed in the gap under the door, Moses had to work to shove the door open. He wore a holey pair of sweatpants and a drunk, apologetic smile.

Moses plopped on the end of the bed. He smelled of alcohol, weed, sweat, and sex.

"Sorry I messed up your night."

Roman reached behind him and tossed one of his pillows at Moses' head, but Moses blocked it and tucked it under his chest to lay on. Roman thought back to his encounter in the alley. As much as he'd enjoyed it, something about what had happened seemed... off. He couldn't put his finger on it. Spicy seemed as equally into him, but something had flashed in the man's eyes right before he'd gone down on Roman.

"It's okay," Roman said at last. "It was probably the hottest blowjob I've ever had, but I don't think it was going anywhere else beyond that."

"You don't know that."

Roman shrugged, too tired for much more.

"Was he at least a little closer to your age this time?"

Again, the shrug, but by Moses' exasperated expression, he read that to be a 'no.'

"He seemed different from the others."

"Only because this time you had your dick in *his* mouth. Isn't it usually the other way around?"

"I like to suck dick. Sue me."

"Hey." Moses' voice dropped, and Roman glanced over at him. "You really liked this guy, didn't you?"

And Roman had no clue why. "I only spent a handful of minutes with him all night."

"Yet you imprinted on him like one of those little ducks that follow the people around in the spotted boots."

"You're such a dick. I didn't 'imprint' on him."

Moses sat up, crossing his legs and hugging the pillow to his bare chest. "Give me his number. I'll apologize to him. I'll make this right. You can invite him back here, and I'll clear out for a night or the whole fucking weekend if you want."

"I don't have his number."

"Then you can—"

"Or his name."

Moses rested his chin in his upturned hand. "Well, fuck."

"Yeah, well, it doesn't look like *that's* ever going to happen. One and done. No big deal, right?"

5

MONDAY MORNING, ON THE FIRST DAY OF THE FALL SEMESTER, Demetri sat at his desk at the back of his art room, watching the students file in one by one. It was his live model class, usually restricted to upperclassmen and typically one of his smaller classes each semester. He glanced down at the paperwork the registrar had given him. Sixteen in this class.

He counted heads. Fourteen students. "Pick any seat," he said as the students settled.

At the front of the room, chairs and empty easels stood in front of a semi-circular dais where the live models sat during class. Like in every class the world over, some students sat in the front row, while others tended toward the back or found a middle ground in between.

In the art department's infinite wisdom, it housed all the art rooms in the bowels of the building. At the beginning of each semester, a few students always got lost trying to find his room.

He waited five minutes past the time class should have started before going to the door and checking to see if there were any stragglers coming. Finding the hall empty, he closed the door. With his hand full of the syllabi, he passed the papers around, then stepped onto the dais and introduced himself.

He recognized some of the students from previous classes. One by one, he read down the list of names that the registrar's office had given him and checked them off when the students answered.

"Roman Reed?" Demetri glanced around the room. "No Roman?"

The students shook their heads. He made a mark by the name and continued down the list. Then came a flash of movement in the narrow rectangle window in the door, and someone fumbled with the handle. The door always seemed to stick. Five years of repair requests to the maintenance department hadn't helped.

The door burst open, and a student stumbled in, his backpack falling from his shoulder and slapping on the ground. "Excuse me. Sorry, I—"

The student glanced Demetri's way. Demetri's heart derailed and slammed into his ribs so hard he heard himself grunt. Even from twenty feet away, those green eyes floored him. The man's wide smile equally as deadly.

Demetri tore his eyes away and stared down at the list of names. Letters jumbled together, and for a minute, he thought he'd lost the ability to read. The man stood there a moment before catching himself and picking up his backpack. He slalomed through the chairs to find an empty seat in the front row.

Clearing his throat, Demetri said, "You don't look like an Emily to me. You must be Roman?"

"Roman Reed," the man confirmed.

"I'm glad that you found us."

Roman grinned. "Same."

In a weird way, the next two hours crawled by. At the same

time, class was over way too fast. Demetri finished the class by rote, going through the introductory material on autopilot, only once hearing a student giggle when Demetri's eyes fell on Roman and lingered there.

Fuck, he was in trouble.

He'd have to talk to the registrar's office and see if he could get Roman transferred out of his class. He couldn't spend the whole semester unable to speak full sentences without catching Roman's eye or thinking about a dark alley and a delicious dick and faltering.

When class ended, the students packed their belongings and filed out the door.

"Mr. Reed," Demetri said before the object of a few of his jack-off sessions could leave. "If I could have a word."

You want more than a word.

But that wasn't going to happen.

Couldn't happen.

Demetri had messed around with some of his live models in the past, that was true. But everything had been consensual. And those models hadn't been students.

Demetri had lines he wouldn't cross. Besides, it being wrong to date a student, he refused to be that old cliché about the professor fucking his students.

Closing the door behind the last of his students, Demetri turned to Roman and got straight to the point. "What happened the other night can't happen again."

"I get it."

"And I'd appreciate it if you didn't tell anybody about..." Demetri motioned between the two of them.

"I hadn't planned to. But to be fair, you were the one who kept staring at me during class and losing your train of thought, so if anyone catches on, I don't think you can blame me."

"Fuck," Demetri muttered as he rubbed at his forehead,

trying to fend off the rager of a headache he had brewing.

"If you ask me, it was kind of adorable."

Demetri scowled, and Roman laughed.

But then again, Roman didn't have a possible tenure he could lose.

Demetri swallowed hard and opened the door a crack. "I think we're done here."

Instead of walking through, Roman put a hand on the door and closed it. The latch clicking home sounded like a shot. Roman had a couple of inches on Demetri and about thirty pounds of pure muscle. Roman leaned in, ducking his head. Demetri knew what was coming. He felt it in the breath he held. He felt it in his bones. In his groin.

He should have stepped aside. He should have made excuses, made an escape, something, anything besides lifting his mouth to Roman's and meeting him halfway. Roman stepped into him, his body pressing Demetri against the door, his hard-on pressing into Demetri's hip.

Demetri should stop. He really should.

Roman broke the kiss, leaning away enough so he could see Demetri's face. "You know, I tried to convince myself that what happened in that alley, what I felt, was an aberration. That it was nothing more than a hot guy on a hot night in a dark alley doing what two horny guys do, but... *fuck*. There's something about you, I—"

Someone bumped into the door. The handle jiggled. Roman and Demetri took a step back. A petite woman with short, spiky red hair and black yoga pants came into the room, glancing pointedly between the two of them.

"Oh, hey, it's you," she said. "Roman, right?"

Heat rushed up Demetri's neck. "You two know each other?"

"She was in one of my sociology classes this morning."

The woman grinned and stuck out her hand to Demetri.

"I'm Emily. I was supposed to be in your two o'clock class."

"I'll catch you later, *professor*," Roman said with a wicked grin.

Demetri gave him a casual nod as if Emily hadn't almost walked in on them sucking on each other's tongues.

What else might she have caught you two sucking if she'd been five minutes later?

Demetri didn't answer that.

"Sorry," Emily said, "I'm a transfer student. I got turned around and couldn't find the room and went all the way back to the registrar's office thinking there was a mistake on my schedule and had to wait there and then find out it was right and—"

Her sentences ran together. Despite her yoga pants and her spiked hair, he knew an overeager student when he met one. They were the type who finished their work on the day it was assigned and came back looking for extra credit.

They were also the type of student whose worst nightmare was missing a class.

"Take a breath," Demetri said. "You didn't miss anything important."

She followed him to his desk, and he handed her a syllabus.

"Sorry. It won't happen again."

"I'm sure it won't."

She started backing out of the room, the hint of a knowing smile on her face. "I'll see you Wednesday."

He waved goodbye and watched her retreat, wondering what she had seen or what she *thought* she had seen when Demetri's back had been pressed against the door's narrow window. He could guess by her grin what she suspected.

In all the art rooms in all the colleges, Roman had to walk into his.

Having Roman in his class all semester wouldn't work.

With no other classes on the schedule for the day, Demetri locked up his room and went in search of a solution to his emerging problem.

DEMETRI KNOCKED ON THE OPEN DOOR OF THE OFFICE NEXT TO his. The art department had been relegated to one of the older buildings on campus. The offices were compact, and the new five-story Engineering and Physics building next door cast them in the shadows.

Lydia Wise glanced up from her computer, her red readers at the end of her nose. She smiled that warm and friendly smile she was known for. She'd had tenure at the college since Demetri was in middle school, but they'd become fast friends.

"Come in, come in." She scooted between her desk and the wall of shelves stuffed with books, photos, and whatnot, and met him with a hug. "How did your first day go?"

Demetri chuckled. "You sound like my dad back in elementary school. How was your day? How many boys and girls in your class?"

"Oh, poo," she said, waving her hand at him. "You know what I meant."

She sat on the edge of her desk, the light shining through her silver hair like a halo.

"Can I talk to you a minute?"

Her smile faded. "What's wrong?"

"Nothing that I hope you can't help me fix."

She removed her glasses and let them dangle from a multicolored cord around her neck. "Close the door."

He did and took the only chair on his side of the desk as she went around to hers. He opened his mouth to speak, but she held up one hand for him to wait.

She pulled out her bottom drawer. Demetri heard glass clacking together, and she came up with two glasses and a bottle of the finest bourbon he'd ever tasted. She poured them each a finger and passed him a glass. "Tell me what's going on."

"I have a favor to ask."

"Anything."

"I have this student. I was hoping we could get him transferred into your class."

She raised her chin and appraised him down the length of her slim nose, her old eyes warm, but shrewd. "It's the first day of the semester. Surely he's not that big of a problem already. And if he's that bad, I'm not sure I want him either."

"It's not that he's bad. It's just..."

How did he tell his friend that he wanted to lock his classroom and fuck one of his students against the wall?

Maybe not in those exact words, asshole.

"Ah," she said after scrutinizing him. "He's a problem for *you.*"

Demetri tossed the bourbon to the back of his throat and swallowed, but he knew it wasn't nearly enough to give him the courage to say what he needed to say. He'd have to power through and spill it. "He trips all my wires. I have zero defenses when it comes to him. I don't want it coming back to haunt me."

"All in one two-hour class?"

Demetri considered lying, but Lydia was his closest work friend. If he couldn't tell her, he couldn't tell anybody.

Keep your fucking mouth shut.

But he couldn't go the whole semester with Roman sitting in the front row of his class every Monday, Wednesday, and Friday.

"We had an... *encounter,*" was the word Demetri finally settled on. "Before school started. I had no idea who he was or that he'd end up in my class."

Lydia didn't even raise a brow. Despite looking like someone's sweet little old grandmother—which she was—she'd been a bit of a hippie in her day. "Of course, you didn't."

"Anyway," Demetri wouldn't go into any more detail than that. He did have *some* discretion, "I need him out."

"I wish I could help, but my emergency sabbatical was approved and—"

"Wait, why is this the first I'm hearing about this?"

"It's unexpected. My Hal was diagnosed with cancer. I'm taking time off to be with him."

"Oh, Lydia. I'm so sorry."

He went to hug her, but she put up a staying hand, her eyes going red and filling with tears.

"He's going to be okay," she said, her voice shaking. She dabbed at her eyes with a tissue and cleared her throat. "Maybe Janet can take him in her class."

Demetri shook his head. "She's only doing 100 level classes this semester."

"Well, fuck," Lydia said, drawing a chuckle of understanding from Demetri. She didn't cuss often but didn't hold back when needed.

"Yeah. Thanks, anyway. And give my best to Hal. If you need anything—"

She nodded and swallowed hard, her voice barely above a whisper when she spoke. "I know."

Demetri left Lydia's office, not even bothering to return to his before heading home for the day. His only hope was that Roman would have mercy on him and agree to drop the class.

Saturday morning, Roman sat at his kitchen table, a plate of bacon and eggs in front of him. He still couldn't believe Grant had offered him the job, and today was the first workday at the

Center's community site. He had to meet early with Grant to go over the plans for the day before they'd head over to start work. He filled his belly, having no idea when he'd get a chance to eat next.

A key fumbled in the front door lock, and Roman glanced over his shoulder as Moses stumbled through the door. He hadn't seen his roommate except in passing the whole week. It wasn't that Moses was a bad student, it was that he was trying to squeeze every last drop of fun out of the few days that remained before his classes kicked in in earnest and he had to buckle down and study.

"You're up early," Moses said as he came into the kitchen, swiped a piece of bacon off Roman's plate, and tore off a chunk with his teeth. Moses turned a light shade of green and dropped the piece of bacon with the bite torn out of it back on Roman's plate. "That's going to make me puke."

"Maybe if you'd put something in your body besides booze and dick for the past week, the food wouldn't turn your stomach."

"The dick had nothing to do with it," Moses said as he went for a cup of coffee instead. "But the alcohol undoubtedly does."

He dropped into the seat across from Roman and hugged his mug of coffee to him like it was a life ring from the Coast Guard. Roman's nose wrinkled when he got a whiff of his roomie.

"Have you been lying in a gutter all night?"

"It was more of a back lane than a gutter, and we were at the club until it closed at two, so I couldn't have passed out there more than an hour or so."

"Look at me." When Moses' heavy-lidded, bloodshot eyes sort of focused on him, Roman said, "You've got to slow down. You're going to either get yourself arrested or killed."

Moses gripped his head and groaned. "I know. Monday. I'm done. Promise."

"Mmm hmm." He'd believe that when he saw it. Maybe rooming with his old friend hadn't been such a good idea after all.

"How are your classes?" Moses asked though Roman couldn't tell if he was trying to fill the awkward silence or if he truly wanted to know.

"You know that guy from last Saturday?"

Moses squinted, his eyes even more unfocused as he mentally flipped through his alcohol, drug, and sex-infused haze of the past week. Then his eyes widened. "Oh, spice boy."

"*Spicy.* And yeah. Him. Turns out, his name is Demetri Stavros."

Moses thought for a minute. It looked painful. "Isn't he—"

"My art professor."

"—related to that porn director."

"What?" They both said at the same time.

"You go first," Moses said. He took another sip of coffee. By the grimace on his face and the burp he held back, it wasn't sitting much better than the bacon had.

"Demetri Stavros, the provider of the best blowjob I've ever had, is my art professor."

Moses threw his head back and laughed. Then he pressed his palms into his temples and groaned. "Shit, don't make me laugh."

"Who did you say he was?"

Moses made a *give it here motion* with his hand. "Phone."

Roman keyed in his code and handed it over. Moses punched around on it until something loaded. "I thought that was him."

Moses handed the phone back, and Roman flicked through the search results. "He's the cousin of Niko Stavros? Black Stallion Studios? *That* Niko?"

"They're well known in the valley," Moses said. "But you'd have had no way of knowing that."

"Well, I'd heard of Black Stallion Studios. But the rest, I had no clue." Not that it mattered. Roman shoveled his now cold scrambled eggs into his mouth, none of the flavor registering.

"I would have thought that having him as your professor would have made you happy. You get to see him again and—"

"First day, he held me after class and flat-out told me nothing else was going to happen."

"What did you say?"

"I said sure... and then I backed him up against the door and kissed him."

Moses held his hand up for a fist bump, but Roman left him hanging.

"And ever since then, he'll barely look at me in class. I'm in the first fucking row, and it's like a cloak of invisibility has wrapped around me."

"Maybe you need to back him up against the wall and show him what little Roman can do for him."

Roman rolled his eyes. "You don't get it. He wants nothing to do with me."

"You can't give up. Not that easily."

"I'm not forcing a guy to be with me who doesn't want me around. There are plenty of other guys out there."

Unfortunately, none of them had snagged Roman's heart the way the professor had.

"I gotta go. I've got a long day ahead of me. Sober up. Then you can come by and help." Roman shoved his remaining breakfast Moses' way.

"Volunteer?" Moses glanced up at him, pure horror on his face. He crossed his fingers in front of him and hissed. "Back, evil one."

Chuckling, Roman said, "That's what I figured."

Roman hopped in his car and threaded his way through traffic. That early on a Saturday morning, it wasn't too hellish. He parked and used the key Grant had given him earlier in the week to let himself into the Center. He headed for the break room and the coffee he knew Grant would have brewing in there.

He turned the corner and came up short at the sight of Demetri sitting at the table in shorts and an old paint-stained T-shirt, his hair still mussed up from sleep as he sucked on a mug of coffee.

Grant turned away from the coffee maker, a fresh mug in his hand. "Oh, hey." He handed the mug to Roman. "Meet Demetri. He volunteered to help with the project."

"Yeah," Demetri said, conspicuously avoiding eye contact. "We've met."

Grant glanced between the two of them, the air in the room thick with a vibe Roman couldn't even begin to describe, though Grant picked up on it right away.

"Is there going to be a problem?" Grant asked.

"Not for me." Demetri watched as Roman took the chair directly across from him, putting himself in Demetri's direct line of sight.

Roman's gaze flicked Demetri's way and then landed on Grant. "No. Everything is copacetic."

"Great." Grant filled his mug, claiming the chair at the head of the table. He pulled some papers out of a manila folder and splayed them out on the table. "Let's get started then."

Grant had several lists of items to be tackled. Roman had driven by the lot earlier in the week. They had to accomplish a lot before the kids could get involved.

Roman took one of the lists. "I'll start with the jackhammer and begin breaking up that sidewalk the tree roots have busted up."

"I'll start power washing the block walls," Demetri said.

"Tavi and I can load the broken-up concrete into the dumpster," Grant said as he shuffled through some papers. "It should already be on site."

"And I've got a friend coming to help later," Roman said.

"A *friend*?" Demetri asked.

For the first time since Roman came into the room, Demetri locked eyes with him. The quick spark of jealousy that flashed in them made Roman smile. Not so immune to Roman, after all.

"A friend," Roman supplied. "From class. Emily. She needs community service hours, and I told her about the project."

"Thanks," Grant said, "We can use all the adult help we can get. It's going to be interesting once the kids get involved. I have a feeling it's going to be like herding hamsters. Let me know if she wants to work with the kids. She'll have to fill out a form so I can run a background check."

"I'll let her know."

Tavi walked into the break room. He was the teen Grant was fostering with his fiancé, Sebastian. Roman had met the kid a few days before. He must have already been in the building because Roman had locked the front door behind him.

Tavi swiped the long, dark bangs out of his face and handed a spiral art book to Grant. "I drew up some ideas for the wall like you asked."

"Hey, kid," Demetri said. "You recovered from the art opening?"

"I think. And Mr. Franklin called yesterday and said he thought he might have a buyer for one of my pieces. Can you believe that?"

"That's awesome," Roman said. He bobbed his chin toward the artbook. "Can we see?"

Grant opened the spiral and set it on the table in front of

Demetri. "Come over here," he said to Roman, "so you can get a better look."

Roman moved around to the other side of the table, his hand on the back of Demetri's chair for balance as he leaned over. The community lot had an ugly concrete block wall on three sides, leaving the front open to the street.

Tavi scooted the artbook closer. "This is the left wall. There are going to be kids of all ages using this space, so I wanted it to function for everyone."

The first page had cartoon drawings of animals. Hippos. Zebra. Lions. Tigers. And a giraffe with his tongue sticking out as if eating the shrubs that draped over the wall.

"This first wall is for the little kids. Obvs." Tavi turned the page. "The back wall will be for some of the elementary age kids. Superheroes and magical dragons."

"That's amazing work," Roman said.

"Thanks. I tried to keep it simple. I thought the older kids could paint the outlines, and the younger ones could fill in the middle, like a giant paint by number."

Grant put his arm around Tavi's shoulders and pulled him to his side. "I'm proud of you, kid."

Red rushed up Tavi's face as he fought the smile.

"I don't see why you need me," Demetri said. "The kid's got it all figured out."

Grant patted Demetri's shoulder. "Don't worry. There's plenty we'll need you for."

"What's going on the third wall?" Roman asked.

Tavi nibbled on his lower lip, picked up the artbook, and turned the page. He held it to his chest so nobody could see. "I don't know if this will fly. It's just an idea I had, and if you don't think it's a good idea, we can do something else. Maybe something that Demetri comes up with and—"

Grant put a hand on Tavi's shoulder and stopped the verbal

vomit. "Take a breath. If we don't like it, we'll come up with something else."

Tavi laid his sketch down. The third and final wall he'd divided into four blocked off sections, with what would be a painted frame around each blank 'canvas.'

"I don't get it," Demetri said.

Grant's brows knit in confusion. "Me neither."

Before Tavi could explain, Roman said, "It's a graffiti wall."

Tavi held out his fist, and Roman bumped it. "At least one of you guys knows where it's at. What do you think?"

"I think it's *sick*," Roman said, but it wasn't his approval that Tavi sought.

"Interesting thought," Demetri added.

Interesting, that's all Demetri could say? Roman cut him a look. And Demetri held up his hands like *what did you expect me to say?*

"It could be a space for local kids to tag," Tavi explained. "Maybe it'll help keep them from tagging the other two walls. Plus, they get to showcase their talents. I figured once a month, we could repaint the area inside the frames, and it can start all over again."

"I like the idea that the art will change and grow each month," Demetri said.

Roman also saw the positives for the city. "And give some of the would-be taggers a place to go besides the railroad tracks or the alleys."

"I like it." Grant tugged at his bottom lip as he considered the idea. "It'll be a living art piece."

"But?" Tavi asked.

"My only concern is the cost. Repainting the graffiti sections every month will—"

"Be covered by Niko," Demetri said. "He's covering the cost of all materials for the community lot project."

"Since when?" Grant couldn't help but be a little suspicious, Roman supposed.

"Since we made a deal."

"See," Tavi said, "It'll work. And if it becomes too much of a problem, we can always redesign that wall and make it something static."

"I say we go for it." Not that anyone had asked Roman, but he got a grin out of the kid, so that was worth it right there.

Grant clapped Tavi on the back. "Me, too."

"Sweet," Tavi said in that understated way teens have when they're stoked but don't want to look uncool and show it.

Grant stuffed the papers into his folder. "Let's get out of here then."

They all broke apart, and Grant turned to Tavi. "I thought Remy was supposed to meet us here this morning."

"Remy?" Roman glanced over. "Does this mean I get to meet this boyfriend you keep talking about?"

"One, I mentioned him like twice, and two, yes. But he had a mandatory meeting this morning at the group home where he lives. Someone keeps swiping all the bars of soap."

"Soap?" Demetri ran his hand absently through his bed-tussled hair, but he only made it worse... and sexier.

Tavi shrugged as he backed out of the break room. "Yeah, I don't get it either."

Grant retrieved his keys from his office. "You're with me, kid. Maybe you two can carpool," he said to Demetri. "I still have to pick up Remy, and I'm packed to the gills with supplies."

Demetri glanced at Roman. Roman watched him bank the flash of terror in his eyes before anyone else could see it. Demetri swallowed hard, but his words still came out strangled. "Yeah, sure."

6

ROMAN OPENED DEMETRI'S PASSENGER DOOR AND LEANED IN. "Look, I can take my car. There's no reason I can't drive myself."

Demetri should accept Roman's offer. The less time they spent confined together, the better.

Or maybe if you spend more time with him, you'll find his fatal flaw and you can stop this stupid, possibly career-ending, infatuation.

"Fatal flaw," Demetri mumbled to himself. Maybe that was the trick.

"What did you say?"

"Nothing. Get in."

Tell him you're poz. I bet you'll find his fatal flaw then.

But Demetri didn't. The part of him that wanted to take Niko's advice and let Roman get to know him better before disclosing warred with the other part that knew getting to know Roman any better would be the stupidest career move he'd ever made.

"We gonna go? Or do you need a minute?" Roman asked.

Demetri shook his head, dislodging some of the mental cobwebs and starting his car.

As soon as Roman buckled in, Demetri backed out. Roman's

wide shoulders bumped into his as they turned corners, his scent that same, mouth-watering hint of the forbidden he remembered so well from the alley.

Demetri tightened his grip on the wheel to prevent himself from parking on a side street, pulling Roman over the center console, and doing some of the naughty things he'd dreamt about.

They drove in near silence, the only sound besides the whirr of the wheels on the road beneath them, and the occasional honk was Roman's middle finger tap, tap, tapping on his armrest.

Roman plucked at the front of his T-shirt. "Is it hot in here?"

Without waiting for a response, Roman buzzed down his window, the cool, early morning air blowing in and buffeting Demetri's eardrums. Demetri lowered his window to equalize the pressure.

They turned the last corner, and the community lot came into view. Parking near the lot came at a premium. Since they didn't have anything to unload, Demetri drove a couple of blocks past and pulled into one of the city parking lots.

"Is it going to be weird like this the whole time we're working together?" Roman asked.

A valid question. "It doesn't have to be."

"It's going to be if you can't look me in the eye, or talk to me without looking the other way, or ignoring me, or—"

"I get it." Demetri scrubbed his hands through his hair and caught his reflection in the side mirror. Shit. He'd left the house without even fixing his hair. Where had his head been?

Up your ass? Where it's been ever since you spent a few magnificent minutes on your knees in a dark alley.

That's helpful.

"I'm sorry." Demetri glanced at Roman—at the line of his jaw, at the dark dusting of scruff on his cheeks, at those magnetic eyes that looked like they wanted so much more. They *deserved* so much more. "I just..."

Demetri didn't know how to articulate his jumbled feelings. Fear over what he had to lose, but also the excitement, the thrill of the forbidden. And all that wasn't even taking into account how Roman made him feel on the inside. How he made Demetri want to spill all his secrets and lay himself bare.

Secrets that would most likely send Roman running.

Here's an idea, brainiac. Tell him. Tell him you're poz and watch him run, and this whole thing will take care of itself. End it before it even starts.

But the hell of it was he didn't want it to end. And it scared the bejesus out of him on so many levels to even start.

"You want to know what I think?"

Demetri shook his head, but still said, "What do you think?"

"I think you're over-thinking things. I think that you should chill. Don't jump twenty squares ahead and plan out every move as if you were in the final round of a grandmaster chess match." Roman paused as if deciding what to say next. His gaze dropped to Demetri's lips for a fraction of a second before locking onto Demetri's eyes again. "And I think you should kiss me."

Roman leaned over, their shoulders brushing, his voice barely a whisper when he said, "We're alone. Nobody has to know."

Demetri couldn't say the devil made him do it. He didn't believe in angels and devils. Only wants and needs and the power of the inevitable.

One kiss. What could it hurt?

"Fuck it," Demetri muttered as he touched his lips to Roman's.

He'd only meant for it to be the briefest of kisses, but like every time he'd been with Roman, things escalated. A brief touch of the lips deepened into this lip-locking, tongue-dueling, heart-tripping kiss that made Demetri's reason turn to mush, and his will bend to Roman's.

"Oh, hey. I thought that was you." Demetri and Roman broke apart as Emily leaned down and rested her forearms on Roman's windowsill. "Hi, professor. I didn't know you'd be here."

"Lucky coincidence." If Emily noticed his voice cracking, she didn't mention it. Like *hey, that was fucking awkward, huh?*

Demetri zipped up the windows and popped his door before Roman could get unbuckled. Emily stepped back, and Roman got out, catching Demetri's eyes over the hood. "You're mad."

"I'm not mad." At least not at Roman.

"Liar." Roman closed the car door and walked off without looking back.

Demetri followed Roman and Emily as they backtracked the couple of blocks to the site. Emily had worn an old pair of cutoff jeans. Long threads dangled down her legs. Her cutoff shirt looked like it had been hacked off with a chainsaw and exposed much of her midriff. She was objectively attractive in a free spirit kind of way.

Roman and Emily talked and laughed, occasionally bumping arms or hips as they walked. An uncomfortable thought landed, hitting Demetri in the gut and making his breakfast want to come back up—was Roman bi?

He hadn't asked.

Hard to do when your lips are wrapped around his dick.

But the thought that Demetri might have competition shoved all his concerns that Emily would take what she'd seen in the car straight to the dean to the back of his mind.

One building away from the lot, Roman stopped and waited for Demetri. Emily kept going.

Roman planted his hands on his hips, then pointed at Demetri's face. "You don't call that mad?"

"I don't know what you're talking about."

"Fine. But you might wanna wipe whatever that expression is off your face, or all day long, everyone will be asking you what's wrong."

Demetri closed his eyes and scrubbed a hand down his face wondering where the hell the reset button for his life was located. Fuck wanting tenure. He wanted his life back on an even keel where each step didn't feel unstable and fraught with unforeseen danger.

Roman took a step closer, his voice measured when he said, "If you're worried about what happened back there, don't be. Emily's cool. She wouldn't say anything."

"You've known her what, five, six days?"

"Sometimes, you just have a good feeling about somebody. I can't explain it."

Roman's voice rumbled. Low. Intimate. Were they even talking about Emily anymore?

Didn't feel like it.

And he'd have to take Roman vouching for Emily at face value. It wasn't like he was going to confront one of his students and ask them to forget what they'd seen.

Unfortunately, unless he wanted to make a complete ass of himself and draw more attention to the kiss in the car, he had no choice but to trust Roman's instincts.

Roman clapped a hand on Demetri's shoulder. "Come on. There's a pressure washer waiting with your name on it."

AROUND NOON, GRANT HAD LUNCH AND DRINKS DELIVERED TO THE site. After several hours wrangling a cantankerous jackhammer, Roman's stomach growled like a starving tiger. He and Emily sat on the curb as Grant rounded up the rest of the crew to give them food.

"Do you two have a thing?" Emily asked.

Roman choked on his bite of pizza. He didn't insult her intelligence by asking who she meant. "I wouldn't call it a thing."

He and Demetri had known each other for only a week, and in Roman's book, you couldn't call a few stolen kisses and a blowjob a 'thing.'

"Why do you think that?" Not only had he not talked to Demetri all morning, but they'd worked on opposite sides of the site.

"Well, there was the kiss in the car that made me hot, and I wasn't even involved. Plus, the professor can't keep his eyes off you. I mean, I get your attraction to him. That lean, body with an artistic vibe, the professor's sexy as fuck."

Roman glanced behind him. Demetri stood with Grant in the middle of the lot, eating their slices, deep in discussion about the work, if the way they kept pointing at different areas gave any indication.

Tavi and his boyfriend Remy had dropped to the ground, sitting cross-legged while they inhaled the contents of the box of pizza Grant had walked over.

"I think you're dehydrated, and your mind is playing tricks on you." Roman grabbed one of the cold bottles of water, twisted off the top, and handed it to her. "This should help."

She laughed but said, "We were power-washing near each other all morning. I know what I saw."

Fortunately, Demetri and Grant walked over, and Roman didn't have to answer. He didn't quite know how to explain, categorize, or unravel the complexities of the draw and fascination he had with Demetri.

Talk turned to plans for the lot. Not only later that day but for Sunday and the next weekend when they hoped to have their first group of kid volunteers from the Center come and help.

In no time, they all demolished three large pizzas. Roman lay back on a whole section of the sidewalk, stretching out his back. The vibrations from the jackhammer ghosted in his hands and arms, and his shoulders had started to stiffen.

"Time to get back to it," Grant said.

The boys groaned but pulled their work gloves out of their back pockets and headed for the wheelbarrow they'd been filling with the broken-up chunks of concrete and dumping in the big blue walk-in dumpster.

Emily stood and gathered up the trash from lunch. Grant mumbled something about calling and checking on Vondra at the Center, leaving Demetri standing over Roman.

Roman raised a hand and shielded his eyes from the high sun. Concrete dust lay in all his sweaty nooks and crannies, and he couldn't wait to go home and shower it off.

If he got lucky, maybe he wouldn't be showering alone.

Demetri held out his hand, and Roman locked wrists with him and allowed Demetri to pull him to his feet. "How are you holding up? You need me to spell you on the jackhammer?"

Roman grinned. "That thing would take you for a ride."

Much like Roman wanted to do with Demetri.

"Oh, and fair warning," Roman said, "if you want to keep us on the down low, you gotta stop staring at me like I'm a chocolate chunk cookie, and you got diagnosed with diabetes."

Demetri's face flamed, and Roman grinned, not because of Demetri's embarrassment, but because Demetri didn't dispel the notion of his attraction. And even better, he didn't reiterate that something between them couldn't happen.

Progress.

"I'd better get back to work," Demetri said.

Roman wanted to lean in and kiss those pouty lips, but even though he had his back to the lot and his body would block the view, standing out on the street, they were still too exposed. He wouldn't do that to Demetri. It wouldn't be fair. "Maybe this time you'll keep your eyes on your work, professor."

When Demetri grinned like that, it lit his face, put a spark in his eyes, and made the sun shine brighter in the sky.

"Don't count on it." Demetri patted Roman's stomach and let his hand trail across Roman's ribs as he stepped past.

The next few hours flew by in a cloud of concrete dust. Numbness gradually creeping up Roman's arms. With the hearing protection, all Roman had to keep him company were the thoughts in his head.

Dirty thoughts.

That hand that Demetri had dragged across Roman's belly burned like a fresh tattoo. All afternoon, Roman had way too much time imagining what those hands would feel like on the rest of his body.

He glanced up from the last section of concrete cracking under his jackhammer, and through the dust-clouded lenses of his eye protection, caught Demetri staring. Emily hadn't been lying. Not that he'd thought she had been.

Roman turned back to his work, the exhaustion taking a back seat to the exhilaration.

When he finished the last square, he turned off the jack-hammer and laid it down, stripping off his eye and ear protection. He bent down to start loading rubble into the wheelbarrow with Grant and the boys, but Grant clapped him on the back and said, "Nope. You're done. Go take a load off. We'll finish up here."

Roman didn't even pretend to argue. "Okay. Thanks."

He boosted himself onto Grant's tailgate, the instant relief of getting the weight off his feet made him groan. Fuck. He couldn't remember a time that he'd worked that hard.

The engine for one of the power washers shut off, quickly followed by the other. Cars still drove by, people walked and talked and went about their day, but the comparable silence was a relief to his ears.

He grabbed one of the leftover bottles of water and drained almost all of it in a few swallows, pouring the last of it over his head. But it wasn't nearly enough to wash all the grit and grime off his face.

"Here, try this." Demetri brought him a clean rag and a five-gallon bucket with water from a nearby spigot. "It's not as good as a shower, but you can at least get some of the grime off you."

"Thanks." Roman took the rag and jumped to the ground.

He ditched his shirt and shoveled the cool, refreshing water over his head and face. With the wet rag, he washed off his arms and chest, not caring that the excess dripped into the waistband of his shorts. He dunked the rag again, squeezing the water over his shoulder. He couldn't reach everywhere, but it was better than nothing.

"Want me to get your back?" Demetri held out his hand for the rag.

Oh, hell, yeah. "Go for it."

7

WANT ME TO GET YOUR BACK?

You're the worst kind of idiot. The kind that can't get out of his own way. If shit hits the fan, if you're fired, you'll have no one to blame but yourself.

When a sexy man he had the hots for turned his back, allowing Demetri to wash it—that great expanse of powerful flesh and muscle and bone—inner Demetri all but jumped up and down with his hands raised yelling *pick me, pick me*, begging for the blame.

From Roman's wide shoulders to his trim waist, Demetri washed the dusting of aerosolized concrete off his skin. Watching a few drops of water disappear down Roman's spine, Demetri wished he could ditch the rag and explore with his hands.

He rinsed and lightly wrung out the rag. He was finished, but he kept going. At the top of Roman's shoulders, he squeezed out the rest of the water, loving the way the droplets jumped and bumped over the dips and valleys of Roman's muscles.

Every place he wanted his lips and tongue to be.

With one finger, he followed the trail of water over the

visible knobs of each vertebra, and Roman's head dropped between his shoulders, goosebumps flashing across his beautiful bare skin.

A throat cleared behind him, and he and Roman both jumped. "Can you toss me one of those waters?"

Roman grabbed one of the waters from the bed of the truck and handed it to Emily. Roman shook the dust out of his shirt and tugged it on over his damp skin.

Grant called out. "Can one of you give me a hand with the jackhammer?"

Demetri held up a staying hand to Roman. "I'll help. You stay here."

Roman had worked hard enough that day and, more importantly, Demetri had no desire to be left alone with Emily, and her questioning looks.

The jackhammer was fucking heavy, making Demetri puff hard by the time they loaded it into the back of the truck for Grant to return it to the rental department at the home center.

"I'll be back," Grant said, then called out to the boys. "You two staying or coming with me?"

Tavi made a face as if he'd rather eat a plateful of Brussels sprouts. "We'll stay."

"Wheel those pressure washers over here," Grant told the boys. "They need to go back, too."

While they waited for the boys, Emily said, "I think I'm going to head out if you're finished with me."

"Yeah." Grant pulled her in for a side hug. "Thanks for all the help. You're welcome back any time."

"Thanks. I have a project for school I have to start tomorrow, but I can come back next Saturday if that works for you."

"That would be great," Demetri said. "That's when the gremlins will be here to help. We could use all the adult supervision we can get."

To Grant, Emily said, "Shoot me that form for the background check tonight, and I'll fill it out, and you can run it before next weekend."

"Will do."

They all said their goodbyes, and Grant closed the tailgate. "Before I forget, Sebastian wanted me to remind you about the family dinner tomorrow night."

Demetri didn't always go to the family dinners on Sundays, but he didn't have a good excuse this time. "I remember."

"Do you two mind waiting with the boys? I shouldn't be too long. They could stay here alone if you have somewhere you need to be."

"I can stay," Roman was first to say.

Demetri didn't have plans for later, and also wasn't ready to say goodbye to Roman either, so he said, "Same."

Grant drove away, and Demetri said, "Want to help me finish loading the rest of the rubble? If we load and the boys dump, we should be able to get it done before Grant gets back."

"Lead the way."

The last of the rubble lay on the side of the lot nearest the church. When Demetri didn't have his eye on Roman, he had his eye out for the pastor from the church next door.

Being Saturday, groups of kids came in and out of the church. He figured they had a well-developed youth program.

But to his surprise—and relief—the pastor never showed his face.

After the boys took the last load to the dumpster, Demetri and Roman stood with their backs to the church, surveying the freshly pressure-washed walls and discussing prioritizing work for the next day.

"We should probably build the forms for the sidewalk first," Roman said, "Didn't Grant say the concrete guys are coming first thing Monday—"

"Hey!" Came a shout from over their shoulders. "Stop that. No one needs to see that kind of sick behavior in public."

Tavi and Remy broke apart. They'd done nothing more than peck each other on the lips and walk hand in hand back toward Roman and Demetri.

The hairs on the back of Demetri's neck danced as he turned around. Demetri opened his mouth to confront the man striding their way. The man's face was flushed, and a vein popped at his temple. Roman placed a staying hand on Demetri's chest and said, "I'll handle this."

"If you have a problem, sir," Roman said, "you can talk to me about it."

The pastor was round and sixty-ish with a comb-over that was the only sin occurring in the immediate vicinity. How Roman remained so calm, Demetri didn't know, not with the blood rushing past Demetri's ears and the heat of anger creeping up the back of his neck. He turned to the boys who'd stopped a few feet behind. "Why don't you guys go chill out by the dumpster? Grant should be back shortly."

"I'm not letting him run me off," Tavi said. "We didn't do anything wrong."

"Show some respect, young man." The man stepped closer and pointed an angry finger at Tavi. "You should—"

Roman took one step to the right, crossing his arms over his chest and blocking the pastor's way. "I think you should move along, sir."

"Move along? While these two sin beside a house of God, in full view of all these innocent children coming and going? What am I supposed to tell their God-fearing mothers, their fathers?"

"Maybe that God loves *all* of his children. Not just the straight ones," Roman said, still without a feather ruffled. "You could start there."

Remy coughed, but it sounded more like a laugh to Demetri.

When the pastor moved to step around Roman, Roman moved in front of him again. If the pastor wanted to get to the boys, he'd have to go through Roman. Demetri rocked back on his heels. The sense of pride he had for Roman made his chest hurt.

"This is an abomination. I'm going to talk to the city council and—"

Roman rested his hands on his hips. "Why don't you call the judge, too, while you're at it. You know, the one who blocked the injunction your church filed to prevent the Center from receiving the lot from the estate. I'm sure he would love to speak with you as well."

"*Hmph.*" The man took a step back but didn't leave before saying, "I'll be watching."

"Better yet," Roman said, "why don't you and your congregation come tomorrow and help? Perhaps after church? This is a community space for all the kids, not only the LGBTQ ones. I'm sure they would love to help out their fellow neighbors."

The pastor turned a shade of red that the fire department might want to adopt for their trucks and spun on his heel, gathering a few of the straggling kids' parents had dropped off in front of the church and ushered them inside.

Roman blew out a breath as the man retreated.

"Holy crap," Tavi said, "that was freaking amazing."

"That was dope. Can I have your autograph?" Remy held out his hands to Roman as if he had a pad of paper and pen.

Roman rolled his eyes. "Shoo, you two."

The boys pushed and shoved each other playfully and jogged over when Grant pulled in at the curb.

Demetri bumped his shoulder against Roman's as they walked to join the others, knowing the next words out of his mouth would be a mistake, but he said them anyway. "Can I buy you a beer?"

ROMAN AND DEMETRI HAD TO WALK THREE BLOCKS PAST WHERE they'd left Demetri's car that morning, and a couple blocks down a quiet, dirty side street to get to the bar.

"Where is this place anyway?" Not a complaint, even with the bottoms of his feet throbbing from standing in work boots all day. If Demetri wanted to buy him a beer at the end of a long, hot day, he'd walk around the city three times if that's what Demetri wanted.

"It's just ahead."

Roman glanced up, but he didn't see a sign or any other indication of an establishment that hadn't gone out of business in the last decade. "Are you sure we're on the right street?"

Demetri grabbed the handle of a glass door, the reflective film so dark you couldn't see inside. There was no sign on or above the door, but Demetri pulled it open and ushered Roman inside.

Roman stopped on the other side of the threshold, and Demetri had to scoot by him. It took a moment for his eyes to adjust as the tinted door behind them swung closed, throwing the place into near darkness again. "What is this place?"

"Sneaky Pete's. It's one of the oldest gay bars in the valley. Niko and I started sneaking into this place back in high school."

Demetri took Roman's hand, and he followed willingly. They ordered at the bar and took their drinks to the farthest table in a dim back corner.

Roman took a seat with his back to the wall. Not because he feared getting jumped, but because he wanted to get a feel for the place.

He took a sip of his peach IPA and stared up at the exposed pipe ceiling, the brick wall that looked like it wouldn't take more than a huff or a puff, and it would blow down.

This wasn't one of those trendy places that spent high dollars to make it look like a hole in the wall. It *was* a hole in the wall. And by all indications, only one or two health code violations shy of a shutdown.

"You trying to hide me?" It was a joke, but by the way Demetri blanched, it hit close to home.

"We can leave if you want," Demetri offered. "I thought this would be a good place where we can be ourselves, and I wouldn't have to worry about running into students or colleagues."

Demetri blew out a breath and stood. "I'm fucking this up. Let's go. There's a sports bar around the corner and—"

"Sit down." Roman took Demetri's hand to prevent him from leaving. "I don't want to go anywhere else."

And it wasn't because the soles of his feet had developed a heartbeat of their own. He liked the bar. Liked the anonymity. Liked that it was a safe space just to be.

But he would have followed Demetri anywhere if it meant he got to spend some one-on-one time with him.

Demetri sat, taking a long swallow of his beer and wiping his mouth on the back of his hand. He glanced at his other hand, the one Roman still held, and the one Demetri hadn't pulled back.

Roman would have held his hand in public, but it was nice that he didn't have to glance around him and make sure there weren't any threats.

Demetri squeezed Roman's hand. "You impressed me back there."

"I have an extremely low tolerance for that kind of bullshit. I'm not about to stand around and let an adult verbally abuse a kid."

"Sounds like there's a story there."

A waiter came over in jeans and a bar branded T-shirt. His

beard was long, and his hair was short. "Want anything off the menu?"

"I'm starved." Demetri let go of Roman's hand and picked up a menu card off the table and gave it a cursory glance. "I'll have the blue-cheese burger and fries."

"Same."

"I'll have it right out."

Roman started where their conversation let off, trying to downplay what he'd revealed. He didn't want to get into all his shit. He didn't need anything else that might potentially scare Demetri away. "Not much of a story."

"Let me guess..." Of course, Demetri didn't take the hint. "Your father was homophobic and—"

Roman shook his head and took another sip of beer, buying him some time. If they were going to go there, he needed to figure out how much he was willing to divulge. His parents were a particularly sore spot in his life. His mother for what she'd done. His father for what he *didn't* do.

"I think my father knew from a very early age that I was gay. He did his best to protect me from my mother, but I came to find out later he had his own demons to battle."

"Was your mother ultra-religious?"

"Only when it suited her. Anyway..." Roman paused until the lump in his throat eased, and he felt certain his voice wouldn't shake and give him away. "My dad eventually... *left*," was the word Roman found to be as close to the truth as he could allow right then. "And she did her complicated best to make the rest of my life a living hell."

"I'm sorry. Did you ever reconnect with your father?"

Wanna know the problem with half-truths? The follow-up questions were a bitch to navigate. "I don't want to lie. I'll just say reconnecting isn't an option."

The food came, and either derailed Demetri's line of questioning, or Demetri decided to have some mercy on him. They both dug into the greasy bar food that may or may not give them food poisoning. At least the flavor was passable, but Roman's standard was a low bar considering he was at the stage of hunger where he would have eaten a can of cat food if it had been his only choice.

Demetri bought them another round of beer and changed the subject to something lighter. By the time they left the bar, darkness had fallen. Demetri linked his fingers with Roman's until they hit the busier main street.

Roman understood Demetri's caution but didn't like the feeling he was being shoved into the closet. For better and for much worse, Roman had been out since before he could remember, and this new secrecy didn't sit well. Even though he knew it had nothing to do with being gay and everything to do with Demetri seeing a student.

Then walk away. It's only going to get worse.

When they arrived back at the Center, only a few cars dotted the parking lot. Demetri got out and walked Roman to his car. Roman unlocked his car, but instead of opening it, he leaned back against his door.

Demetri stuffed his hands into his pockets as he glanced around. He didn't seem nervous, more like he had something to say, and didn't know how to say it.

"I'd ask you back to my place," Roman said, "but I have a roommate, and I already know the answer will be no."

Demetri leaned against the car beside him and kicked at a bottle cap laying on the chipped white line. "If things were different..."

"But they're not." Then Roman admitted something he hadn't wanted to because it showed how invested he already was. "I checked with the art department to see if I could transfer out, but you're the only professor offering this class this semester. And when I tried to switch to a different class entirely, they were full, or I didn't have the right prerequisite."

Demetri glanced up, a sad smile softened his features. "One of the professors is taking an unexpected sabbatical. I imagine having to cancel her classes has added a bit of chaos to the schedule."

"If I didn't need the class for my minor, I would—"

"No. I wouldn't ask you to jeopardize your ability to graduate on time for..." Demetri gestured between the two of them as if he didn't know how to define their relationship.

"Dick?" Roman said, filling in the blank.

Demetri laughed but turned to him. "But it's more than that. Right?"

"Yeah." But they didn't have to define it. They only had to figure out a way to make it work if they both wanted it to. "There are no departmental rules about being friends, is there?"

"No." Demetri brightened, his smile now more genuine than guarded. "We can take things slow. If at the end of the semester, we want to see where things can go, then we can do that."

"Slow." Roman chuckled. "I think we surpassed slow that first night when you went down on your knees and sucked me off in the alley."

Demetri sucked in a breath. "Fuck. That's not helping. You're going to make me hard just thinking about it."

"I'm already hard."

Demetri glanced down. In a pair of athletic shorts, Roman had no way to hide what Demetri did to him. Demetri pushed off the car. "I'm going to go before I help you out with that."

Roman waited and watched while Demetri pulled away, adjusting himself before he got into his car. The whole drive home Roman tried to navigate the fine line between appropriate friendship and an inappropriate relationship.

A few months in the grand scheme of things wasn't all bad,

but he'd have the biggest case of blue balls by the end of it. He'd already jacked off more in the past week than he had since he'd first figured out how good it felt to come.

Back at his apartment after spending his drive manufacturing ways to engineer more alone time with Demetri, he glanced at Moses sitting on the couch. Judging from the stack of beer cans, the pizza box, and the empty chip bags, Moses hadn't moved from that cushion all day.

Roman plucked one of the earpieces away from Moses' head and said, "You need to disappear tomorrow night."

"What?" Moses did a double-take, then paused his game and tugged his headset down to his neck.

"I need the apartment tomorrow night."

Moses grinned. Chip crumbs fell from his shirt when he shifted to get a better look at Roman. "You and the professor going to get naked?"

"No. But I don't want him to see another student here and have you scare him off."

8

"You hungry?" Roman asked.

It was Sunday night, and Demetri walked Roman to his car at the Center after a long day at the community lot. Roman had spent his day making concrete forms for the sidewalk and a flat-top area where the kids would be able to play games like hopscotch and foursquare, as well as helping Grant and the boys build above-ground planters for gardening.

After painting a primer coat on the concrete walls, Demetri had tiny white flecks of overspray on his old T-shirt, in his hair, and on his face.

"Starved." Demetri glanced down at himself. "But I'm not dressed for anything fancier than a drive-through."

"I know a place where they don't care what you wear, and the food is… passable."

Demetri's brow went up. "Where?"

"You're going to have to follow me to find out."

"I'm supposed to be having dinner with my extended family tonight, but—"

Damn. Roman had forgotten about that. "Another night, then?"

"I'd rather have dinner with you."

"Won't they be mad you missed?"

Demetri shrugged. "They'll get over it."

Roman couldn't help the grin that broke out across his face. If he'd been going for cool and detached, he'd totally blown it. "Great. Follow me."

In his car, Roman waited for Demetri to fire off a text to let whoever know he had other plans. When Demetri gave him the thumbs up, he pulled out of the parking lot with Demetri on his tail.

He should have thought the whole dinner thing through a bit better. He wasn't even sure what he had back at the apartment. They may have to order out if he couldn't find anything to throw together.

Ten minutes later, they parked in front of his apartment block. Demetri smiled as he got out, locked his car, and met Roman on the sidewalk in front of the stairs. "Is this how you lure all your men back to your place? Promise them dinner?"

Roman chuckled. "You make it sound like I have a long string of men knocking on my door every night."

"Valid question."

Roman started up the stairs and glanced back to find Demetri a couple of steps behind. "The answer is no. I don't have a string of men knocking at my door. And it's not because I'm new in town."

"Then, why?"

At the door, Roman ushered Demetri in ahead of him, hoping like hell Moses hadn't left the apartment looking like a herd of beer-drinking, pizza-gobbling, weed-smoking wildebeest had run through it. He let out a relieved breath when the apartment appeared relatively intact.

"Excuse the apartment," Roman said as he continued past

Demetri and went into the kitchen to check the freezer for options. "My roommate is only marginally housetrained."

"Your place isn't so bad." Demetri gave the kitchen a quick scan. "I don't see any rats or roaches. I've seen plenty of college apartments that were closer to a biohazard than this one."

How many other college guys had Demetri hooked up with, despite how concerned he seemed to be about dating a student? Maybe it was all a show. Maybe Demetri did this all the time, like a new guy every semester kind of thing.

That light, flighty feeling he'd gotten in his gut when Demetri had said yes to dinner dropped with a nearly audible *thud*.

His thoughts must have shown on his face because Demetri quickly added, "Not that I see a lot of my students' apartments. Or any of them. What I'm trying to say is..." Demetri took a breath and blew it out again. "What I'm trying to say is I've never seen a student before."

Before sort of indicated he was seeing one *now*.

That goofy, feather-light feeling roared back, and Roman took Demetri's hips in his hand and backed him against the counter. Demetri's breath caught when Roman leaned close, loving that he had that effect on him. "Oh, yeah? What makes me so special?"

Demetri swallowed hard. "That's what I'm trying to figure out."

Any other time, any other man, and Roman would have taken their hand and led them back to his bedroom—especially when they looked up at him with unadulterated need and want in their eyes—and shown them exactly what made him so special. But, he wanted to respect Demetri's boundaries.

As much as Roman wanted a chance to get his hands and lips and teeth and tongue all over Demetri's body, he understood Demetri's concerns.

Demetri's nose wrinkled, and then he sniffed himself. "I reek. Maybe a drive-through would have been better."

"I'm a fan of the way you smell, but you can take a shower while I cook if you want to get some of the grime off. Tacos sound good to you?"

"Tacos always sound good."

"You'll want to use my bathroom. The guest bathroom in the hall is also attached to Moses' room, and I'm afraid if you go in there, you'll need a hazmat suit."

"That way?" Demetri pointed to the hall on the left.

"Yes. I'd show you the way, but I'm afraid if I get you in my bedroom, I won't let you out again."

SOMEWHERE DEEP DOWN, DEMETRI FOUND THE STRENGTH TO NOT invite Roman into the shower with him. Three and a half months. One semester. That's all he had to get through. If Roman were still interested then, they'd have plenty of time for dual showers and everything else that went along with them.

He didn't waste time washing up, even though he could have used the extra minutes to jack himself off so he could keep his hands to himself the rest of the night. But since his spank bank for the past week consisted of nothing but Roman, jacking off to him while in his apartment—in his shower—might push Demetri to do what he knew he shouldn't.

After all the grime rinsed down the drain, Demetri cut off the water and wrapped a towel around his waist, dreading the thought of having to put his dirty clothes back on after getting clean.

He stared at himself in the mirror. *What are you doing standing naked in your student's bathroom?*

A bathroom with pictures of Roman with several older men stuck to the frame around the mirror. Old friends? Old lovers?

He pushed that out of his mind. Roman's past relationships weren't any of his business.

He glanced into the bedroom. When he'd left to take his shower, he'd only closed the door to the bedroom and had left the door to the bathroom open. He walked out of the bathroom to find the dirty clothes he'd left on the floor were gone and, on the bed, lay a clean pair of sweatpants and a T-shirt.

Demetri turned on his heel and glanced into the bathroom. The way the bathroom was designed, he had a direct line of sight to the shower with the frosted shower curtain on the back wall.

Had Roman stood there and watched Demetri shower in silhouette?

"Down boy," Demetri said as his dick woke beneath the towel. That's the last thing he needed when all he had to wear was a pair of sweatpants.

He got dressed in Roman's borrowed clothes. The sweats were too big, and the short sleeves on the T-shirt went nearly to his elbows.

At least the shirt's long hem covered his semi.

He lifted the fabric to his nose and breathed in, the clean scent reminding him of Roman, making the situation beneath the sweats more immediate.

Maybe he should have jacked off in the shower after all.

The smell of ground beef and spices cooking met him as soon as he opened the bedroom door. He followed his nose to the kitchen and found Roman stirring and swaying his hips to some song he had playing through his earbuds.

He tapped Roman on the shoulder, and Roman plucked one of the buds out of his ear and turned, his grin going wide. He loved the way Roman's smile bunched up his cheeks and crinkled the skin around his eyes.

But what Demetri loved most about Roman's smile was how it made Demetri feel, like he was the beginning and end to Roman's world. That he made Roman's world brighter by existing. That all battles could be won. That all trials could be overcome.

"Thanks for the clothes. Even if they do make me feel like I'm ten years old and wearing my father's clothes."

Roman raked his eyes up and down Demetri's body. His smile turned smoldering and salacious. "When I look at you, I don't see a kid."

He should have let the thread of conversation stop there, but Demetri didn't always do what was best for him. "What do you see?"

Roman cut the heat on the burner and pushed the frying pan to the back of the stove. "I see a man who I want."

Shit. Demetri shouldn't have led him on like that. "*Roman...*"

Roman took a step back, and Demetri wanted to follow but didn't. "I know. You about ready to eat? The beef's cooked, and the shells are about to come out of the oven. All we need to do is put the condiments on the table."

Demetri could think of other things to do with that table, like bend Roman over it and—

Roman cleared his throat. "When your eyes get all smoky and half-lidded like that, it makes me want to ask you what you're thinking."

"For both of our sakes, I think I'll keep it to myself."

"Probably best," Roman said, though the way he said it, all sad and melancholy, made Demetri think that Roman didn't agree with the very words he'd said.

They each grabbed a beer from the fridge, served their plates, and sat down across from each other at the four-top table. Demetri loaded his tacos up with grated cheese, diced tomatoes, and sour cream and dug in.

They didn't talk much while they ate, each too hungry after a long day of work. The tightness had already started to settle into his shoulders from working the paint roller. At the rate his muscles were stiffening up, he'd be lucky to be able to lift his arms over his head in the morning.

Good thing you don't need to raise your hands above your waist to jack off.

No one has to know. You could have sex right now, and no one would ever find out.

Except *he* would know.

And even if he got past the havoc having sex with a student could wreak on his career, he still had to get past the whole HIV disclosure thing.

Fuck.

HIV wasn't something he could outrun. It would tag along with him for the rest of his life. It had gotten easier, day to day, living with his diagnosis, but the disclosures never got easier.

Neither did the rejection.

And the hell of it was, he *liked* Roman. Making whatever potential reaction Roman might have to the news even more consequential. It was one thing for some dude on the apps Demetri had never met to turn him down, but it was entirely different telling someone you had a connection with. The potential rejection was much more devastating.

"What's the matter?" Roman asked.

"Nothing."

"You still have a taco left, and you haven't touched your refried beans. I know I'm not a Cordon Bleu chef, but this isn't half bad, so what's eating you?"

Say it. I'm poz. Two words. Easy.

"I'm..." The words wouldn't come. They latched onto his

tongue with tiny barbed hooks he couldn't dislodge. "I'm wondering when your roommate is due back."

"Liar." Roman dropped half a half-eaten taco onto his plate and carefully wiped his mouth. "Wanna try again?"

"Do you always date older guys?"

Roman barked out a laugh, tossing his napkin on his plate. "Okay. You don't have to tell me."

Demetri sent him an apologetic smile. "Thanks."

Roman picked at his taco shell and broke off a corner and chomped it between his molars. "You really want to know the answer to that question?"

The question had been asked as a diversion, but Demetri did want to know the answer. "If you don't mind."

"Yes." Roman met his eyes and didn't look away, as if he wanted to see every nuance of Demetri's reaction. He'd have to disappoint Roman because, in the grand scheme of things, the age thing didn't bother Demetri one bit.

"Daddy issues?" Demetri was only half kidding.

"Some people say I have an old soul. I seem to relate better to people older than me." Roman shrugged. "But truthfully, I do have some abandonment issues playing a part, but not in the way you might think. My father didn't reject me... But let's say it taught me that one of the most important things in this life is honesty."

Demetri picked up the taco he'd laid down and started eating again, not wanting Roman to feel self-conscious that Demetri focused all of his attention on him.

Filling the void in conversation, Roman continued, "Don't worry, I'm not going to make you promise never to leave me."

Demetri choked and chuckled. "No?"

"This is only our second date. I usually save that for the third."

Demetri swallowed. "This isn't a date."

"Great. Then there isn't an issue." He stood and placed his plate next to the sink.

"I'll get the dishes. Why don't you get a shower while I clean up?"

"That mean you're going to be here when I get back?"

Demetri brought his plate to the sink as well, snagging the front of Roman's shirt and pulling him in for a brief kiss. He tasted of beer and ground beef and the forbidden. Fuck.

That kiss wasn't even close to enough.

"I'm not going anywhere."

Before Roman returned from his shower, Demetri finished with the dishes and walked to Roman's bedroom door, his hand on the knob before he stopped himself.

He rested his forehead on the door, the exhaustion of the day catching up with him. He knew if he opened that door, he wouldn't stop until he had Roman beneath him. And without a disclosure, that couldn't happen.

You're undetectable. You're untransmittable. You wouldn't be putting his health in danger.

Yet Demetri had made that promise to himself.

The same way you promised yourself you'd never get involved with a student?

Jesusfuckingchrist.

Demetri thumped his forehead on the door. One. Twice. Trying to knock some sense into himself before he got himself into insurmountable trouble.

"Come in."

Demetri turned the knob, even though that hadn't been his intention. The door opened in his hand, and Roman stood there in a pair of athletic shorts, his chest still dotted with drops of water. "Um... I... Dishes are done."

Roman opened the door wider and stepped back, a clear invitation.

For a college professor, Demetri was remarkably short on words. "I could turn the television on." He sounded like an idiot. Maybe he should grab his things and leave. "Or I could go."

"I threw your clothes in the wash, so unless you want to go home in my clothes or naked, you're going to have to wait."

"You washed my clothes?"

"Like dinner, it's all part of the evil plan when I lure unsuspecting men back to my place. Stealing their clothes makes it nearly impossible for them to leave."

"Tricky."

Roman took Demetri's hand, and his heart spun up, the acceleration making his head spin. If Roman pulled him into the bedroom, he wouldn't fight it. Instead, Roman led him back into the living room, killing the overhead lights as he went.

With the kitchen lights on, they had ample light. Roman sat, and when Demetri went for the opposite end of the couch, Roman pulled him onto the cushion beside him. "I'm not going to bite. No promises about licking, kissing, and sucking, though."

That should have been Demetri's clue to leave, but he couldn't make his feet move toward the door.

He settled beside Roman, their thighs touching hip to knee. Roman clicked on the television and started searching. "Star Trek?"

"Original or Next Generation?"

"Original," Roman said, "I'm old school."

Demetri shook his head. "Next Generation is where it's at, but I can deal."

Roman blindly chose an episode. After all, it wasn't about the show, now was it?

They hadn't even made it through the opening credits when Roman tugged on Demetri's hand and patted his thigh. "Come here, old man. You're about to fall asleep sitting up."

"Old man, my ass." Demetri followed Roman's guiding hand and laid out on the couch, his feet stuffed into the crack by the opposite armrest, his head in Roman's lap.

He snuggled in, as Roman's hand absently went to Demetri's head and started lightly scratching.

Demetri groaned. "That feels good."

Roman laughed. "If you think that feels good, you should see what I can do with my tongue."

9

Demetri rolled to his back and looked up at Roman. Roman knew better than to bait Demetri. He was lucky that Demetri had accepted his offer for dinner. He shouldn't push it. He knew how Demetri felt about a relationship with a student, and if he didn't back the fuck off, he'd risk Demetri running.

Roman brushed the damp hair off Demetri's forehead. "I shouldn't have said that. My dick gets ahead of my brain sometimes."

"And you don't think mine does?" Demetri took Roman's hand and laid it on top of his hard cock. "I've been walking around like this for more than a week. I wouldn't be here, questioning my sanity if my brain wasn't lagging so far behind it might never catch up."

Roman stroked Demetri through the thin cotton of the old borrowed sweatpants. "Christ, I want that dick."

Demetri sat up and straddled Roman's lap, pulling Roman's shirt off over his head and tossing it away. Then he stopped, his breaths coming quick. "Tell me to go home. Tell me I'm making a big mistake."

"I can't tell you no. But I also won't tell anyone. It should go without saying, but I want to make that clear. No one is going to find out."

He tugged on the hem of Demetri's shirt, and when Demetri nodded, Roman stripped it off him. He ran his hands down Demetri's chest, through the smattering of short-cropped hair there, his fingers skimming over the ridges of his ribs.

"You shave your chest?" Roman liked the roughness and the thought of watching Demetri take a shaver to his body.

"Greek heritage," Demetri said. "I haven't learned to embrace all the hair yet."

Demetri scooched closer. Their hard cocks lined up beneath their clothes, effectively shutting down that train of thought as Roman bucked his hips, grinding against Demetri. Their lips met. Roman opened immediately, wanting to devour, but holding back. He didn't want to overwhelm Demetri with his intensity.

Demetri must have sensed it because he broke the kiss and said, "I'm not fragile or afraid. I want this as much as you do."

"What about school?" Roman hated to bring it up, but one of them needed to be the voice of reason. He'd hate for Demetri to resent him for pushing too hard, too fast.

"Shut up."

And to make sure Roman did just that, Demetri covered Roman's mouth with his and slipped a hand beneath Roman's shorts. The groan that crawled up the back of Roman's throat escaped, egging Demetri on.

Precum welled at Roman's slit, and Demetri slicked it up and down his shaft. Roman hooked his thumbs into the waistband of his shorts and shoved them to mid-thigh. He hadn't bothered with underwear, so they didn't get in the way.

"When I got out of the shower and saw the clothes you'd laid out..." Demetri worked Roman with practiced ease. "How long did you stand there watching me shower?"

The heat rose in Roman's cheeks. With his darker complexion, most people never noticed unless they knew him well.

Sitting back, Demetri turned on the lamp on the end table and scrutinized Roman's face. Demetri's eyes lit. "You're fucking adorable when you blush."

Unless that person had an eye for detail, for subtle colors and shades the way an artist would.

Roman ran his hands down Demetri's back and cupped his beautiful, tight ass and snugged him tighter against him. "Long enough to get an eyeful, but not long enough to get my fill."

Demetri kissed him again, his tongue stroking in and out of his mouth in concert with his hand on Roman's dick, making Roman's synapses misfire, nearly stealing his ability to think. Demetri broke the kiss long enough for Roman to say, "What would you have done if you'd known?"

Demetri stilled and met Roman's eyes. "I'm not sure. *Then*, I might have run."

Roman dragged a finger up the crack of Demetri's marvelous ass, loving the way the man shuddered at this touch. "And now?"

"I don't want to run. Not away anyway. But, fuck, this is getting way more complicated than I ever thought it would."

Which sounded a lot like regret. Already.

"Would you have sucked me off in that alley if you'd known what was to come?"

"Honestly, I don't know."

At least Demetri didn't hide his ambivalence, and Roman appreciated that they could talk about it. Even if it was a bit of a boner killer.

"But I did," Demetri said.

"And here we are with my dick in your hand again."

"So it seems." Demetri grinned. "A very nice dick. Thick and long and tasty."

Demetri started kissing his way down Roman's neck. Roman

let his head fall back and allowed himself to feel. Demetri's words were all laced with an undercurrent of caution that Roman completely understood.

But his hands...

His mouth...

His kisses...

His tongue... completely contradicted Demetri's words.

His touch was bold, his mouth devouring, his kisses hungry, his tongue teasing, giving every indication that Demetri's heart and his head had disconnected.

Roman did the only thing he could, he blocked out the words and let his body listen to what Demetri's body told his— that he was wanted.

But for how long?

Even as that question surfaced, Demetri shifted, going to his knees on the floor where his talented tongue worked its magic on Roman's dick. The sensation Roman's mind blank out, only allowing for sensory input.

Roman's hand fisted in Demetri's hair as Demetri worked Roman's dick from balls to tip and back again. He turned his concentration to Roman's sensitive tip, Demetri's wet, warm tongue working its way across the ridge as his hand reached down and cupped Roman's balls, a finger reaching back and grazing his taint.

"*Fuuuck.*" Roman's hips thrust, driving himself deep to the back of Demetri's throat, the groan he pulled from Demetri making his balls draw up and the base of his spine tingle.

Horny all week, he was in no shape to last. Roman shoved his shorts down his legs and sank lower on the couch, spreading his legs wider for easier access. Demetri kept up the exquisite torment, taking him so impossibly deep that he didn't know how Demetri didn't gag.

As much as he enjoyed a mind-numbing blowjob, he

couldn't wait to repay the favor. Demetri had had his mouth on Roman twice, and he'd done nothing more than cupped Demetri through his clothes and ground up against him.

It wasn't enough. Not nearly. He wanted to taste him. To suck him. To fuck him.

But before he could pull Demetri off him, the first blinding pulses of his orgasm hit. His head dropped to the back of the couch, his hips working, his hands behind Demetri's head, encouraging.

That finger working his taint slipped back, grazing his hole.

He lost it.

Demetri chuckled, knowing full damn well what he'd done. The vibrations from Demetri's laughter rushed down Roman's dick, and he came with a roar, his fingers and toes tingling, his heart crashing like a tsunami against his ribs.

He didn't let a drop of cum go to waste before he pulled off, his hands lightly encircling Roman's softening dick, gently guiding him back to earth.

"Com'ere," Roman grumbled when he'd found enough oxygen to make his lungs function again.

Getting off his knees, Demetri straddled Roman. Roman's hands went to Demetri's ass as if his hands were magnets, and Demetri's ass was steel. "I want that hole. I want my dick in—"

Demetri stilled. "I want that more than anything. It's... I need... What I'm trying to say is..."

He stumbled over his words worse than Moses did after a bender. But Demetri's expression wasn't that blissed-out, red-eyed, slack-faced expression that comes with someone who'd imbibed too much.

Roman wouldn't describe Demetri's expression as *distraught*, but the emotion had to be related, like its younger, slightly less intense cousin.

The front doorknob jiggled, and Demetri jumped off

Roman's lap, the coffee table tripping him up. He landed on it with a jolt.

Roman yanked up his shorts as Moses stumbled into the apartment two fucking hours early.

Moses stopped short as if surprised to find Roman there. Moses' heavy-lidded eyes fell on Demetri—high or drunk. Or both. Roman couldn't tell any more.

"'Zis the prof—professor?"

"Mo, what the actual fuck are you doing here?"

Demetri scoured around, searching for his shirt, finally finding it on top of the lampshade on the other end of the couch.

"I live 'ere?" It came out as a question as if Moses didn't know for certain.

"You were supposed to disappear until midnight."

"It's not?" Moses came into the living room, leaving the front door wide-ass open.

Roman scrubbed his hand down his face. He had to rethink his roommate situation. "No, man. It's fucking not."

In the few seconds it took for Roman to close the door and turn around, Moses had managed to cross the room to Demetri without falling on his face. He stepped in close, and Demetri had to take a step back.

"Hey," Moses waggled his finger at Demetri. "Is this the professor?"

"I'm sorry," Roman said to Demetri as he took Moses by the shoulder and steered him toward his roommate's side of the apartment.

"He's fucking hot. Why aren't my professors hot?"

Drunk and high Moses had no volume control. It was set on blast, and if every neighbor in the complex hadn't heard, it was because they weren't home. "Wanna three-way?"

"No," Roman said, though it was just a guess. He and

Demetri had a chance to discuss things like monogamy or inviting special guest stars into their sex lives.

That's because you aren't even supposed to be seeing each other. How can you have a conversation about openness or exclusivity when you aren't supposed to be together?

Roman opened Moses' door and pushed him inside, admonishing him to stay there before closing the door behind him.

He got three steps down the hall before Moses opened the door and said, "Tell him I have a friend who could join us. We could—"

Roman spun on his heel and got in his friend's face, his voice more of a growl when he said, "So help me, Mo, if you don't get your ass back in there..."

He let the rest of the threat drop. The murder must have been clear in his eyes even with Moses blitzed out of his mind because Moses backed into his bedroom and quietly closed the door.

Roman hoped like hell that Demetri hadn't left while he had his back turned.

In the living room, Roman found Demetri dressed and leaning against the back of the couch, his arms braced on either side of him, his head dropped between his shoulders.

If Wikipedia needed a picture of inner turmoil and conflict, Roman could snap a quick picture and upload it for them.

Was Roman being selfish, unfair? Would it be more considerate to agree not to see each other again?

Something in his chest pinched, and he winced.

That would hurt like hell.

But it would hurt a hell of a lot less than letting him go later.

"I'm sorry," Roman said as he entered the room.

Demetri's head popped up, and a sad smile ghosted across his lips. "Not your fault."

Sure as shit felt like it was.

Roman leaned against the couch beside him, then took Demetri's hand and pulled him between his legs, his hands linking behind Demetri's waist. Their foreheads came together, and they stood there, breathing each other in. And damn if even that most innocent of touches didn't have Roman's cock starting to rouse and press against Demetri.

Demetri lightly pressed his hips into Roman's. A dark, rueful chuckle rumbled out of Demetri's throat. "I guess youth has its advantages."

"We need to talk," Roman said. "And not about hard-ons."

Demetri glanced up. "What's there to say? We both know this can't end well. If one person talks, if—"

"Moses is so baked he's not even going to remember this tomorrow."

"*This* time. But what about the next time, or the one after that?"

A question popped into Roman's head. It made his throat tight at the thought of voicing it. "You want to quit us then?"

Us? Do two blowjobs make an 'us'?

Demetri met Roman's eyes. Roman hoped his didn't shine with the stupid-ass tears that wanted to gather there. "I don't know what I want."

A mix of emotions swirled in Demetri's eyes. Uncertainty. Fear. Ambivalence. Attraction. Lust. So many, that Roman feared they'd swamp Demetri.

To break the vortex, Roman said, "How about I return the favor?"

Demetri huffed out a laugh, though humor only licked at the edges. "As much as it pains me to say this, I think I have to pass."

"You've sucked me off twice. I haven't even—"

"I'm not keeping score. I did what I wanted to do." The conviction in Demetri's voice rang true, but something else lingered there.

Something untold.

More of Demetri's apprehension about getting caught with his hands down Roman's pants?

Or was it something else?

Roman gave Demetri a little shake. "What aren't you telling me?"

Demetri deflected the question. "I thought you didn't make demands of people until the third date."

If Demetri wanted to pivot, Roman would let him. For now. "Third date, yes. But there is a sub-clause attached to the second blowjob."

A semblance of a smile almost reached Demetri's eyes. "You never said anything about a sub-clause."

"Fine print."

"Maybe you should have been a lawyer." Demetri cupped Roman's cheek and pressed a kiss to his lips before stepping out of Roman's arms.

Roman could have held him in place, but forcing someone to stay when they wanted to leave was never the answer.

Only a step away, but those inches felt cold and miles long.

"I like breaking the rules too much to be a lawyer," Roman said.

"I should go." But it sounded more like Demetri said, *ask me to stay.*

But they both needed some space to figure this out. "We'll talk tomorrow."

Roman walked Demetri to the door and saw him out, standing on the second-floor landing and watching until Demetri drove away, leaving Roman with the nagging feeling that there was something Demetri was hiding.

10

For the rest of the night, Demetri divided his time between staring at his messaging app. His thumbs hovered over the keyboard while he tried to come up with the words to tell Roman about his HIV status. At the same time, he tried to convince himself that there was no reason to disclose if he had no intention of seeing Roman again.

Not when the risks of disclosing were astronomically high.

You really think you can break it off? You've got a raging case of blue balls that begs to differ.

He wanted to be pissed at Moses for interrupting them. Then again, he wanted to kiss Moses' drunk ass for saving him from doing something stupid.

But most of all, he wanted to tell Roman the truth.

Demetri: *You're an asshole.*

Three little dots appeared, then disappeared, then reappeared again before the return text came through.

Niko: *Usually, people wait until after five in the morning to tell me that.*

Shit. Was it that early? Demetri rolled out of bed, the grit in his eyes made his lids scrape across his corneas, and the stiffness in his shoulders made him groan.

The mild soreness in his jaw an erotic reminder of taking Roman to the back of his throat.

His morning wood got impossibly harder. He went to brush his teeth, and his phone buzzed in his hand.

Niko: *Okay. I'll bite. Why am I an asshole?*

Demetri: *You said I shouldn't tell him.*

Demetri didn't have to explain who *him* was.

Niko: *And?*

Demetri: *He has this thing about honesty.*

Niko: *You haven't lied. Unless he asked your status, and you denied it.*

Demetri: *I wouldn't do that.*

Niko: *Then, I don't see the problem.*

And maybe that wasn't the problem. If Demetri didn't see him anymore...

That's not going to happen. Roman's already under your skin.

Meaning it wasn't a matter of *if* he was going to tell Roman, it was a matter of *how* and *when*.

And telling Roman with a text wasn't the way to do it. Demetri leaned on the counter and stared at himself in the mirror, his hair all disheveled from a sleepless night.

And then Roman will leave.

Demetri: *I should tell him before I'm more invested. Before it rips my heart out when he runs.*

Niko: *Don't be an idiot.*

That was the great thing about Niko... undying support. Before Demetri could reply, Niko texted back.

Niko: *The more he gets to know you, the more he'll have to think twice about walking away. You're a good man, Dem. You deserve to find love.*

Demetri's throat tightened as he pocketed the phone, glad

that he didn't have to face Niko in person right then. The 'idiot' was a lot easier to take than the affirmation.

Compliments had never been Niko's strong suit.

Until he'd found Vin.

Now Niko thought he was the expert on everyone else's love life and relationships.

Demetri: *Maybe I should break it off.*

His cell rang, and he almost didn't pick up when Niko's name flashed across the screen. "What?"

"What I have to say is too long to type," Niko said. "Get your head out of your ass. Are you going to break off something good before it gets started because you're afraid of rejection?"

"I—"

"That's asinine. You break it off, you lose him. You tell him— and when I say *you tell him* I'm saying you tell him way the fuck later—then you have a chance it could all work out. Don't let your fear of rejection make you sabotage your relationship."

What Demetri had to say would hurt to admit out loud. "Maybe you're right."

"I am. Look, I have to go. Hang in there and call your mother, she missed you last night."

He should have texted his mother instead of Niko when he'd canceled, but he hadn't wanted to fend off his mother's probing questions. "Yeah. Thanks, I will."

Demetri's front door opened and closed, and a heavy toolbox thunked down on the tiles in the entryway. He'd given Joss a key at the start of the renovation. Demetri knew that Joss's ability to work depended on the schedule of his skydiving business and that he'd be coming and going at unorthodox times.

Luckily for Demetri and his bathroom, the winds still blew too strong and consistent for Joss to take any clients up.

Demetri showered and dressed. He might as well head to his office early and get a few things done before classes started.

He peeked in on Joss, already at work in the bathroom, stripping the old broken tiles off the wall and preparing to go down to the studs. Joss would probably have to saw the old tub in half to get it through the door.

"Making progress," Demetri said.

Joss was standing in the tub, the pry bar stilled in his hand when he glanced over his shoulder. "What the hell happened to you?"

"Nothing happened."

"Right," Joss said as he went back to work. Some of the old tiles popped off with minimal effort. Others required a little more persuasion. "The last time I saw someone looking that rough was at a bachelor party in Vegas."

"I had one beer and no sleep."

"Everything okay?"

"Can I ask you a personal question?"

"You can always ask." Though the way he said it, Joss might not answer.

But Demetri needed another perspective, someone who might help him get his head on straight.

"When you date, do you tell people you're a widower upfront, or do you let men get to know you a bit first?"

Joss tossed his pry bar in a five-gallon bucket and gave Demetri his full attention. "It's a fine line. You disclose too early, and they think you're still hung up on them. You disclose too late, and they get butt-hurt that you didn't tell them something so important from the start. Honestly, I can't win." Joss smiled, but it looked bittersweet. "That help?"

Demetri shook his head. "Not a bit."

"Bottom line, Dan's death is something I'm going to have to live with and deal with for the rest of my life. I've learned some people can't handle the truth. But what they don't understand is that life is complicated and messy and ugly and a beautiful gift all at the same time. All anyone is trying to do is make it to the next day the best way they know how. In my book, that's all anyone can ask of you."

"That's sweet."

Joss huffed out a laugh. "Yeah, well, Vin taught me that. He also taught me I could love again. But I'm not looking."

Demetri and Joss said their goodbyes, and Demetri headed off to the college, still unsure of what he planned on doing about Roman. But after the talk with Joss, the possibilities didn't seem so dark.

There had to be a path he could navigate their budding relationship through if he searched hard enough.

As he climbed into his car, the wind nearly stole his door out of his hand. But the sun shined bright like it always did in the valley, giving him hope.

While he drove, his phone vibrated with an incoming email. He waited until he parked on campus and pulled his leather briefcase out of the backseat before checking it.

His stomach plummeted.

A department-wide email from Michael Pittman, the head of the art department, concerning a mandatory meeting that afternoon to address rumors of a student-teacher affair.

In the teacher's lounge down the hall from his office, Demetri poured himself a cup of much-needed coffee. His hand holding the pot shook, and he had to set his cup on the counter to keep from splashing hot coffee on his fingers.

Taking his mug back to the office, he locked the door behind him. He opened his blinds, but the far-off, hazy view over to the San Gabriel mountains didn't fill him with the same sense of peace that it normally did.

Come five o'clock that afternoon, that space may no longer be his office.

He took a sip of his coffee, forgetting to blow on it. It scalded a trail down to his stomach where the crosscurrents of bubbling acid sloshed it around until it nearly came back up.

Maybe he should get in front of the problem. He could go by Dean Pittman's office early. He didn't want to wait until the end of the day and sit through the revelation and humiliation in front of his colleagues. Besides, who wanted to wait around for the death knell?

A thump came from the office next door. Had Lydia gone to the dean and told him what Demetri had confided about Roman?

Demetri hadn't said anything to anyone else besides Niko, and he'd have no reason to tell *anyone*, much less his dean.

And the email had come way too early for him to suspect that Roman's roommate had somehow made a report. Chances were the kid was still sleeping it off.

Stepping into the hall, he worked his head from side to side, easing the tension in his neck before knocking on Lydia's door.

"Come in."

Play it cool.

He stuck his head in as if he were on his way somewhere else and had only popped in to ask a quick question. "I thought you started your sabbatical already?"

"I forgot a few things." She glanced up from the desk drawer she was scrounging through. "Don't stand out in the hall, come on in."

"I've got a thing. I can't stay," Demetri said cryptically. "I just wondered if you knew anything about the meeting Pittman called this afternoon?"

"What meeting?"

"I don't know. Something about a teacher-student affair. He

sent it out this morning." He tried for a carefree, casual tone, but the tension in his voice made it come out weird.

Lydia stopped what she was doing and closed the drawer. "Demetri, what you told me, I've held in the strictest confidence. If this meeting has to do with you, it didn't come from me."

That hadn't been what he'd asked, but it had been what he needed to hear. He felt relieved and more nervous at the same time. If Lydia hadn't said anything, then who had?

His gaze fell to the floor, and when he glanced back up, Lydia stood in front of him. "If you need an ear, I—"

"Thanks. I'll keep that in mind. If you'll excuse me, I think I'll try to find Pittman."

"Good luck," she said, with one of those sympathetic faces that somehow also said, *you're going to need it.*

Demetri's heart rate and blood pressure ramped up. His pulse pounded at his temples while his stomach sank so low he almost tripped over it on the way to the dean's office.

Claudia, Pittman's secretary, since way before the Mesozoic era, sat behind her desk. She was slight and silver-haired, but you didn't want to let her diminutive size and grandmotherly look fool you. She was an old battle-ax. And from some of the rumors going around, may have personally responsible for the dinosaurs' demise.

"You're looking nice this morning, Claudia—"

"If you've come here to see Dean Pittman, you're wasting your time. He's booked solid with meetings all day."

"But if I could have a quick word, it won't take more than a minute or two." If that. How long would it take Pittman to tell him he's fired?

She stared over the rims of her readers perched on the end of her nose. "I can put you down for tomorrow afternoon."

"I'm afraid that will be too late."

"Then I'm sorry, I can't help you." She didn't look sorry. She looked apathetic.

He didn't dare storm the dean's door the way they do in all the movies. She had to hide that battle-ax somewhere. She probably had it strapped to her back to keep it within easy reach.

Then Pittman strode through his inner office door, buttoning his suit coat. Claudia cut Demetri a *don't you dare* look, but Demetri took advantage of his one chance.

"Dean Pittman, if I could have a minute."

A good head taller than Demetri, Pittman was the tallest man with a Napoleon complex that Demetri had ever known.

"I don't have time. Claudia can put you on the schedule." Pittman kept walking past Demetri, headed for the hall. He stopped short when Demetri fell into step beside him.

"I wanted to talk to you about the meeting this afternoon."

Pittman looked him up and down. The disapproval sat on his face as permanent as a birthmark. It was no secret Pittman didn't like Demetri, and he couldn't tell if those rheumy eyes held more contempt than usual.

Demetri wasn't quick to blame Pittman's animus on homophobia because there were others in the department who Pittman had developed a profound dislike for as well, and they were straight.

And the only reason he could think that Pittman didn't ream him out right there in the hall for his indiscretion was that Pittman preferred to humiliate people when he had an audience.

"If I'd wanted to talk to everyone individually, I wouldn't have called a meeting. Now, if you'll excuse me."

Pittman didn't wait for Demetri's response before walking away, leaving Demetri to stew in his turmoil.

Roman walked into his art class, laughing and joking with Emily. Being new in town, he appreciated meeting a new friend who seemed to get him and have the same sense of humor and dirty mind. They'd had similar backgrounds with conservative families, and they'd both enjoyed exploring their newfound sex lives now that they lived on their own.

Scoping out guys together made it that much more fun.

"I'm telling you," Emily said as she took her seat next to him, "this guy had the most magnificent di—" Emily caught Demetri's stormy expression. "Whoa, professor, you look…"

She let the sentence trail off as Demetri's scowl deepened. She leaned into Roman and grumbled low enough that only he could hear. "I think teacher needs a nice blowy to put a smile on his beautiful face."

She glanced at Demetri. His back was turned to them as he put something on the whiteboard. "I mean, I'd do it, but I don't think it's me he wants."

Roman elbowed her to shut her up. They still had five minutes before class started, and only about a third of the students had made it in so far, but he knew how private Demetri was, and he didn't want to take a chance anyone would overhear even if Emily were just joking around.

She narrowed her eyes at Roman, the *WTF* unspoken. She couldn't know what had happened between him and Demetri, but she'd been at the community lot. She had eyes. And she hadn't been slow to connect the dots.

A couple of his classmates came in, two girls chatting animatedly about something. He didn't pay much attention. He was too focused on getting his notebook out of his backpack while trying not looking like he was staring at Demetri's biteable ass.

"…all I'm saying," one of the girls said, Cheryl, he thought her name was, "is if you're going to fuck your professor, you should—"

Demetri spun around, and Cheryl didn't finish her sentence. When Demetri turned away again, Cheryl poked Roman and mouthed, "What's with him?"

"How am I supposed to know?" Roman whispered. What the hell was going on? Had someone found out about him and Demetri? "What are you guys talking about?"

Rita, the girl Cheryl had been talking to, piped in, "A professor's getting fired." She rolled her eyes. Roman's mother would have knocked that eye roll out of him if he'd done that to her. "Couldn't keep it in his pants."

Even though Roman hadn't had time for lunch before class, his stomach still soured. He didn't want to ask, but he had to. "Who?"

Rita shrugged her shoulders.

Cheryl said, "I don't know. All I heard was there was some sort of department meeting after classes this afternoon."

The students finished filing in, and Demetri started his lecture at the front of the class, giving some sort of instructions for their next project. Roman didn't hear a word.

Had he gotten Demetri fired?

Demetri must have finished because he walked to the back of the class, leaving the live model on the dais. The rest of the students weaved around Roman on the way to their art lockers to get whatever they were supposed to get.

He sat there in his seat, feeling Demetri's eyes on his back. Should he turn and look, or would that make it worse?

Emily sat back down beside him, placing a new twelve-by-twelve canvas on her easel. "Aren't you going to get your stuff?"

"What? Uh... yeah. I was waiting for the crowd to die down."

He took quick stock of the supplies his classmates had gathered and went to get his own. On his way back to his chair, he chanced a look at the back of the room, but as soon as his eyes met Demetri's, Demetri looked away.

Shit. Did Demetri blame Roman?

He started to walk toward Demetri, but Demetri's head popped up, and he gave Roman the most imperceptible shake of his head. Roman detoured to his art locker.

He doesn't want to talk to you. This is your fault. You shouldn't have invited him over for dinner. You should have taken his concerns to heart.

Roman dropped down in his seat and tossed the rest of his supplies at his feet. He wrapped his head in his hands and took a couple of deep breaths trying to swallow down the excess saliva pooling in his mouth before his nausea got worse, and he had to make a mad dash for the men's room.

Emily leaned in, her hand on his back and whispered, "What's wrong with you?"

He snuck a glance at the back of the room. Demetri didn't notice, his attention on his computer screen.

"What?" Emily followed Roman's gaze. Her eyes going wide as she mouthed, "You and..." She jerked her head toward the back of the class.

He didn't have to confirm her suspicion. He assumed his guilt was an easy read. Demetri had said he could get fired, but the stupid part of Roman, the *horny part of Roman*, hadn't taken the concern overly seriously. He knew that professors had affairs and got caught, but that was *those* people. That wasn't him. That wasn't Demetri.

Only now, it probably was.

Class ended, and everyone put their supplies away. Roman remained in his seat, his canvas untouched, his paints unopened.

Emily shouldered her backpack. "You coming?"

"No. I—" Fuck, he didn't know what he was going to do. "I'll see you in class tomorrow, yeah?"

"Sure. It's my turn to bring the coffee."

He nodded, though at this point, who brought coffee was his least concern.

"Mr. Reed," Demetri called from the back of the room after the model and the last student had left, the words cold, formal, *dismissive.* "I believe class is over."

Roman snagged his backpack off the floor. The backpack with the grocery store bag stuffed with Demetri's clean clothes from the night before. Maybe if Roman told the dean he'd been the one to pressure Demetri into seeing him, he wouldn't lose his job.

Roman stopped in front of Demetri's desk, his finger tapping on the top. "Will you look at me?"

"I'm a little busy." Demetri refused to glance up from his screen as he typed away. "You can set up office hours online if you need to talk—"

"Fuck that."

Demetri didn't owe Roman much, but he owed him the decency of looking at him. Roman unzipped his backpack and dropped the baggie of clothes on Demetri's desk. "You left these last night."

Demetri glanced around the classroom, his eyes furtive as if Roman had thrown a kilo of cocaine on his desk and not a bag of clothes. He snatched them off his desk and tossed the bag into his bottom drawer, kicking it closed with his foot.

"We'll find a way to fix this," Roman said.

Demetri huffed out a rueful laugh. "There's no fixing something like this."

"I'm an adult. What we did was consensual. I'm not some snot-nosed kid fresh out of high school with stars in their eyes.

You didn't take advantage of me. I don't understand how this is a problem."

"The college has rules. I was stupid enough to lose sight of that." Demetri laid his hands on his keyboard again, his eyes returning to his screen. The only outward sign that he wasn't as cool and composed as he looked was the muscle jumping at the corner of his jaw and the deep furrow between his brows.

"For what it's worth, I'm sorry."

11

Demetri didn't accept Roman's apology. Instead, he sat there at a loss for words.

"So that's how it's going to be? Radio silence?" The anger seeped into Roman's expression.

It was better this way. If Roman were angry, then he'd stay away. "I think you should go."

"Fuck you."

Roman left. Without looking back, he yanked on the classroom door. It slammed against the wall, the crack echoing throughout the classroom before the door slammed closed.

Fuck.

Now who's the asshole? Roman didn't deserve the way you treated him. You are as responsible as he is for what happened between you two. Scratch that. More responsible.

Demetri laid his elbows on his desk and held his head in his hands, staring down at the scarred metal surface. All those years teaching at Winston college down the drain for what? Sucking a guy off?

And Demetri hadn't even come.

Unless you call all the jacking off he'd done at home with Roman at the center of his fantasies.

Demetri didn't know how he'd pivot from this. How do you recover when you have destroyed your good name? No other university or college would hire him. And the local high schools wouldn't even go so far as to read his résumé.

His art sold, but not well enough to pay his mortgage.

Too bad Niko only used straight guys to shoot his gay porn.

The calendar notice on his phone binged, reminding him the dean's meeting was in ten minutes. He stood and glanced around the room at the array of easels and the supplies Roman hadn't put away. Demetri loved this room even if it was windowless and in the bowels of the building.

Would this be the last time he saw his room?

Would he be escorted to his office after the meeting by security to get his things?

Jesus Christ. What had he done?

The long walk to the conference room on the second floor of the art building felt like a convicted killer's final walk down dingy corridors to the execution chamber.

He slipped into the half-filled classroom and found a spot at the back. If he were smart, he would have found a place near the front so that he could make an easy escape after all the humiliation Pittman would deal him ended.

The room filled, and sweat beaded on his brow and dripped down the length of his spine, his dick so shriveled he'd need a microscope and a pair of tweezers if he ever hoped to find it again.

Voices buzzed in the room, a quiet cacophony of intrigue and excitement. Nothing this scandalous had hit the art department in his memory. If this were the theater department, it would have been just another day. Or the science department. Turns out those science nerds were kind of kinky.

Pittman came in and nodded his head for the person closest to the door to close it since he was too important to do it himself as he came through.

He mounted the podium and stood at a lectern, an expression on his face that Demetri couldn't quite read. Somewhere between barely contained excitement and glee, as if Pittman couldn't wait to deliver the news.

Demetri's colleagues quieted. Pittman always refused to use a mic, but he had one of those voices that carried.

"These are unfortunate circumstances," Pittman said, his grip tight on the lectern. "One that brings embarrassment to the department and to our sacred home here at Winston College."

"If I could say something first," Demetri raised his hand, trying in vain, it would seem, to minimize the public scalding he was about to receive.

"You'll have a chance to speak at the end." Pittman glanced around the room. "And I would appreciate it if the rest of you will hold your questions until then."

Demetri sank lower into his seat and dried his sweaty, clammy palms on his pants legs.

"Following rumors of impropriety, I spoke with Professor Chadwick, and to minimize embarrassing the department, he has agreed to step down as the art department chair and render his resignation after confirming to me that the rumors of an affair with a freshman student of his were true."

In the middle of the room, Sampson, who taught sculpture and pottery, laughed. "Mr. Rogers' doppelganger? Are you kidding me? He's, like, ninety."

Chadwick, the art history professor, was so old that people joked the historical artists were his contemporaries. And Chadwick's likeness to a certain children's show host from the late sixties was uncanny. Apparently, there were unplumbed depths beneath that button-up sweater that no one had been privy to, except an unsuspecting coed.

"That Viagra prescription must be working well for him," someone muttered.

Light laughter rolled around the room. Pittman's scowl deepened, and his complexion turned ruddy.

Pittman started talking again, but Demetri couldn't hear over the buzzing in his ears. It sounded as if a hive of industrious bees had taken up shop. Had his heart stopped? Or would the relief washing over him make him pass out?

The nausea that had been rooting around in his belly all day intensified instead of eased.

He dashed out of the classroom, the door to the men's room slapped against the rubber stop as he crashed through and entered the first available stall. He leaned over the toilet and emptied everything in his stomach. Someone in the next stall over coughed, then flushed, leaving Demetri to his misery.

Demetri leaned against the stall wall until the heaves passed. He could practically feel the whoosh of air next to his skull as the bullet he'd dodged skimmed by him with millimeters to spare.

He wretched again, but he came up dry.

Finally, he straightened and rinsed his mouth at the sink. He couldn't remember a time he'd felt so physically and emotionally drained. The anxiety that had clawed and fought with him all day had been a formidable foe.

Instead of returning to the meeting, he walked to his car in a daze and drove straight home. He ended up in his driveway beside Joss's Jeep sometime later, not even remembering how he'd gotten home.

He walked through the unlocked door as Joss came down the hall. "Hey, I thought that was y—"

Joss did a double-take as Demetri walked by him headed for the refrigerator. "What the hell happened to you?"

Demetri stood in front of the open refrigerator door, staring blankly at the shelves. What had he been looking for?

Joss moved him out of the way, grabbed a couple of beers, and herded him outside to the loungers on the pool deck. "Sit."

Demetri sat, and Joss twisted off a top and handed him a bottle. Demetri took a long swallow and then another. When he'd drained it, Joss gave him his beer and disappeared inside.

When he returned, he had what must have been his lunch cooler stuffed with ice and a few more beers. The bottles prevented the lid from closing, but they could always get more ice if needed. But at the rate Demetri was sucking the beer down, running out of ice first wouldn't be an issue.

Joss pulled up the lounger beside him, construction dust on his face, the ghost of his mask and eye protection still visible. Resting his elbows on his knees, Joss took more conservative sips of his beer. "I'm happy to sit here all night. You don't have to talk. But if you want to, I'm here."

All of Demetri's thoughts swirled around in his head, a tornado and a hurricane coming together in an epic storm of chaotic emotions.

"I almost got fired today."

"What did you do?" Joss's tone held no judgment. He didn't seem like that kind of man.

Demetri shook his head, not knowing how to begin. When he'd been that big of an idiot, when he'd made many poor decisions, where did he start unraveling the shit show that had become his life?

"I'm kind of seeing this student of mine."

"The naked kid that was here the other day? Not my type, but good on you."

Demetri huffed out a laugh. "No. Not him. A kid—a *man* in

my life drawing class." And maybe it was the beer hitting Demetri fast on an empty stomach or maybe it was because it felt so good to talk about something he'd been holding inside, but he told Joss everything from the back-alley blowjob to following Roman home for 'dinner.' He didn't care what secrets he divulged, not anymore.

Not when he didn't plan on seeing Roman again outside of class.

When he finished, Joss deadpanned, "Maybe I need to go to more art openings."

Demetri threw back his head and laughed, the tension easing. He supposed that had been Joss's goal all along. "Jesus Christ. If that's what you got out of that..."

He didn't know how to finish that thought, so he didn't.

"What I got out of that was that you're human. That you're not immune to being led around by your heart."

"Or my dick."

The look Joss shot him landed somewhere between reproach and *ain't that the truth*. "I don't think if it were your dick talking you would have let it get that far. If that were true, I think when you found out Roman was a student, you would have shut it down. But apparently, there's something more to him than his charm or his good looks."

"I wish I knew what the hell it was. Maybe then I could get one of my friends from the science department to find a way to inoculate me against it. I can't afford to lose my job."

"After losing Dan, all I know is that some things, some people, some *connections* are worth more than your job. Finding that special person can be more important than all the rest."

"Does that mean you'd give up flying if the right guy came along?"

"*Touché.*" Joss polished off his beer, reached into the cooler, and twisted the top off another. He offered it to Demetri. He didn't turn it down, not when he had a good buzz going and no good reason to stop it.

"And there's a twist to this saga, that makes sacrificing my job for a man that much more craptastic."

The sun had started to set, the colors shifting until it lit the horizon ablaze with pinks and oranges. Out of sight behind his fence, the sliding glass door of the neighbor behind him open and closed. A splash and the rhythmic strokes of a swimmer. A classic rock station playing the Eagles' "Wasting Time" came through his neighbor's outdoor speakers, soothing him.

Demetri didn't hem or haw or beat around the bush about what he had to say. He came right out with the truth. "I'm poz."

How had that been so easy when telling Roman had proven impossible?

Because you have nothing to lose by telling Joss.

Joss connected the dots. "And he doesn't know it."

"Bingo."

"Well..." Joss sighed and pulled a long swallow of beer from his bottle. "Fuck."

They both fell silent, and Joss turned and put his legs up on the lounger, his beer between his thighs and his hands behind his head as he stared up at the darkening sky.

Sometime later, after Demetri's neighbor finished his swim, the speakers went quiet, and the sky went dark, Joss said, "I lost a lot of friends back in the day. I'll be honest, back then, I never thought I'd live to make it to my forties."

Demetri grunted. He was younger than Joss, so the worst of the bad years of AIDs had passed by the time he'd started dating. That he'd gotten infected now, in this day and age of screening and PrEP—pre-exposure prophylaxis—he almost couldn't believe it. But that's what happened when your ex was a lying, cheating piece of shit.

"I also have quite a few friends who have been in serodiscordant relationships for years. Being poz with a negative partner doesn't mean it can't work out."

Intellectually, Demetri knew that. But Demetri had known many more relationships that hadn't survived the disclosure.

"I'd wanted to disclose at the beginning, but I let Niko talk me out of it. Now the thought of disclosing fucking terrifies me."

Now that he'd decided to tell Roman they couldn't see each other anymore, he still wrestled with disclosing even though now it shouldn't matter. It went to show how screwed up he was.

Then again, after how unfairly he'd treated Roman, were they even together?

"Rejection's not easy. Take it from a guy whose relationships have consisted of anonymous hookups for far longer than I care to contemplate. You're navigating this thing the best way you know how. You don't need my approval or consent."

Joss should have been a diplomat, not a pilot.

"It seems like no matter what I do, I'm equally fucked."

***

Roman typed in another message to Demetri. Well, not a message. More of a *WTF* with a bunch of question marks after the previous four texts he'd sent over the last several hours hadn't been answered.

Which should have been answer enough.

He doesn't want to talk to you. He made that clear in class and by his radio silence. Do you need him to turn his rejection into a club and clobber you with it for you to take the hint?

But his father had taught Roman never to give up on people. The way his father hadn't given up on Roman when he'd tried to distance himself from him and do more things with his friends even when his father kept trying to find common ground something, anything that they could do together.

His father's truth was probably the one thing Roman could probably never forgive him for. If his father had been honest with him, if Roman had known he was dying, that he was so sick, Roman would have spent what little time his father had left with him while he had the chance. And if his father had told him that he, too, was gay, that might have changed his experience of living at home with his homophobic, angry mother. It might not have made his life *easier*, but maybe it would have made everything easier to understand.

Roman sent off another text. To Grant this time. The response came with no questions. Roman appreciated Grant minding his business.

Plugging in the address Grant had given him into his map app, he drove a few miles away from campus and pulled in front of Demetri's house. A Jeep sat in the driveway next to Demetri's car. Demetri's mid-century modern had huge windows in the front and rear, allowing him to see all the way through to the backyard.

Without the shades drawn, Roman saw a watery reflection off the windows from the gentle glow of the pool lights.

He almost drove away. But he couldn't leave. Not without knowing if he'd destroyed Demetri's career. He couldn't stand the thought of waiting until his next class to find a substitute teacher in Demetri's place.

Besides, if Demetri *had* lost his job, Roman owed him a huge apology.

He got out of his car and walked up the sidewalk to the front door. The doorbell didn't work, so he knocked. And waited. And knocked again. Either Demetri couldn't hear him, or he was refusing to answer the door.

Go home. He doesn't want you here.

Probably. But Roman wasn't leaving until he knew that for certain.

Roman backed away from the front door and went to the side gate, promising himself if it were locked, he'd drive away. He grabbed the latch, and the gate opened.

His heart rate jacked up. His stomach had been flipping and flopping since class. Now it performed a couple of back hand-springs and topped it off with a cartwheel that left his head spinning. He caught his hand on the fence for support. Maybe this wasn't his best idea.

But no, if he needed to apologize, he would. If he could salvage anything, he'd damn well try.

He walked through the side yard and turned the corner to find Demetri and another man relaxing in a couple of loungers, drinking beer.

"Hey," Roman called out as he approached. He didn't want to risk Demetri spotting him lurking in the shadows like some kind of creeper. Demetri and the other guy sat up, swinging their feet to the pool deck. "I tried the door, but there was no answer."

Roman stopped a few feet from Demetri. Demetri still wore the clothes he'd had on in class, though he'd unbuttoned the top button, the collar of his shirt laying open, exposing his white T-shirt beneath.

Roman wanted to unbutton all those buttons and tug the undershirt out of Demetri's pants and get him naked in the pool. A stupid fantasy. "I wanted to talk, but if... if you'd rather I go..."

Demetri sat there, his mouth hanging open in surprise. The man on the other lounger stood and offered his hand.

"I'm Joss Kincaid," the man said. "I'm the carpenter, and I was just leaving."

"You don't have to go," Demetri said, more of a plea than an offer.

"I should get back up the hill. I've got some parachutes that need repair." He patted Demetri on the shoulder. "I'll be back in the morning."

Roman waited until Joss disappeared inside before taking the abandoned lounger. "You wouldn't answer my texts. What happened at the meeting. How much trouble are you in? Did you get suspended? Fired? Do you have any recourse, any way to let me speak to them and explain—"

"You going to let me talk sometime? Or should I let you keep going?" Demetri reached into a tiny cooler and handed Roman a bottle of whatever the two men had been drinking. "Here, I think you need this as much as I did."

Roman tossed the bottle cap into the cooler on top of the half-melted ice. "Okay." He took a sip and let the cold liquid slide down. "Talk."

"It wasn't me."

It wasn't him who wanted a relationship? It wasn't him who'd made the first move? Tilting his head, Roman said, "What wasn't you?"

"The professor who had an affair. Well, to be fair, it was, but it wasn't me the department caught."

"Oh, thank fuck." Roman didn't bother asking who. All that he cared about was that it hadn't been them who'd been found out. Roman let his head fall between his shoulders, his stomach finally settling, and the knot of muscle at the back of his neck relaxing.

"I can't..." In the quiet of the backyard, with nothing but a few insects and the low hum of the pool skimmer, Roman heard the quiver in Demetri's voice. He glanced up, and Demetri's confliction reflected back. "I can't do this."

"I get it." Roman didn't hesitate.

"It's not what I want."

"Same."

"You're not mad?"

Mad didn't even register in his mix of turbulent emotions. Relief being the foremost. Sadness. Regret for what couldn't be.

At least not yet. "I'm not mad. I'm glad you didn't lose your job. That's the best news I've heard in a long time."

But he couldn't sit there all night looking at Demetri and not want him. He needed to leave before he did or said anything he shouldn't. He stood and backed away, intending to leave the way he'd come. "I'll see you in class on Wednesday?"

Demetri stood as well. "You're allowed to leave through the front. Come on."

At the back door, Demetri cut off the pool lights, and Roman followed him through the dim house, a hall light providing some illumination. At the front door, he willed himself to grab the handle and leave, but he couldn't do it.

"I'll see you this weekend at the community lot, right?" Demetri asked.

"I'll be there." Roman leaned in one last time, brushing his lips against Demetri's. He tasted of the beer they'd shared.

Light from the streetlight down the road highlighted the relief on Demetri's face. Or was that desire?

Fuck.

No.

Leave.

"Stay."

If Roman had taken a breath, he wouldn't have heard it.

Even though the house remained silent, Roman wondered if he'd heard correctly. That one word had to be a figment of Roman's over-indulgent imagination. He hadn't even seen Demetri's lips move.

"Stay," Demetri said again, louder, surer, and more forceful this time.

Damn him.

The only thing in recent memory that Roman had wanted more had been getting out of Utah and finding a new life in California. A new life with room for a man like Demetri.

Roman's heart couldn't take the pull and the push, the no and then yes. But his heart also couldn't stand to leave. Time for a few honest words before he got in too deep.

"I can only imagine how scary today must have been for you. I'm falling hard, and I'm falling fast, and as much as I want to be with you, I'll wait until the end of the semester if I have to. But you can't keep coming at me and then backing off. You choose once and for all, and I'll abide by your decision. But I can't stay tonight and have you act like you don't know me tomorrow. That's not going to work."

"First, you didn't deserve the way I treated you today. Second, I'm so fucking sorry." Demetri stepped closer and cupped the back of Roman's neck, pressing their foreheads together. "And third, I'm done pushing you away. I'm not sure I know how to balance us against my career. But I know I don't want to stop seeing you. Not even for a few months."

Roman leaned back so he could see Demetri's face, the sincerity and vulnerability staring back at him clogged his throat. His voice croaked, but he had no desire to hide his emotions. "What if it's you they're coming after the next time they call a meeting?"

"We'll be careful. That's all we can do. If there's fallout, I'll deal with that when it comes."

"*We'll* deal with that."

"We..." Demetri's sweet, shy, sexy grin wrapped around Roman's heart like a warm hug. "I like the sound of that."

Demetri took Roman's hand, tugged at it, and started walking backward. Toward the bedroom, Roman assumed. He didn't need any encouragement, not when the invitation came from Demetri. If Roman were a good man, he'd remind Demetri of everything he stood to lose, of the bullet he'd dodged.

If Roman were a good man, he'd refuse.

ONE LIGHT TUG HAD ROMAN SILENTLY FOLLOWING DEMETRI.

What Roman saw in him, Demetri didn't know, but he wouldn't question that now.

As sure as Demetri had been when he'd sat out by his pool that he had to break things off with Roman, having him in his house, trailing behind him toward the darkened bedroom, Demetri tossed all logic away, grinding it into the tile floors with the heel of his shoe as he passed.

Logic had no place where sex was concerned.

And even though no neighbors could see in through the sliding glass door in his bedroom that led out to the pool deck from his bedroom, his concern with being caught with a student had him closing the blinds. He'd never bothered to close them before when men had come over, and doing so now felt wrong.

A naughty secret he had to hide from the world.

Roman bumped against the corner of the bed in the dark, tripping and falling onto the mattress. In his mind, Demetri had imagined a slow seduction as they both stood in front of each other, taking off their clothes item by item, but he could adapt.

And crawling on his knees until Roman's hips lay bracketed by Demetri's thighs, that worked too.

Roman wasted no time stripping off his shirt and shorts, taking his underwear with them. Two *thunks* came next as Roman's running shoes hit the floor. "Your turn."

"Fuck, you're beautiful," Demetri said, as Roman's muscles flexed and quivered beneath Demetri's hands.

"You can't even see me."

"I don't have to see you, or even feel you, to know you're beautiful." Demetri put his hand to the center of Roman's chest. "Not here. Where it counts."

Roman pulled Demetri in for a kiss, their lips brushing before Roman nipped and licked Demetri's bottom lip. "Are you telling me I could have skipped all the workouts?"

Chuckling, Demetri said, "Not gonna lie. As an artist, I can appreciate all your hard work."

"As an artist." Clearly, Roman saw through Demetri's bullshit. But it wasn't *all* bullshit.

If Roman were only a hot body, Demetri would never have put his career in jeopardy, but so much more than firm muscles and a thick dick made the man. His compassion, his passion, shined bright.

Roman would have been the kind of man Demetri could have looked up to as a kid. Grant and the Center were so lucky to have found him.

With open-mouthed kisses, Demetri worked his way from the hollow of Roman's neck down between the thick slabs of pectoral muscles. "I would love to draw you in my den as the afternoon sun sets over my fence, painting your body with golden light."

"R-really?"

The hesitation came not from disbelief, but from his words catching as Demetri's hand brushed a broad stroke across

Roman's lower abdomen. He continued that movement down to the base of that sumptuous cock.

Between Roman's legs, Demetri sat on his haunches, his fingers skimming down muscled thighs. "Besides what I'm doing now, it's hard to think of much else."

"You gotta get naked." Roman reached down and tugged at the shirt still tucked into Demetri's waistband. "It's way past my turn to get my hands on you."

If Roman noticed Demetri's moment of hesitation, he didn't comment on it before Demetri pushed off the bed and took off all his clothes. When Demetri went to get back on the bed, Roman said, "We need light. I want to see you."

Whatever Roman wanted, Demetri couldn't deny him. At least when it came to something as simple as turning on a light.

What about when he wants to blow you?

Or fuck you?

Are you going to deny him then?

Demetri's secret wasn't sustainable. Not if he hoped their relationship would be going anywhere.

Demetri walked around the bed and turned on his bedside lamp. It had a rheostat on the wall, and he turned down the brightness until it cast the room in a soft glow. "Better?"

Roman rolled to his side, propping his head on his hand. "*Daaumn.*"

Demetri grinned. "Is that good?"

"Get over here. I need to get my hands on you."

The head of Demetri's dick glistened with precum as he crawled over the side of the bed. Roman wasted no time getting his hand on Demetri. Demetri nearly collapsed at the intimate touch, his head dropping between his shoulders as Roman stroked his cock with a strong, sure hand.

But Demetri couldn't take the chance that Roman would

replace his hand with his tongue, so he shifted out of reach and took Roman into his mouth.

Roman bucked. The harsh guttural sound made Demetri's balls buzz as he took Roman to the back of his throat. He took advantage of Roman's distraction and moved back between his legs.

Demetri couldn't get enough of this man. His scent, his taste, the way he muttered unintelligible curses as Demetri sucked and licked and worked the full length of that girthy shaft.

Slicking his fingers with spit, Demetri skimmed a finger down Roman's taint and across his hole. Roman shivered. Goosebumps broke out over his skin.

"You like that?"

"Fuck me."

Demetri chuckled, loving Roman's responsiveness.

Roman braced himself on his elbows. "That wasn't rhetorical. That was a command."

Demetri gently bit Roman's inner thigh, along that sexy muscle that joined his leg to his groin, and worked his way up from there. He laid on top of Roman, their cocks aligned, his hands going beneath Roman so he could hook his hands over Roman's shoulders for leverage as he ground against him.

He nipped at Roman's jaw and licked away the pain. "Did you bring condoms?"

The hands Roman had on Demetri's ass stilled. "I didn't come here to fuck you. I came here to make sure you were okay."

Roman blew out an exasperated breath. "You seriously don't have any condoms?"

Demetri ducked his head and flicked his tongue across Roman's nipple so that Roman wouldn't see the lie in his eyes. "No."

"What gay man doesn't have condoms?"

"It's been a while since I've hooked up with anyone." Which

wasn't a lie, and he had no problem meeting Roman's curious gaze.

A half-smile slid across Roman's face. "I find that hard to believe."

"Does it matter that I haven't?"

Roman hesitated. Demetri saw the question in his eyes, the one that asked *why not.* "I guess not."

"But if I can't use my dick, I can still use my mouth and my fingers."

Or you could tell him the fucking truth.

Demetri needed to tell him. But not right then when they were naked and enjoying each other's bodies. "If you're game."

Roman thrust up against him. "I won't say no to that."

Demetri kissed him on the lips and leaned across him, opening the nightstand drawer, reaching past the unopened box of condoms that had been sitting in his drawer for months, and grabbed the bottle of lube.

Sitting up, he laid the bottle of lube by his leg so it would be handy when he needed it. Then Demetri lifted Roman's legs over his shoulders and licked and tasted his way from Roman's heavy balls to his taint, and finally to that pucker of muscle Demetri had been dying to get his mouth on.

Roman grunted, his legs quivering at the contact as he reached down and stroked his own dick. The sight down Roman's body from between his legs over the short-cropped pubes, the hills and valleys of his abdominals, to the puckered peaks of his nipples had Demetri almost confessing the truth.

He wanted this man.

And as much as he loved his taste, loved the way he groaned and the unabashed way he pleasured himself, Demetri wanted to be balls deep, pounding away at that glorious ass. Instead, his tongue did all the work. Roman's musk working its way into his nose, making Demetri's dick ache.

Reaching for the lube, he slicked up the fingers of one hand and worked it down the crease of Roman's ass, teasing his hole while he sucked on those balls. He let Roman's legs fall to the bed on either side of him as one finger breached the tight ring of muscle.

Roman's head fell back, and he pushed against the intrusion begging for more. "Is that all you've got?"

When Roman relaxed around his finger, Demetri added a second and thrust his fingers in and out. Roman's hand stroked faster on his cock. His balls drew up tight, his breath short, and his moans long.

He was close.

But not close enough.

Demetri found Roman's prostate.

"*Jesus fucking Christ.*" The words ripped from Roman's throat —an epitaph or a prayer?—as Roman fucked himself on Demetri's fingers, hitting that sweet spot over and over again until Roman's head thrashed side to side and air sawed in and out of his lungs.

He loved seeing Roman like this, at his wit's end, hanging on that cliff. He wanted to go with him, but he wanted to give Roman his pleasure more. There would be plenty of time for Demetri to come later because he wasn't inclined to let Roman go.

Not tonight.

Or any night?

Forever wasn't guaranteed. Or even a likely possibility. Demetri pushed that thought out of his mind and let his fingers do what his dick wanted to.

"More." Roman pushed back against Demetri, the muscles in Demetri's forearm strained and fatigued in the best, most amazing way.

He added a third finger to Roman's greedy hole, stretching

him wide before knocking Roman's hand away from his own dick and taking Roman into his mouth and shoving him off the cliff.

Glancing up, he watched Roman's epic fall, felt the pulsing tightness around his fingers, felt the first strains of Roman's orgasm as he sucked.

Roman held Demetri's head in his hands, thrusting into his mouth, once, twice, before that saltiness hit Demetri's tongue, and he swallowed and swallowed. Slowly, he eased his fingers out as Roman landed, a low, harsh chuckle rumbling from Roman's chest.

Roman panted, sweat slicking his body, his chest heaving as his legs flopped and splayed out on the bed. On all fours now, Demetri leaned over Roman. Roman pulled him in tight, laying lazy kisses across his jaw, his cheeks, the slight stubble raking beneath Roman's teeth.

Then Roman shifted and had the lube in his hand. "Squirt some in my palm."

Demetri obeyed. When he finished and tossed the bottle aside, Roman used his strength to flip them. Demetri landed on his back with a bounce and a grin. The grin turned into a moan as soon as Roman's hand went around Demetri's dick.

Having Roman's hands on him felt like heaven in a touch. He'd denied himself long enough.

Concentrating his attention on Demetri's cock and nipples, Roman licked and nibbled, the taut flesh sending lightning strikes straight to his dick. It had been so long since someone had taken him in his hand or even touched him more than casually that Demetri lost himself in the sensation.

Blood quickly pooled in his groin, Roman's fingers working Demetri's dick like a maestro, expertly reading his body cues, his shivers and quivers and sighs. For a man who'd jacked off more in the past couple weeks than he had since puberty, it surprisingly only took seconds to drive Demetri to the precipice.

Cupping a hand behind Roman's neck, Demetri pulled him in for a kiss. He needed to taste him and let their tongues do what his dick wanted to.

Roman's slow ministrations turned into exquisite torture. A touch too light to ignite. The devilish grin on Roman's sweet face catastrophic to Demetri's control.

"You're such a fucking tease." Demetri fisted his hand around Roman's and took over, thrusting into their joined hands, Roman's fingers and palm working Demetri's sensitive head.

Demetri bucked, the pulses building at the base of his cock. Roman had to have felt it as he teased Demetri's nipple between his teeth.

Lost.

Utterly. Completely.

And he had no map to find his way back.

And didn't care to either.

He shot his load, his nerves singing, the lights flashing behind his tightly closed lids. Warm, wetness landed on his abdomen and chest. He shouldn't have been able to shoot that far, not with the number of loads he'd wasted on himself, but then that's what Roman did to him. He took him to the edge...

...and destroyed him.

Roman stretched out beside Demetri, settling into the crook of Demetri's arm while Demetri tried to catch his breath. The air felt rough in his lungs, and his heart kicked and punched.

He pulled Roman in and pressed a kiss to his temple. "That was amazing."

"The only thing that would have made this better was having you inside me."

Demetri grunted in agreement, but he must not have

sounded convincing because Roman rolled up on his elbow and said, "*If* that's something you're into. I mean, we don't have to. I know not everyone is into it. And if you're not, it's not a deal-breaker. It's—"

Demetri shut him up with another kiss. "It's not that."

With his finger, Roman drew a small circle through the drying cum on Demetri's skin. "Then what is it?"

ROMAN WAITED FOR DEMETRI TO RESPOND, HIS HEART RATE kicking up the longer it took Demetri to form the words. Way, way back in a deep dark corner of Roman's mind, he heard that grating whisper. The one that said he wasn't good enough, wasn't worthy enough, wasn't *deserving* enough.

All those inconvenient truths his father's lies had taught him came bubbling up. Those stupid insecurities. Slippery bastards that resisted any strategy to tie them down or drown them with confidence.

Then what is it?

Demetri took a deep breath. Why was that such a difficult question to answer? "For once, I'd like to take things slow."

Not a lie, but it certainly wasn't the whole truth. What was Demetri hiding?

A steel door shuttered over Roman's heart. Above all else, he had to protect himself. "Yeah. I heard you the first time you said that. But you're the one who asked me to stay."

"I meant it. Though that was great," Demetri quickly added. "Just having you here, laying in my arms, would have been more than I could have imagined for myself a few weeks ago."

"You make it sound like you're some antisocial troll that no one in their right mind would want in their life. I don't get it. You're sexy as fuck. You're smart. You're not always an asshole..."

Demetri chuckled like Roman hoped he would, then the smile fell from Demetri's lips. "I feel like I owe you an apology."

"For not dicking me down, maybe. Though as soon as I can run by the pharmacy, I'll let you make it up to me."

Something flashed behind Demetri's eyes as he said, "Very generous of you."

Roman took another swipe through the jizz on Demetri's belly, already getting aroused again at the thought of Demetri fucking him. He brought his finger to his lips to get a taste of Demetri, but Demetri caught his hand.

Demetri sucked Roman's finger clean, giving him a wink, then rolled out of bed. "Come on. We could both use a shower."

They showered together. A perfunctory, utilitarian task and not the least bit sexy. Roman washed Demetri's back, but when he got to the good bits, Demetri stepped away spewing some bullshit about having had a long day and being tired and blah, blah, blah.

Something was wrong.

That knowledge burned into Roman's bones. Melted into his marrow. As they climbed into bed, he wanted to press Demetri for more, but the sadness and melancholy in Demetri's eyes had Roman swallowing down the words. Whatever Demetri was hiding gnawed at him, too.

He had mercy on Demetri and let the matter drop. At least for now.

"Roll over," Demetri said.

Roman rolled to his other side. Demetri lay behind him and curled up against Roman's body. With Roman's size, he usually played the big spoon. But something about having Demetri's arms around him holding him tight, his lips pressing into the space between Roman's shoulder blades, soothed the unease that had begun brewing in his belly.

Maybe he'd read Demetri wrong. The fright of almost losing

his job had to have hit Demetri hard. He couldn't imagine how he'd react if the roles were reversed and it was his life and career that had narrowly avoided disaster.

Reaching over, Roman clicked off the lamp and snuggled back against Demetri.

If anything, Demetri's hold only got tighter as if he feared Roman would disappear.

Little did Demetri know, Roman had no plans to go anywhere.

They woke in the same position that they'd fallen asleep, though sometime in the night, they'd kicked the covers away. Two men in one bed produced a hell of a lot of body heat, and Roman welcomed the cool air when the air conditioning clicked on.

"What time do you have class," they both said at the same time.

Demetri laughed and pulled Roman in tighter, his morning wood lining up with the crack of Roman's ass. "I don't have to be anywhere until ten." He stroked a lazy hand down the length of Roman's thigh. "What about you?"

"I have an eight o'clock class." Roman wiped the sleep from his eyes and glanced around the room. "What the hell time is it anyway?"

Demetri rolled to the other side of the bed and checked his phone. "Almost seven."

Roman groaned and flopped onto his belly, trapping the cold bottle of lube beneath him. He left it. He could sleep for another ten hours, easy.

Demetri bit him playfully on the ass and climbed out of bed. "I've got to piss."

Roman sat up as Demetri padded into the bathroom.

Palming the bottle of lube, he opened the nightstand drawer and tossed it in. Something caught his eye, and he opened the drawer wider. There. In the back. He picked up the unopened box of condoms. The bottom dropped out of his stomach. All those old insecurities slipped free of their bonds and thumbed their noses at him.

Demetri could have forgotten they were in there.

Maybe.

Maybe not.

The toilet flushed, and Roman tossed the box of condoms to the back of the drawer.

"I'll make you some coffee for the road," Demetri said as he walked into the room naked, his hair sleep tussled.

With his thigh, Roman quietly slid the nightstand drawer closed.

Demetri drew up short. "Everything okay?"

"Why wouldn't it be?" Roman retrieved his clothes from the floor and quickly dressed. "I need to go. I'll take a rain check on that coffee, yeah?"

13

Demetri didn't know what happened. One minute everything seemed fine, and then he'd flushed, and it seemed like everything positive that had happened the night before had flushed down the pipes as well.

Roman was... *off*.

Demetri padded after Roman, down the hall and into the den wearing nothing but a pair of boxer briefs he'd thrown on as Joss walked through the front door with his toolbox.

"Hey." Joss bobbed his chin as Roman passed by.

Roman did the head-bob thing as well, catching the front door before it closed.

"Wait up." Demetri hurried through the den and stopped Roman before he could leave. "I'll call you later?"

Roman's sour expression softened. "That would be great."

Demetri pulled him in for a lingering kiss but broke it before he got a full-blown hard-on. He lowered his voice so Joss wouldn't overhear. "Thank you for staying."

Roman gave him a quick peck in answer and headed for his car. Demetri stood there in the open doorway and watched him leave.

"If you're trying to keep this thing with Roman on the down low, you might not want to make out with him in full view of the neighbors while you're half-naked. Just a thought."

Demetri closed the door, shaking some sense into himself. "Am I thinking with the wrong head?"

Joss buckled his tool belt around his waist. "I don't know if you can blame all of this on your dick. Maybe your heart is partially responsible."

Joss had a bathroom to finish. He didn't wait around for a reply. With the Santa Anas expected to come to an end soon, he'd be up flying again and have much less time for his side job.

Demetri prepared a pot of coffee and left Joss to his work. Despite his colleague getting caught having an affair, Demetri felt optimistic about him and Roman for reasons he couldn't quite explain. But Joss was right: he couldn't spend the next months until the semester ended sending Roman off in the morning standing at his front door in his underwear. They'd have to be more discreet than that.

While the coffee brewed, Demetri put on a pair of shorts and took the kitchen garbage into his single-car garage. A garage that had never seen a car, at least not in the time Demetri had owned it. He had too much junk strewn about. Art supplies, mainly, that he'd meant to organize a year ago.

He dumped the garbage into the bigger can, opened his garage door, and took the can to the curb. On his way back, he glanced up and down his quiet street. Mostly working families. Out early. Back late. But Demetri didn't think for a moment that if Roman's car were at his place every night that someone wouldn't notice.

And if they noticed, they might ask questions.

But if he showed up at Roman's apartment, the consequences could be worse. Roman's apartment complex was only a few blocks from the college. Demetri couldn't expect to go there often and not see another one of his students.

He returned through the garage, tripping over the leg of an old easel laying on the floor. He hit the button for the garage door opener. Slowly, the door came down, closing him off from the rest of the world.

And potentially nosy neighbors.

Then again, if Roman parked in his garage...

Demetri pulled his phone out of the pocket of his shorts. He still had a couple of hours before he had to leave for campus. He put on some tunes and went to work organizing his garage and making room for Roman's car.

Later that morning, he walked onto campus with a spring in his step and an optimism he hadn't felt for a long time. Maybe it was the garage remote in his pocket he'd brought to give to a certain someone who made his heart giddy and his dick hard that would account for his optimism.

He didn't have a class with Roman that day, but he knew Roman hung out at the coffee shop near the student center between classes the same way half of the student body did.

The student center wasn't on Demetri's way to the art building, but he veered off and headed for it. He'd stop for a coffee even though he'd drunk a pot all by himself as he'd cleaned and organized. He hadn't had enough time to make the garage perfect, but it was enough to squeeze in a small car.

Demetri paid for a coffee at the counter and glanced around while he waited for his order. He immediately spotted Roman in the corner by the front window, his laptop open as he typed away.

"Demetri," the barista called out as she set his cup on the counter.

Out of the corner of his eye, he saw Roman's head pop up and a smile slide across his beautiful face. Demetri wound his way through the tables, some occupied, some empty. None of the students paid him any attention except the man who'd warmed his bed the night before.

"Mr. Reed," Demetri said as he stood by Roman's table.

"Fancy meeting you here, Professor Stavros."

"I have class coming up, but..." Demetri set the garage door opener on the table, his body blocking the view from the other students.

He put a finger on it and slid it over to Roman, dropping his voice when he said, "I figured you could use this."

Roman palmed the clicker, and Demetri wanted to kiss that mischievous smile off Roman's face. Roman must have seen it in his eyes because he gave a little shake of his head and said, "Later."

Demetri set his coffee on the table. "Promise?"

Roman nodded and commandeered Demetri's coffee.

He left Roman with coffee in his hand and a promise in his eyes. Night couldn't come fast enough.

DEMETRI PUSHED THROUGH EXETER'S FRONT DOOR FRIDAY evening, fifteen minutes early. And if Niko's shoot ran late, Demetri could be waiting a while.

He bellied up to the bar, nodded to acquaintances, and casually eyed a few of the scantily clad men as he waited for his rum and coke. Not that the men particularly interested him. Not when Roman had warmed his bed most nights that week.

"What's up with you?" Phil, the bartender, said as he handed Demetri his drink. "You look mighty pleased with yourself."

"It's been a good week."

Hard for it not to be when he thought he had the answer to his *dating a student* problem. And add to that, a few nights of cooking dinner with Roman, of chilling out and snuggling on the couch.

And the sex.

World-tilting, star-exploding, all-consuming sex.

Even if it was getting harder and harder to come up with ways to have sex that didn't cross the personal lines Demetri had set.

A few more men came through the front door, the pop music coming through the speakers set a booming beat in Demetri's blood. Phil waved at the guys who came in. "Looks like it's going to be a decent night, too."

As small as Sneaky Pete's was, it didn't take many people before bar stools and tables filled, and people had to stand elbow to elbow. He kept his spot at the end of the bar, with a clear view down the back hall to the dark backroom. A place where men liked to go to grope and suck and fuck.

With the popularity of the apps, not many of the gay bars had a back room anymore, and he appreciated that Sneaky Pete's and its patrons protected theirs. Even as he thought that, two guys he didn't know hurried down the hall and disappeared behind the curtain.

A hand landed on Demetri's shoulder. "You wishing that was you back there?"

Demetri turned around, making room for Niko to take the open seat beside him. "Makes me nostalgic more than anything." He glanced behind Niko, but no one had come with him. "Where's Vin? You leave him tied up at the house?"

"Not in the way he'd like. He's editing the shoot from this morning. We have a quick turn around on that one, and he wanted to get started."

"You know it's the weekend, right?"

"That was his decision. I tried to get him to come."

"You need to try harder. Vin will work himself to death trying to please you, and you know it."

"You're right." Niko pulled his phone out of his pocket and hit Vin's number. Vin must have answered because Niko said, "Stop what you're doing and get your ass down here." Then Niko chuckled. "They've got a backroom. Why don't you come down here and show me who's boss?"

He hit end. Demetri couldn't tell for sure because of the dim lighting, but it looked like a blush rose to Niko's cheeks. Niko refused to meet Demetri's gaze and instead raised a hand and caught Phil's attention.

When his whiskey arrived, Niko took a sip. "You figure out your little problem?"

"I think." Demetri swirled his glass, and the ice cubes clinked together. Without a good way to ease into it, Demetri spit out his plan. "I'm going to resign at the college and work for Abe Franklin at Premier."

"The art gallery?" Niko sputtered and wiped his chin with the cocktail napkin. "You've got to be fucking kidding me. Did Roman suck so hard that your brains came out of your dick?"

"Don't be an asshole." Demetri didn't put much heat behind the words because now that he'd voiced the plan, it did sound kind of crazy, not to mention a rash solution to a temporary problem.

Niko leaned in, even though between the din of voices and the music, the people standing near had little likelihood of overhearing. Not that anyone at the bar would give a flying fig who Demetri fucked, student or not. "What's gotten into you, besides Roman's dick?"

Demetri shot Niko a look, but it bounced off Niko's Teflon shield without leaving a scratch. "It's not like that."

"You haven't told him yet." It wasn't a question, and Niko wasn't referring to the job offer.

Demetri shook his head, feeling like the kid who'd hidden his bad grades from his parents. It's one of those things that you couldn't keep secret, not from the people who mattered.

"You have to tell him."

Demetri sat back, his mouth gaping open before he caught it. "You're the one who told me *not* to disclose."

"This is different. You're about to make a huge mistake. You're so close to getting tenure, and you're about to throw all that away for a man who is operating under false assumptions and partial truths. And you would fucking hate the gallery. You're a teacher, Dem. That's what you do. You'd wilt under the hot, stifling lights of a gallery, discussing someone else's work instead of making your own and showing others how to make theirs."

"You think I'm being hasty."

"I think you're being stupid."

Demetri drained his rum and coke and asked for another while he stewed. Niko stayed beside him, giving him the space to think. He hadn't realized how long they'd both sat there in silence until Vin squeezed in between them.

"If I'd known this was a funeral, I would have stayed at home."

"Sorry, babe," Niko said. He gave up his seat and called Phil over to get Vin a drink.

Demetri shoved his half-finished drink across the bar and stood. "Hey, Vin. Glad you could come, but I need to go."

He headed for the door. Neither the raised voices nor the music could drown out Niko's parting words. "You know I'm right."

Demetri flipped Niko off over his shoulder without looking back.

Whoever said you shouldn't drink alone didn't have an opinionated cousin who thought he knew best.

14

"You're quiet," Roman said. He'd driven over that morning having left his car in Demetri's garage so they could carpool to the community lot. Today would be the first day that kids came to help, and it was going to be a long, exhausting, fun day.

"Didn't sleep well last night." Demetri turned past the community lot and pulled into the parking space.

"I would have thought without me there, you would've been able to get a lot more sleep."

"You would think."

After the great week they'd had, sliding into Demetri's car that morning to find him in some kind of mood, smudged a little bit of light off Roman's. That feeling that Demetri was holding out on him refused to go away.

As a kid, he'd had the same buzz in his brain, like someone tapping his shoulder trying to tell him to look, to pay attention, that something wasn't right with his father. That he should have asked more questions when his father started losing weight, and his energy had declined until he could hardly get out of bed.

Though Demetri looked as good as he always did, Roman couldn't deny Demetri's issue felt as world crushing. Roman had hoped that the more time he and Demetri spent together that that feeling would ease, but it had only intensified.

And every time he pressed Demetri, asking him if he were okay or if he wanted to talk, Demetri brushed him off. As bad as the push and pull had been with Demetri trying to decide if they were going to see each other or not, this was worse.

At the city parking lot, Demetri shifted into park, leaving the car running. For a second, Roman feared he'd drop him off instead of staying for the day to work.

Demetri stared out the windshield. "We need to talk."

Roman settled back into his seat. "It's about time."

Locking eyes with Roman, Demetri said, "Tonight. Promise."

He wanted to shake Demetri and maybe make those words spill out unguarded. Working all day knowing he had this *thing* hanging over his head would make the hours long and his temper short. Just when he needed patience the most working with the kids. But Roman saw Demetri's resolution flaring as strongly. If Roman pushed now, he'd be unlikely to get any answers.

So he'd agree.

And he'd wait.

As difficult as that would be.

"I'm going to hold you to that."

"I hope that you do." Demetri leaned in, threading his hand behind Roman's neck and pulling him in for a kiss. "I missed those lips last night."

"I missed a lot more than your lips."

Demetri chuckled, some of the tension easing. "We can make it up to each other tonight."

———

ROMAN AND DEMETRI SPENT MOST OF THE DAY APART, WORKING

on different aspects of the project. Except for lunch. And the demonstration Demetri gave the kids showing them the best way to hold the brush and showing some of the older kids basic painting techniques such as blending and shadows.

The kids had the adults outnumbered, even with Grant's fiancé tagging along and closing the Center so Vondra could help. Tavi and Remy took a couple of the older kids to work on the superhero wall, outlining the superheroes and the buildings so the younger kids could paint between the lines.

Demetri, Grant, and Sebastian worked with some of the younger kids on the animal wall while Roman corralled a couple of kids as they worked on the frames for the graffiti wall.

The sun was high and hot, but at least the Santa Anas had died down quite a bit, so the wind didn't whip up the dirt and ruin all the paint.

By five in the afternoon, most of the parents had come to pick up their kids. Vondra entertained the few that remained on one of the concrete pads that had been poured during the week. There was still more concrete that needed to be poured, but the concrete company was backed up and didn't yet know when they could come back.

They still had to paint the four-square boxes and the hopscotch lines, but they were going to wait until they didn't have so many kids running around that they would have to worry about one of them accidentally running through it.

Roman gathered up the pans of paint and started pouring them into their respective cans. A little girl walked up, maybe four or five, her blond hair sweaty and sticking to her forehead. She hadn't been one of the kids helping with the wall. Roman assumed she'd come from the churchyard next door.

"Watcha doin'?" She squatted down beside him and watched him pour. "It's so pretty. Gween's my favorite color."

"Are you here alone?" Roman glanced around. Parents were

driving up to the front of the church, picking up kids, but none of them appeared to belong to the little girl.

"I'm with Jakey. He's my bubba."

"Your brother?"

The little girl nodded.

"Malorie!" A boy of about ten came running up and grabbed her hand. "I told you not to leave the playground."

"I wanted to see the pretty colors."

Roman handed her the green brush. It still had some paint on it that hadn't dried. He pointed to the short stack of newspapers. "Wipe the brush on there. You can help me use up the paint."

Malorie painted the newspaper, and before Roman could put the top back on the green paint can, she dunked the brush into the can almost up to her hand and slathered on more.

The brother slapped a hand on his equally sweaty forehead. "I'm sorry." He tugged her hand. "Put it down, Mal. Mom's gonna be here any minute."

Roman held up a staying hand. "It's okay. She's not hurting anything."

"What are you guys doing here, anyway?"

Roman gave him the basics. "The lot is for the whole community, even though The Cory Center owns the lot. If it's okay with your parents, you're more than welcome to come another day and help."

"That would be cool."

Malorie dipped her brush again, and Roman laughed. "I think your sister would want to come, too."

Over Jake's shoulder, Roman watched the pastor start walking their way, that pickled expression plastered on his face that he always seemed to have every time he glanced over at the lot.

The man put his hands on the boy's shoulders, and to

Roman said, "You need to leave these kids alone. It's not right what you're doing here."

The confusion on the boy's face had him looking up at the pastor.

"They're making the ugly lot nice for everyone. What's wrong with that?"

Demetri must have noticed the pastor had wandered over because he showed up beside Roman and casually linked a couple of fingers with him. Subtle, but enough to let Roman know he wasn't facing the pastor alone.

"We don't appreciate your kind recruiting young children into a life of sin. They are impressionable and—"

"Is there a problem, Pastor Tom?" A woman walked up, and Malorie put her brush down and took the woman's hand.

"I caught these men talking to your children. Don't worry. I'll speak to the city council and—"

"He only asked if we wanted to come help paint sometime," the boy told his mother.

"Is he your boyfriend?" Malorie asked Roman.

Demetri squeezed Roman's hand. "Yes, he is."

The pastor became apoplectic, his face turning red. "That's preposterous. Why would you say that to them? How do you explain to a young child—" The pastor waved his hand in the general direction of Roman and Demetri's linked hands as if voicing their hand-holding was a sin.

"Well," the mother said, "Let's see." She squatted down next to her daughter. "All kinds of people fall in love. Sometimes it's a mommy and a daddy. But sometimes guys love other guys, and girls love other girls."

"Like Julia? She has two daddies."

The mother grinned. "Yeah, like that."

Malorie looked like she was thinking about it for a second, then she said, "Can I get a Happy Meal on the way home?"

"Sure." The mother held out her hand, and Roman shook it. "Thank you for letting her paint. That was very sweet of you." Then she turned to the pastor. "I think tomorrow's sermon on *love thy neighbor* is particularly timely, don't you think?"

The boy giggled and ran ahead to his car. The pastor stormed off, and Malorie turned and waved at Roman. He waved back.

"You have a way with kids," Demetri said. "You attract them like bees to honey."

"I'm sure the pastor doesn't think I'm so sweet. But I fucking loved that mother."

"She was amazing. For a minute there, I thought the pastor had stroked out, the way he stood there with his mouth agape, his eyes blinking rapidly in confusion."

"We should be so lucky. I know I shouldn't be so surprised when a person is filled with irrational hate." Like his mother. But Roman didn't want to bring her into this. The more he didn't think about her, the better. "But I'm surprised every time."

"I'm sorry I didn't get over here sooner."

Roman squeezed Demetri's hand before letting go. "Thanks. It's nice to know someone has my back."

He squatted down and started hammering the lids onto the paint cans before Demetri could see the moisture pooling in his eyes. He hadn't expected that discovering he wasn't alone in the world would hit him so hard it would make his eyes leak and his chest refuse to expand.

"Always." Demetri leaned over and dunked all the brushes into the water bucket and started rinsing them.

"And that whole boyfriend thing. You didn't have to say that when we're only..."

Roman didn't know how to finish that sentence, so he let it hang out there. Maybe Demetri wouldn't notice he didn't have the words.

"I figured calling us fuck buddies was too reductive, and lovers sounds like something my mother would say." Demetri fake shivered. "I don't need that thought in my head. Besides, that's what we are, right?"

"You're not afraid the pastor is going to tell the college?"

"He has no reason to know who the hell I am, or even that you're in one of my classes. I'm not worried about him. And I might have found a workaround for that pesky student-teacher problem, too."

They picked up the paint cans and old newspaper and started carrying them toward Grant's truck. "What is it?"

"I'll tell you tonight."

Sounded like they had a lot to talk about. The potential solution to their biggest problem, and whatever the hell had been eating at Demetri that morning. Maybe once they got everything out into the open, that twist in Roman's gut would finally unwind, and he could appreciate the fact that he had a boyfriend.

DEMETRI LED ROMAN THROUGH HIS FRONT DOOR. THE exhausting day should have put a damper on his libido, but Roman always managed to rev his engines and get him hard no matter how sore or tired he was. His horniness even penetrated through his personal mindfuck of knowing he'd disclose later that night.

That anxiety should have kept him soft, but short of being neutered, Demetri didn't think that was possible with Roman in his house. As soon as the door closed, Roman pulled Demetri back and trapped him against the door, his hard cock pressed into Demetri's hip.

"I've been waiting all day to get you like this."

For the first time since he'd bought the house, Demetri reached out and closed the front blinds. He'd never bothered before, loving the way the light came through the house.

He'd been an open book, and living in a fishbowl hadn't been a problem.

Until he had something to hide. Or rather, *someone.*

Closing those blinds went against Demetri's nature, like a thief walking past a stack of hundred dollar bills and not taking them, but until they had everything figured out, he wanted to limit the chances of word about him and Roman getting out.

That, and he liked the idea of keeping Roman naked as much as humanly possible.

Roman kissed him slow and deep until the goosebumps flashed across Demetri's flesh, and his cock developed a life of its own. He ground against Roman, and his resolve to not have sex until they talked faltered.

Breaking the kiss, through heavy breaths, Roman said, "I think we need to hop in the shower and get clean so we can get dirty."

Roman didn't wait for an answer. He took Demetri's hand and headed for his shower, stepping around some of Joss's construction debris in the hallway as he went.

Demetri took his time washing Roman, loving the play of Roman's thick muscles under his soaped-up hands. He cleaned every inch of Roman's magnificent body, from his broad shoulders to his narrow waist to the two little indents above the most mouth-watering ass he'd ever gotten his hands on.

He tried to memorize the form and the shading and the play of light and suds over Roman's skin so he could paint him later, even though he knew that not even Michelangelo possessed the skill to do Roman justice.

Because Demetri knew something Michelangelo didn't. As

classically beautiful as Roman was on the outside, it was the inside of the man that made him stunning.

Next, Roman had his turn, and Demetri braced his hands on the cool tile. Water sluiced off his back from the rain shower head above. Roman liberally applied the soap, using his hands instead of a washcloth. He got into all the nooks and crannies and the crack of Demetri's ass.

"I love your ass." Roman's slick finger slid up and down Demetri's crack, his finger lingering around his hole, teasing and torturing.

Demetri groaned. "I love having your hands on my ass."

Roman shifted to the side so he could continue playing with Demetri's hole and stroke Demetri's dick at the same time. All thought and reason left Demetri, the way it always did when Roman put his hands on him.

Demetri's head fell between his shoulders. Roman worked his cock with expert hands until Demetri's balls drew up, and he started thrusting into Roman's fist.

Roman chuckled and nipped at the tender skin at the base of Demetri's neck. "You're so fucking sexy when you're at the brink of losing control, when your breath catches, and your hips lose all rhythm."

"You're a wizard who's cast a spell I can't break."

Roman spun him around, shoving him against the tile, Roman's hot breath in Demetri's ear. "Don't you forget it. You're mine."

"Fuck," Demetri muttered as Roman's hand started jacking him again. "I'm so fucking gone for you." He opened his eyes and met Roman's heated, heavy gaze. "You know that, right?"

Demetri almost didn't notice that fractional hesitation, before Roman nibbled on Demetri's ear and said, "Same."

Their words weren't a declaration of love. It seemed too early for that, but those exact feelings held Demetri's heart hostage. Even if Demetri had wanted, he couldn't break free.

As Roman brought Demetri to the brink, his quads quivering and his locked legs threatening to buckle, Roman sank to his knees. "I want to taste you. I want you to fill my mouth and—"

Fuck. Demetri shoved Roman's shoulders too hard. Roman landed on his ass on the shower floor. Anger flashed in Roman's eyes, but the hurt beneath it slashed Demetri's heart.

"What the hell is wrong with you?" Slowly, Roman stood and cut off the taps, water cascading down the wide expanse of his chest.

Demetri stepped out of the shower, grabbed two towels, and tossed one to Roman. Roman threw it aside, not caring that he dripped water all over the bathroom while Demetri hurriedly dried himself.

Roman caught his arm. "I asked you a question."

Demetri wrapped the towel around his waist and his still-hard cock. He didn't know who was more pissed, Roman or Demetri's dick. "I should get dinner started."

Roman's head dropped as he shook it in disbelief. When he glanced up, he couldn't hide the pain and the confusion, or the anger. But the disappointment in Roman's eyes added a few more cuts to Demetri's already shredded heart. "I'm going to take a few laps in the pool and blow off some steam. Unless you need my help."

At least Roman wasn't running. Roman was a reasonable man. The fact that he hadn't already left proved that. Demetri could fix this.

You can't fix it. It's not spilled paint or a torn canvas Roman already knows something's wrong. He just doesn't know how *wrong.*

"No. I've got this."

"Great." Though by Roman's clouded expression, it was

anything but. "You don't need my help with dinner *or* getting off. Noted." Roman brushed past him, their shoulders bumping as he went by.

Demetri wanted to call out and tell him it wasn't like that. But talking to Roman when both of their emotions lay ragged couldn't work in their favor. He'd let Roman calm down, get a little food in his belly, then they would talk.

Before starting dinner, he set a towel on one of the loungers for when Roman finished swimming. Demetri stood there on the threshold of the sliding glass door and watched Roman's powerful arms churn through the water. The wave in front of him sloshing over the ends of the pool with each turn.

He left Roman to start dinner.

Sometime later, as he added the ground beef to the spaghetti sauce and the timer on the garlic bread beeped, Roman opened the slider as he dried his face and head with the towel.

Demetri turned the heat down on the bubbling sauce. Roman came up behind him and threaded his arms around Demetri's waist, his breathing still elevated from what had looked like a brutal workout.

The calm vibes rolling off Roman were what Demetri noticed first. Roman rested his chin on Demetri's shoulder. "Smells good."

"Thanks."

Neither apologized. Demetri didn't because then he'd have to explain. Roman didn't because he had nothing to apologize for.

Roman patted Demetri's belly and took a step back. "You have any shorts I can borrow? I forgot to bring a change of clothes with me this morning."

Demetri turned and sized him up. "I don't think anything of mine will fit you, but I think there is a blue pair of athletic shorts in the bottom drawer of my dresser his ex had left behind ages ago.

A pair of shorts wasn't all he'd left you with.

Demetri set the table and dished out the food. Still no sign of Roman. Demetri almost went to rescue him. His drawers weren't exactly the best organized, and those shorts might be in a different drawer.

As he set the Parmesan cheese on the table, Roman returned with something in his hand. On the table in front of him, Roman dropped a handful of Polaroids, his expression inscrutable.

Demetri didn't see the trap even as he walked into it.

He picked up the photos and shuffled through them, garnering a chuckle. Fuck, he'd been wild when he was younger. All the photos were of him and some of the guys he'd hooked up with—sometimes one-on-one, sometimes three or more—all back in the day. As much fun and adventure and experimenting he'd done in college, his sex life since then would appear tame.

If anything, he should have caught HIV then. Before the age of PrEP. Back when he'd been horny and reckless. Not when he'd been in a *supposedly* monogamous relationship.

Karma's a bitch.

Demetri didn't even know if he believed in Karma. But it had bitten him on the ass anyway.

"Coachella and Burning Man," Demetri said, naming the annual art and music festivals where sex with friends and randos was just another day. "I had some fun in college."

Roman's lips went flat, and his hands went to his hips.

"You're mad because I had sex with random people fifteen years ago?"

Roman rolled his eyes. "I don't care about that."

Demetri found it hard to keep his anger in check. He didn't

see the problem. "Then what is it?" It didn't exactly come out as a snarl, but it didn't sound exactly civil either.

Roman gathered up the photos. He held the first one up. "You getting fucked." He threw it down onto the table and held up the next. "You fucking someone." He held up another. "This one's nice, you're fucking someone at the same time someone is fucking you." Then the next photo. "You being spit-roasted."

"I like fucking and being fucked. I told you that. Why is that such a big surprise?"

Roman blew out a breath. His frustration glittered in his eyes, along with a darker emotion Demetri couldn't read. "Right. Then it's me you won't fuck."

"Wait. It's not like that."

"You are so full of shit." Roman ran his hand over his short hair, seemingly at a loss for words. "You know what. Fuck dinner. And fuck you, too. I'm out of here."

He grabbed his keys out of the bowl on the kitchen island and headed for the door.

"*Roman*, wait."

But Roman didn't wait. He didn't even slow as he strode out the door to the garage, not even bothering to close it behind him. He hit the button for the garage door opener, and Demetri hollered out. "I'm poz."

He ran after Roman.

Roman had his car door open, one foot on the floorboard as the grinding gears of the garage door opener came to a stop. "What did you say?"

Demetri's heart thudded so hard it made his ribs shudder, and his breath catch in his chest. The air felt too thin to breathe. "I'm poz. I have HIV. I didn't want to fuck until I told you."

Roman didn't move. If it weren't for his eyes blinking, Demetri might have thought he'd turned to stone.

"I'm undetectable."

"Great." Roman laughed. Without humor, the sound came out harsh, judgmental. "That makes all the lies better then."

Yeah, Demetri had lied. And he couldn't even say it had been to protect Roman because the only one the lies had protected from the pain of rejection was himself. It had been stupid and selfish. He saw that in full HD clarity now.

He'd never wanted to hurt Roman. But that's what he'd done. Outside, one of his neighbors strode by walking two dogs. The setting sun threw beautiful hues of pinks and oranges and reds over the horizon, but that light couldn't penetrate the dark cloud surrounding him.

"Come in. We can talk."

"Did you ever see me as a person, or have I always been a pawn?"

"That's not fair."

"No. What's not fair is you not treating me as if I had the right to know this about you. Know this about my *boyfriend*." Roman shook his head. "You're a fucking piece of work."

He climbed into his car, started the engine with a roar, and backed out of the driveway. All Demetri could do was watch Roman drive away with his heart held hostage.

Punching the button on the wall, the garage door slowly lowered. Demetri went back into the kitchen, picked up his phone, and dialed Niko's number.

When Niko picked up, Demetri had to clear the clog out of his throat before he said, "I'm never taking advice from you again."

15

ROMAN TOOK A LONG DRIVE UP THE COAST AND BACK DOWN, HIS windows wide open, his speakers blaring. He didn't listen to what was playing. He only needed it to drown out the voices in his head. The ones that told him he wasn't good enough, that he wasn't trustworthy enough, that he wasn't deserving enough.

It was his father all over again.

That old, festering wound now a gaping hole in the middle of his heart. How it kept beating, he didn't know. If it stopped, would anyone notice? Would they care?

The hours passed in a stream of headlights and taillights and honking horns. Most of the honks he'd earned. Sometime in the night, he ended up on campus. He prowled the grounds, his long stride eating up the trail that looped around all the buildings and dorms. When he couldn't walk fast enough to outpace his thoughts, he started running, his bare feet slapping on the concrete, the sweat pouring down his bare chest.

When he couldn't go another step, he got back into his car and drove home. He unlocked the door to find Moses and two other guys in various stages of nakedness, the smell of weed thick in the air, and empty beer bottles on every surface.

"Oh, hey, man." Moses took a drag from the joint and held it out to him. "You want a hit?"

"Get that the fuck out of my face." Roman batted Moses' hand away and headed for his bedroom, slamming and locking the door behind him. If he'd had anywhere else he could go, he would have gone there.

He flopped on his bed and rolled to his back, staring up at the dark ceiling as music played in the den, and the distinct sounds of people fucking came through the door. He held his hands over his ears to block the sound, but it wasn't nearly enough.

How could he have put so much trust in one person so fast? How had he let his guard down? Everything had felt so right, and—

Bullshit. You knew something was off. That knot in your gut? It tried to warn you, but you refused to listen.

Because he'd wanted so badly for it to be real. For someone to love him without condition.

But unconditional love was a lie.

Or a myth.

It didn't exist except within the cover of a book of fiction. A place where tales are spun, and people suspended all disbelief. Perhaps that's why all the famous old poets and authors were drunks. They needed the alcohol to trick their numb minds and hearts into suspending their disbelief, even in the fantastical.

Roman didn't know how long he lay there. Long enough for his sweat to dry and the burn of built-up lactic acid to dissipate from his muscles. At some point, he realized the music and the fucking had stopped. Odd. It wasn't morning yet.

A knock came at his bedroom door.

"Go away."

He heard the scrape of metal on metal, then the push button

lock on his door popped, and Moses walked in, a straightened metal hanger in his hand. "What the hell happened?"

Roman groaned and rolled to his side, facing away from his friend. He didn't want to think about it. And he *definitely* didn't want to talk about it.

Moses didn't take the hint and climbed onto the foot of the bed, sitting cross-legged. The light from the hall shined on his face, and Roman saw the heavy-lidded eyes and the slack face of a guy who looked too high and drunk to be vertical.

Moses pushed Roman's legs out of the way and lay down on his stomach across the foot of the bed, his chin in his hands, his legs hanging over the side. Roman's nose wrinkled. Moses smelled like pot and sex.

"The professor?"

Roman grunted.

"You get dumped? I mean, not a surprise. They like to fuck around, but that's all it is. You can't let your heart get involved. I figured you were smart enough to know that."

Maybe Moses wasn't as drugged out of his mind as Roman had at first thought. But in Roman's defense, it was a Saturday—or Sunday, actually. Moses and sobriety usually didn't reconnect until Monday came along.

Roman cradled his head in his arms. "Too late."

"He cheat on you?"

Was he going to talk about this? With Moses of all people?

But who else could he talk to? Not Emily. She knew too much already, and though she liked Demetri, she had a protective streak, and Roman feared what she might do or say if she knew the truth.

Not the truth about Demetri's HIV status. That wasn't something Roman would tell anyone, no matter how mad he was.

"He lied. I thought I could trust him."

Moses fell quiet for a long time. Roman thought he'd passed

out, then Moses finally said, "You know. Not everything is about your father."

But Moses couldn't know that, not without knowing the truth about Demetri's lie. "You don't know what you're talking about."

"That's where you're wrong. I probably know better than anybody. Maybe even you. I was there for a lot of it. At least the immediate aftermath. I watched as you pushed all your friends away, thinking that if you didn't let anyone close that you wouldn't get hurt again."

Roman let Moses ramble. Not so much because Moses was right, or that Roman agreed, but because he was so fascinated that someone so clearly wasted could string a few coherent words together, much less make any sense.

"Well, it's all bullshit," Moses rattled on. "Life doesn't work that way. People are going to disappoint you. They're going to lie to you. They're going to hurt you. And it's going to feel like none of it is worth it..." Moses' eyes rolled closed but opened again. "Maybe it isn't. Fuck. I don't know. Don't listen to me. But bottom line, people fuck up."

But some fuck-ups you couldn't take back.

Roman didn't know what to do or what to feel. All he knew was that he couldn't face Demetri in... he checked the time on his phone, the battery at two percent. He couldn't face Demetri at the community lot in three hours.

He fired off a text to Grant, so his boss would see it first thing when he woke up.

Roman: *I'm not feeling well. I won't be able to make it today.*

The battery died, the phone powered down, and Roman didn't bother to charge it. There wasn't anyone he wanted to talk to anyway.

While Roman's text skirted the lines of truth, it wasn't a flat-out lie. He felt like crap. His insides flattened as if he'd been steamrolled and left in the Mojave Desert sun to bake all day.

Tomorrow, after he'd had a chance to sleep and think more clearly, he'd come up with a plan.

DEMETRI WAS LATE, AND HE DIDN'T MUCH CARE. HE'D WAITED FOR Roman at the Center for thirty minutes, not that he'd expected Roman to show. Not after what Demetri had told him the night before.

You act like this is a surprise. You knew this would happen all along.

Instead of bypassing the lot, he ran the tires on the right side of his car over the curb behind Grant's truck and lurched to a stop. Shouldering his door open, he shoved his sunglasses up his nose against the harsh glare of the sun to hide his bloodshot eyes and the bruised puffiness beneath them.

Grant turned and leaned against the tailgate, crossing his arms over his chest. "What did you do?"

"I just came here to work."

"Hey Grant, I—*whoa.*" Tavi stopped mid-sentence, backed up a few steps, and went back to wherever he'd come from.

Demetri tried to brush past Grant, but Grant caught his shoulder. "Roman called in sick this morning. You know anything about that?"

"Should I?" Demetri shook off Grant's hand. He considered Grant family now that Grant and Sebastian were engaged, but that only gave Grant a few privileges. A window into Demetri's sex life wasn't one of them.

"Roman's a valuable member of my team. Whatever's going on between you two, you need to fix."

"Apparently, there's nothing between us. I'm sure Roman will be feeling better by tomorrow."

At least that's what Demetri told himself. And kept telling himself the next afternoon as he waited, his gut twisted in knots, for Roman to walk into class. He kept his eye on the door, even as Emily came in alone, and as the minutes dragged on and on until class ended, and everyone left.

He almost stopped Emily at the door, but she hadn't shot him a shitty look during class the way Grant had when he'd showed up to the community site the day before, so maybe Roman *was* sick.

By Wednesday, when Roman didn't show up for class again, Demetri began to worry. He hadn't called or texted Roman, wanting to give him space. If Roman had wanted to talk to Demetri, he knew how to get hold of him.

You say that like you haven't spent every night with your thumb hovering above the keyboard on your phone, crafting your apology in your head.

He owed Roman an explanation, but he didn't want to do it over text or to force one on Roman if he was done with Demetri. With the radio silence since Saturday night, it looked like Roman was.

Anything you say will be an excuse for the inexcusable.

Demetri should have gone with his gut and not listened to Niko. Not that any of this mess was Niko's fault. His cousin had only been trying to help.

At the back of the class, Demetri sat staring at the empty seat and easel where Roman should be. The rest of the students worked diligently on their shading project due the next week. At this rate, Roman might miss turning in the assignment altogether. Demetri didn't want Roman's grade affected by something that he'd caused.

Or maybe Roman is in the hospital. You could have at least texted to find out if he was okay.

Class was coming to an end, and the students started cleaning up. The door to the classroom opened. Demetri's heart stumbled for a beat. A student aide. Not Roman. Demetri drew a breath in through his nose and out through his mouth, steadying himself so his hand wouldn't shake when he took the paper from the aide.

"What's this?"

"Updated class roster." The aide looked at him as if he'd lost one of his marbles, and it had fallen on the floor and rolled away. "Add/Drop ended Monday."

Of course. Which probably explained why another one of his students had missed his classes that week. He'd totally spaced on the date. "Thanks."

He hardly noticed the students or the aide leave as he held his breath and scanned the Add/Drop sheet for Roman's name. There, near the bottom. *Roman Reed.*

He blew out the breath, part relief, part frustration. At least Roman hadn't missed his class because he was in the hospital. But it meant that Demetri had hurt Roman so profoundly that he couldn't stand to be in the same class with Demetri for the remainder of the semester. A class that Demetri knew Roman needed to graduate.

Demetri dropped into his desk chair before his knees gave way as nausea rolled through his belly. If Roman couldn't graduate on time because of *him*, it would be hard to forgive himself for that.

This after promising Roman that sleeping with him wouldn't affect his grade.

Demetri had hesitated to text Roman before, now he pulled out his phone and immediately fired one off. They were adults.

They could work something out so that Roman could get the credit he needed for graduation.

Demetri: *We need to talk.*

He dropped his phone in the pocket of his pants, not expecting to hear from Roman for hours. The near-immediate chirp of his phone from an incoming text made his heart race and his palms get sweaty.

Roman: Now *you want to talk.*

Demetri: *It's about class.*

And so many other things, but Demetri figured his greatest chance of getting a reply was if he kept things professional.

Like you should have from the moment you found out he was a student.

But in the seconds it took Demetri to fire off his response, Roman had blocked him.

Fuck.

Demetri strode to the registrar's office to convince a friend to give him a copy of Roman's schedule. Maybe if he could orchestrate a 'chance meeting' on campus after one of Roman's classes, he could get somewhere face-to-face.

But somewhere between his classroom and the registrar's office, some speck of sanity crept in, and he walked right past the registrar's door. Demetri had office hours that afternoon, but with no one scheduled to come in, he skipped out on that and headed for his car. He needed to get as far away from campus as he could.

An hour later, like some sick, creepy stalker, he pulled into the parking lot of the apartment complex across the street from Roman's unit. He palmed his phone and pressed the number under one of his favorites.

When Niko answered on the second ring, Demetri said, "Stop me from doing something brain-numbingly stupid."

"One second," Niko said into the phone. Then all Demetri

heard were a few muffled orders Niko gave to someone. Probably Vin. Then Niko uncovered his phone. "What's going on?"

Demetri rubbed at the ache in his forehead. "You're shooting, aren't you? I'll let you go. I—"

"We're finishing up. Vin's got it covered. He knows what I want anyway." There was an echo to Niko's voice, and Demetri pictured him going up the back stairwell at the studio to the wing that held Niko's office and home. He heard a door open and close, and the background noise went silent. "What am I supposed to stop you from doing?"

"Roman wasn't in class Monday or today. I got my roster update, and he dropped my class."

"I guess I don't have to worry about that gallery job sucking out your soul anymore."

"You're an asshole." But Demetri couldn't help the half-strangled laugh. That job would have been like combining water torture with peeling back his skin layer by layer.

Because if Roman hadn't run? As ill-advised as it would have been, Demetri probably would have taken the job.

"I texted Roman and told him we needed to talk. He blocked me. Now I'm sitting in my car across from his apartment. It doesn't look like he's home, but..."

Demetri let the sentence trail off. He didn't know where he'd planned on going with that. He grimaced and dug his thumb and forefinger into his temples again, trying to alleviate the searing headache that had signed a lease and set up permanent residence.

"I know you told me the other night that you don't want any more of my bad advice, but I'm just going to say this one thing. Him running when you disclosed told you everything important you needed to know about him as a person."

'But Roman's not like that,' Demetri wanted to say. But the

fact that Roman had left, that he'd dropped the class and blocked his number, said that he was *exactly* like that.

Demetri blew out a breath through the stricture in his throat. "It still fucking hurts."

"I know." Niko's voice went soft, and Demetri waited for whatever else he had to say. "He's not the right man for you. No matter how good he made you feel."

Demetri grunted, the hit coming hard even though Niko spoke the truth.

"Now put the car in reverse and go home, Demetri. Or come here, we can—"

"No." The last thing Demetri wanted was an audience to his meltdown. And the way his head pounded, all he wanted to do was crawl beneath the covers and not wake up until next semester. "No. I'm going. Thanks. I think."

Niko softly chuckled. "Anytime. And Demetri?"

"Yeah?"

"I really am sorry."

Demetri cleared his throat and only managed another mangled, "Yeah. Me, too."

16

Roman made it to the end of the school week and blindly loaded up his lunch tray with food he wasn't hungry for. He poured himself a giant cup of sweet tea for a much-needed sugar rush. At the cashier, he scanned his card, giving the lady a half-hearted nod as he took his tray and went to find a table.

He hadn't heard a thing from Demetri since the day before when he'd blocked him. But some heart-sick part of Roman thought that if Demetri wanted to talk to him badly enough, he would have found a way to contact him.

But he hadn't.

There's your answer.

Two women vacated a two-top table by one of the front windows, and Roman headed straight for it before anyone else could snag it.

From across the cafeteria, he heard Demetri call his name. Roman's steps faltered, then he caught himself and kept going. Only someone paying close attention would have seen how that voice had affected him.

And while three seconds ago he'd lamented that Demetri

hadn't found a way to contact him, he was pissed that Demetri had chosen the cafeteria for that confrontation.

Roman wanted to eat the tasteless food, space out in his next class, and go home to hibernate before he had to do it all over again the next day.

"Roman, would you wait up?" Demetri caught Roman's arm as Roman made it to the table.

All the hurt, all the sense of betrayal that he'd tried to keep strapped down so he could at least function on autopilot for most of the day broke free and welled to the surface as anger. He slammed his tray on the table. The hamburger bounced, and his tea dumped over. "What do you want?"

The buzz of conversation in the cafeteria died as all the curious students eyeballed them. There were a few giggles and embarrassed smiles before most everyone looked away again, and their conversations picked back up.

Demetri caught Roman's cup. The tea had drenched Roman's food and spilled onto the floor, splashing Demetri's dress shoes. Roman tossed his napkin on top of the mess, but it was like trying to sop up the Great Flood with a Q-tip.

"I want you back in my class."

"It's too late for that." And Roman wasn't just talking about the fact that the Add/Drop deadline had passed.

He couldn't get back into Demetri's class even if he wanted to. He'd suffer through Landscape Drawing for the remainder of the semester. He'd been lucky someone had dropped it at the last minute, allowing him to pick it up. He hated the class, but it fulfilled his requirement for graduation, so that's all that mattered.

"Can we go somewhere and talk?" Demetri kept his voice low, but with some undue attention still on them, more people than Roman cared to had to have heard him.

"Now you want to talk? *Now?*" Anger, as well as his voice,

rose like super-heated steam. He poked Demetri in the chest. "Fuck. You."

Roman heard the squeak of the rusty wheel of the mop bucket rolling their way and turned as the janitor appeared to clean up his mess.

"I never meant to hurt you," Demetri said.

Those words only made it worse. Demetri reached out to him, but Roman stepped away. "You were right from the start. This wasn't a good idea. I didn't listen. My bad. This is my fault as much as it is yours."

Roman pasted on a plastic smile for anyone still watching. He didn't know if he believed his own words, but he knew there had to be a nugget of truth to them, even if he hated to admit it.

You know everything isn't about your father.

Moses' surprisingly insightful words popped back into Roman's head, though they hadn't been far from his consciousness since they'd fallen out of his roommate's mouth. The crazy part? Roman doubted Moses remembered uttering them.

"Can we—" Demetri huffed out a breath as the janitor wedged between them and started cleaning up the mess. "Can you give us a minute?" he asked the older gentleman.

Roman took hold of the mop handle. "It's my mess. I'll clean it up."

The man looked between Roman and Demetri and must have sensed the tension because he said, "I'll be back in five."

Ignoring Demetri, Roman squeezed the excess water out of the mop and tackled the puddle on the floor. Demetri put a staying hand on his arm, but Roman shook him off, unable to keep the emotion from his voice when he said, "Leave me alone, Demetri."

It came out more like a plea than the command Roman had intended.

Demetri took the mop from Roman's hand and bobbed his chin toward the cafeteria doors. "Go. I've got this."

Roman only made it a few steps before Demetri called out to him. "Roman?"

He should have kept walking. He knew that's what was best for his head and his heart, but his feet betrayed him and stopped. "What?"

"You going to be at the community lot tomorrow?"

All week, Roman had managed to avoid Demetri. He couldn't think with him near, which hadn't differed much when they were apart. If he didn't get his head on straight soon, his job and his grades would suffer. If he said yes, would Demetri not go?

"It's my job."

When Roman started walking again, Demetri didn't stop him. That's what Roman wanted.

Right?

Demetri approached the community lot on Saturday with equal amounts of excitement and dread, not knowing what to expect from Roman. He walked up to Grant, who had already arrived with Tavi and Remy in tow. Even Sebastian had made it.

Of course, with a group of kids expected to help, it was an all-hands-on-deck sort of day. Luckily, the kids weren't due to arrive for a little bit, giving him time to drink his extra-large, extra-caffeinated coffee.

Grant and Sebastian were in the middle of building what would be ten waist-high planters for the community garden section of the lot.

"Hand me the crescent wrench," Grant said, his hand stuck

out like a surgeon waiting for a scalpel, a circular saw in several pieces on the ground by his knees.

Sebastian slapped something into his hand.

"That's a box wrench."

Sebastian pulled out another tool.

"Those are vice grips."

Sebastian tossed them back in. "You're gonna have to give me a clue."

"God, I love you." Grant chuckled and looped an arm around Sebastian's neck and planted a kiss on his cheek. He released Sebastian, pulled the tool bag closer, and held up the tool he'd wanted.

"To be fair," Sebastian said, "If you'd needed a fully catered dinner or flowers for a venue, I'd be a lot more useful."

"You were certainly useful this morning."

The grin on Sebastian's face and the red creeping up his neck told Demetri they weren't talking about planter construction anymore.

Grant held Sebastian's chin and kissed him. It was slow and deliberate and so intimate that it made Demetri want to turn away. "I'm glad you're here. Thanks for coming."

Demetri tried his damnedest not to feel jealous over Grant and Sebastian's relationship. But fuck it hurt to see them so happy. Even though he knew their relationship hadn't come easy. Neither had Niko and Vin's.

Isn't everything good worth fighting for?

Then why have you given up on Roman? Isn't he *worth the fight?*

Demetri couldn't watch the two of them anymore. He turned away, giving them some privacy, and bumped into a wall of muscle.

"Ow." Roman shook the hot coffee from his hand, his to-go coffee cup falling and dumping all over the dirt.

"You okay?"

Roman sucked at a spot on his hand that must have received the brunt of the burn. He held Demetri's eyes, his throat rough when he said, "I will be."

And, fuck, that answer had zero to do with Demetri's immediate question. The hurt in Roman's eyes had replaced the anger from the cafeteria the day before, and all Demetri wanted to do was pull him in for a hug and tell him everything would be okay, even though he'd been the one to cause the hurt.

Instead, Demetri held out his cup of coffee to Roman. "Take mine. Two creams and a raw sugar, the way you like it."

Roman took it, more out of necessity for the caffeine probably than anything else, but Roman didn't throw it back in Demetri's face so he'd call it a win. "Thanks."

"Look," Demetri started, "Can we—"

"Work together?"

That wasn't where Demetri was going with that. His thoughts had gone more towards a conversation they could have in private, but maybe being able to spend the day together without having a fight or causing a scene was a good place to start. "I can do that. You?"

Roman took a sip of his coffee, and Demetri tried not to look longingly at it as if it were a prized treasure he'd lost. If it took relinquishing his coffee to have Roman speak to him again, it had been well worth the monumental sacrifice.

"I can." Demetri picked up Roman's spilled coffee cup and tossed it into a wheely bin trash can that Grant had brought to the site. "Sorry about the coffee."

Roman's gaze went past Demetri to the church behind him. Demetri was almost afraid to turn around and see who was coming. He'd about had enough of the pastor. "What happened over there?"

Demetri spun around. The front door of the church lay wide open, and two firemen in their turnout gear walked out with the pastor. Demetri hadn't noticed when he'd walked up the non-existent loading and unloading of kids at the church's entrance.

"Hey, Grant," Demetri called out, "What happened at the church?"

The pastor shook hands with the firemen and sat on the church steps, looking utterly defeated as the men walked around the corner to their truck parked on the side street near the hydrant.

Grant stood and brushed the dirt off his legs. "There was a fire in the kitchen in their community room. Most of the fire crew were packing up the hoses by the time we got here, though."

Now that Demetri paid closer attention, a faint smell of smoke lingered in the air, but Demetri had figured one of the local barbecue joints had started up their cookers earlier than usual.

"Anybody hurt?" Roman took another sip of his coffee.

Demetri had to catch himself from watching the play of Roman's Adam's apple bob up and down. Who would think something so innocuous would be so damn sexy? Especially on a man who'd reached deep down and fucked with Demetri's heart.

"Sounds like it happened in the middle of the night when the building was empty, luckily," Sebastian said.

Vondra arrived as cars started pulling up, and parents started dropping off their kids to work on the project. She'd done a good job, scheduling out the kids into two-hour time slots spread out over the day so that the younger ones, especially, wouldn't get too tired or lose focus.

Demetri's group consisted of a revolving door of tweens who kept him laughing and reminded him how much art brought people together. Roman had been saddled with some of the younger kids, but his energy and playfulness kept them all engaged. If the kids lost focus, Roman gave them a break and miraculously redirected that innocent energy onto Tavi's paint-by-number wall, turning it into a masterpiece instead of something that looked like a two-year-old's finger-painting project.

And fuck if the way those kids grinned up at Roman didn't make Demetri's heart shift in his chest. He couldn't reconcile the man who'd run out on him when he'd found out Demetri had HIV to the man in front of him directing a bunch of paint-splattered kids like a graffiti conductor.

But the pain of Roman's rejection shifted Demetri's heart back into place. Demetri yanked his eyes away from the play of Roman's sweat-slicked muscles his tank top couldn't hide and tried to concentrate on his kids and his art wall. Wishing things were different couldn't change what had happened.

Lesson learned.

Time to move on.

That thought should have felt relieving or refreshing or something other than a chunk of lead ballast in his gut.

"Hey, Mister Demetri." One of the kids, a boy about eight years old with wide brown eyes and an innocence Demetri hadn't seen in a kid that age in a while, interrupted his thoughts. "Why do you keep staring at that man?"

"That's Roman. And I wasn't staring."

The kid leaned in. "It's okay. I used to stare at a girl in class all the time, and now she's my girlfriend."

Demetri swallowed down the bubble of laughter. Since when did eight-year-olds have girlfriends and boyfriends? "What does that mean when you're in what, third grade?"

"She makes me eat lunch with her, and I have to let her cut in line in front of me when we are buying lunch or lining up for recess. Maybe if you asked really, really nice, Mister Roman would eat lunch with you, too."

If only it were that easy. Demetri ruffled the kid's shaggy hair. "Maybe, kid, maybe."

By the end of the day, they'd made significant progress on the walls. All the bright colors made the once dirty, dilapidated eyesore of a lot cheery. A place you would want to play and spend time. Grant and Sebastian had made significant progress on the planters, and Tavi and Remy had filled them with wheelbarrow after wheelbarrow of rich, dark soil.

The volunteer kids had finally gone home, and now all that remained was a little cleaning up before they started it all over again the next day. Roman dunked the paint-covered brushes into a pail of water and carried the small, plastic containers of paint over to Demetri to pour back into the paint cans.

"Here are a few more," Roman said as he set the containers down next to Demetri.

"Thanks." Without glancing up from where he knelt on the ground, Demetri started combining the paint.

"You're not even going to look at me?"

Demetri shaded his eyes with one hand as he finally gazed up at Roman. "One of my kids accused me of staring at you too much today."

Demetri had been staring at him?

Roman's heart twirled in his chest, but he beat it into submission.

"Apparently, from what one of my kids said, I'm supposed to share my lunch with you, and then you'll be my boyfriend, and I will have to let you cut in line in front of me."

"Seems legit. What did you tell him?" Roman couldn't keep the amusement out of his voice. God, he loved those kids.

Demetri returned his focus to the paint cans, but not before

Roman saw the flash of darkness in his eyes as his mood shifted. "Look, Roman. You're the one who wanted space. I'm trying to give it to you."

He dug at the lip of the paint can with the head of a screwdriver, the soft metal giving way to the prying because the dried-up paint along the rim had sealed it closed.

"*Space* doesn't mean pretending I don't exist when I'm standing in front of you."

The screwdriver slipped, catching Demetri in the web of his hand between his thumb and forefinger. "Damn it." He tossed the screwdriver aside and stood, sucking on his hand.

"Let me see."

Demetri cautiously allowed Roman to take his hand. Without Demetri's mouth covering the wound, it bled freely. He'd be lucky if he didn't need stitches.

"Let's get that cleaned up."

"I'm fine."

"The Center can't afford the lawsuit when your hand turns gangrenous and falls off. So do Grant and I a favor and stop being macho."

Demetri chuckled, and damn if that soft, rolling sound didn't make Roman want to wrap Demetri in his arms and kiss all the pain away. But kissing a boo-boo wouldn't make what happened between them any better.

"No one has ever accused me of being macho before."

Roman raised a brow at him. "How about stubborn then?"

"That word may have been thrown around a time or two in my general direction."

Roman huffed and, under his breath, said, "Tell me about it."

He didn't let go of Demetri's wrist as he led Demetri back to Grant's truck to scrounge around for the first aid kit. He lowered the tailgate. "Sit."

Demetri sat, the blood dripping down his fingers and splattering on the asphalt.

Roman riffled through the first aid kit but couldn't find any gloves. "You're undetectable, right?"

Demetri wiped a hand down his face and muttered, "What am I thinking?" more to himself than Roman. "Here, let me do it."

Reclaiming Demetri's wrist, Roman said, "If you're undetectable, you can't infect me. Even with an open, bleeding wound like this."

"Well, no, but..." Demetri cocked his head, a hint of confusion lining his face. He let the rest of the sentence fall off, and Roman was too busy wiping off the blood and cleaning the wound to press the matter.

It didn't look like the wound needed stitches after all, so Roman applied some antibiotic salve, a few gauze squares, and wrapped his hand with soft cling gauze. "There. All better."

"Thanks, I—"

"Everything okay, here?" Grant had several paint cans in each hand. He lifted them over the side of the truck and set them in the truck bed behind Demetri.

"Industrial accident," Demetri teased as he held up his hand. "All taken care of."

The boys dropped the tools into the truck and climbed into the rear seats, while Sebastian brought the last of the painting supplies. "We're going out for pizza. You two coming?"

Demetri raised a questioning brow at Roman, but Roman didn't think a night staring across the table at Demetri would do his battered heart any good. "I think I'll head home."

Hopping off the tailgate, Demetri closed it. "I think I will, too. See you all in the morning."

"Night, everyone!" Vondra called out. She left with a friend who'd met her at the lot.

"Night!" They all waved back.

Grant and Sebastian said their goodbyes, got in the truck, and pulled away, leaving Roman and Demetri standing by the sidewalk.

Roman didn't have much to say to Demetri, especially with the hurt so fresh, but damn it, he didn't want Demetri to leave either.

Demetri shoved his hands in his pockets, his eyes going to the ground, not making a move to return to his car. A noise came from the church behind Roman, and Demetri's attention shifted over Roman's shoulder.

"What's the pastor doing?"

The hair on the back of Roman's neck stood on end, not quite knowing what to expect when he turned around. He doubted it would be anything good. Prepared for a confrontation, he turned. The pastor, who'd at some point changed into old work clothes, carried a water-logged cardboard box out of the front of the church and dropped it at his feet next to several other similar boxes on the church's neatly manicured front lawn.

Even from a distance, Roman could see the pastor's sweaty hair plastered to his head and the dark sweat stain down the front of his shirt. Roman started walking his way.

Demetri jogged to catch up. "Where are you going? You remember he doesn't like us, right?"

"The man needs help. I don't want him to have a heart attack on the street. This is me turning the other cheek."

"You're a better man than me," Demetri said, though he kept walking with Roman instead of returning to his car.

The pastor stiffened as Roman and Demetri approached. Roman half expected the man to hurry back inside to avoid them, but he didn't. "Can I help you," the man said in a tone that indicated he'd rather do anything but help them.

Roman stopped, his hands on his hips, paint splattered and

smudged on his clothes and skin. He probably looked a sight. He bobbed his chin toward the boxes. "We've come to see if we can help you."

The man's jaw dropped, and Roman schooled his smile.

"I'm... um..." He glanced behind him at the church. "We'd stored our food for the food drive in the basement. Unfortunately, water from the fire seeped through the old floor and flooded the basement. I've separated all the can goods, but all these dry goods are ruined. I need to carry them to the curb for trash pickup."

"With the three of us, we should be able to knock it out in no time," Roman said.

The pastor glanced at Demetri, who only nodded. Considering how the pastor had treated them, Roman knew Demetri's heart wasn't in it, but Roman had to hand it to Demetri for offering to help anyway. Though Roman had the distinct impression he was doing it for Roman and not the man in front of them.

"I— You—" The pastor blew out a breath and used the collar of his T-shirt to wipe the dripping sweat off the side of his face. "I would appreciate the help is what I'm trying to say."

"Lead the way," Demetri said.

It took several hours to dispose of the water-damaged food to the curb, relocate the canned goods to a drier location, help the pastor squeegee and mop the excess water off the floor, and set up fans to help dry everything out.

Roman's stomach grumbled on the way out of the church. He needed food before he collapsed. Demetri looked like he could use the calories too.

On the church's porch, the pastor offered his hand to Roman and Demetri. "I don't know how to thank you. You didn't have to help."

"We're going to be neighbors. And that's what neighbors do. They help each other."

They all shook hands, and Roman and Demetri headed to the parking lot a few blocks over to get their cars. Demetri put a staying hand on Roman's arm before Roman could climb into his car.

"Can we talk?"

Roman closed his car door and leaned against it. "Today was a good day. Maybe we shouldn't fuck it up by talking."

Demetri nodded, but by his exasperated expression, it didn't look like he agreed. Then he did the unexpected. He moved in close, and though no one else was within hearing distanced, his dropped his voice and whispered, "I miss the fucking out of you."

It took several seconds for Demetri to meet Roman's gaze to gauge the effect his words had. If Demetri stepped even an inch closer, he'd be able to feel the rap of Roman's heart against his sternum without having to lay a hand on him.

Demetri stood there, the vulnerability staring back at him. Roman almost let the truth slip out and said, 'I miss you, too.' But he swallowed the words down before they could betray his true feelings.

Demetri closed the gap, laying his hand on Roman's chest as if he needed to feel what his words had done to him. But would he be able to feel the way his heart had ripped? Could he feel it bleeding out into his chest?

"And I know I shouldn't. And I understand if you don't want it, too. But I'd like to kiss you."

It took every ounce of willpower Roman had ever possessed in his life not to dip his head and taste those lips. The lips that had been in his dreams every night. Lips on his lips, his chin, his chest, his co—

Roman leaned away, practically becoming one with his car door. "I don't think that's a good idea."

Retreating a step, a soft, humorless chuckle ripped from Demetri's throat. "Look, I understand if you hate me right now."

"Fuck, Demetri." Roman shook his head and laid his hand on his chest where Demetri's hand had been. "I don't hate you. All of this would be a hell of a lot easier if I did."

"We need to talk then."

"I'm not sure it will help."

"I'm willing to risk that. Are you?"

17

"WE CAN GO TO MY PLACE," DEMETRI SUGGESTED, BUT HELL, HE'D go wherever Roman wanted to go as long as they talked. Would it all work out? He didn't know. But he didn't want to walk away without putting in the work.

Because if anything, their time apart had shown Demetri that what he felt for Roman wasn't fleeting. It was building. Despite Roman running away. Despite the time apart.

And that wasn't just his dick talking.

Roman glanced down at his crotch. At the tenting in his shorts. "I don't think that's a good idea."

Though he knew Roman's roommate had a good chance of being at Roman's apartment, he said, "Yours then."

Roman shifted out of reach. "That's even worse. Maybe someplace that I won't try to get you naked."

"You still want to get me naked?"

That had to be a good thing, right? Roman's admission brought a flutter to Demetri's chest that had been missing since his disastrous disclosure. That flutter turned into a thumping when Roman's shy smile spread across his face.

"Wanting you naked has never been the problem, though now it's more of a complicating factor. I can't think when all I want to do is hold you, and kiss you, and..."

"Fuck me?"

Roman chuckled. "Definitely that too. None of this is about me not wanting you. It's about—"

The grumbling of Roman's stomach made Demetri's growl in response. The sun was setting low over the valley, and night would soon fall. "Hold that thought."

Demetri unlocked his car and held the passenger door open. "Get in the car. I know where we can get some food and have a little privacy, but not so much privacy it'll get us into trouble."

He waited out Roman's hesitation, his heart lodged in his throat, hoping like hell Roman wouldn't come to his senses before he climbed in.

Finally, Roman pushed off his car, locked it, and mumbled, "I hope I'm not going to regret this."

Demetri closed his door and to himself said, "You and me both."

They found a gourmet drive-through diner with burgers so thick you practically had to unhinge your jaw to eat them. The aroma of cooked beef, honey-glazed bacon, and fresh fries filled the interior of Demetri's car.

By tacit agreement, they didn't talk much along the way. They sipped on their chocolate shakes as Demetri drove to a park in the foothills overlooking the city. They climbed out with their food as dusk turned to darkness, the city lights shimmering below, the breeze mild as the Santa Anas finally relented.

They boosted themselves onto the hood of Demetri's car, the bag of food between them.

"Nice spot," Roman said as Demetri squirted hand sanitizer

into Roman's palm. The hand sanitizer wasn't ideal, considering they'd been working with their hands all day, but it would do.

Demetri carefully worked the sanitizer around his bandage. "This was one of my favorite places to go when I first got my driver's license."

"You bring any boys up here?"

Demetri chuckled. "One or two maybe."

He glanced over at the big tree on the other side of the guardrail, where a kid from his class had given him his first blowjob. It had been sloppy and lacked all skill, but any doubts Demetri had had about being gay vanished that night.

"One or two?" Roman took another slurp of his shake. "Why do I think that number needs a multiplier in front of it?"

Those were much simpler times. All any of them cared about was getting off as often as possible. Sure, feelings were involved, but not all the time, and they hadn't seemed so consequential.

Not like now.

"It was hard to find any kind of privacy when my mom didn't work outside the home. We did what we had to do. Where'd you go?"

"The desert. Lots of open land in Utah. Lots of sand in crevices on my body I'd like to forget."

"I'll bet." Demetri bit into his burger before it got completely cold. They weren't talking about what they'd come up there to talk about, but they *were* talking. Hard for someone to block you in person. And he had the car keys, so it would be harder for Roman to run if the conversation got too messy.

One for the win column.

"How's the hand?" Roman unwrapped his burger, dumped both containers of fries into the middle of his wrapper, and squeezed out all the ketchup packets.

Demetri opened and closed his hand. It hardly hurt. "I'll live."

Much like the car ride up, they mostly ate in silence, starved, and each unsure what to say. At least the food tasted delicious.

Roman finished first, dumping his empty cup and his ketchup-smeared wrapper into the bag. He leaned back on the hood of the car, bracing his weight on his elbows as he stared up at the sky. A few of the brighter stars popped out, but the light pollution hid most of them.

He pointed at the sky. "Shooting star."

Demetri caught the end of it out of the corner of his eye. "You're supposed to make a wish."

"Done."

He threw his trash into the bag with Roman's and turned, one foot on the bumper, the folded up on the hood. "What was your wish?"

Roman blew out a heated breath and held Demetri's gaze. "I wished you hadn't lied to me."

"FUCK, ROMAN," DEMETRI GLANCED DOWN AT THE HOOD, MAKING abstract designs in the fine layer of dirt with his finger. Then he glanced up. "Don't you think I wish I could take it all back and do it all differently?"

"I don't know what you wish. All I know is that I knew something was wrong, and you wouldn't open up to me no matter how many times I asked." Roman sat up. "There are many things I can forgive and forget, but dishonesty... that's not one of them."

"Who hurt you?" Demetri asked at last.

This was supposed to be Demetri's chance to explain himself, not that Roman had expected the explanation to make any difference in the end, but he'd resigned himself to at least listen.

"This isn't about me."

"It's as much about your baggage as it is mine. Don't deny that to my face."

The kicker? Demetri wasn't wrong. Roman jumped off the car and started pacing, the milkshake souring in his stomach, and that scar on his heart his father's lies and deceptions and half-truths had left him with broke open again.

He stopped in front of Demetri, the backdrop of the city behind him, the warm wind rising off the valley floor, whipping his shirt. He had to clear his throat. "My father."

Demetri tilted his head as if confused. "I thought your father knew you were gay. I thought the two of you got along."

He shoved his hands into his pockets. "He did. And we did. Except…"

How could Roman explain something he'd never been able to explain to himself fully?

"He loved me. I know he did. But as much as I felt his love and acceptance, there was a barrier between us. But as thin as it was, it was also impenetrable. I thought I knew my father. As it turns out, I didn't know him at all."

Demetri shifted, both feet on the bumper now, and leaned forward, his forearms on his knees as if he didn't want to miss a single word.

"He was gay. And he died of AIDS when I was fourteen."

Demetri sat up straight. "Wait. *What?*"

A soured laugh escaped Roman, though he found nothing funny about growing up being deceived. "I didn't find out about it until after we'd put him in the ground. My mother knew. About his orientation. About him being poz. I don't know if that's why she's so bitter, or why she hated me so much—because I was so much like him."

As his words flowed, the righteous indignation that had fueled him leached out of his body. His knees became weak, and he sat down on the thin edge of the metal guardrail, bracing his hands on either side of him.

"Why... why didn't he tell you?"

"I'm not sure. I think that as much as my father accepted me, I don't think he'd ever accepted himself, and I think getting the diagnosis only made him more ashamed of who and what he was."

Roman's anger started building again as he thought back on his father's silence. "Do you have any fucking idea how much it ripped me apart to know he couldn't tell me? How ashamed it made me? How could I believe that he loved me when I was the same as him, and he—he couldn't love himself?"

Roman held his head in his hands, trying to keep it from exploding as his heart drummed in his chest. "I watched him get thinner and thinner. Watched him waste away in front of my eyes. All the while, he told me he would be fine, that nothing serious was wrong with him. That he wouldn't die. That was the biggest lie of all. Coming from a man who'd taken it upon himself to stop taking his meds. To leave his son in the care of a woman who couldn't stand the sight of him."

"Jesus Christ," Demetri muttered, the words almost drowned out by a jet flying low overhead on its approach into LAX.

Demetri stared down at the gravel, his mouth working, but it didn't look like he had any idea what to say or how to make it better.

But nothing would make what Roman's father had done to him any easier to swallow.

Roman had to live with that. He'd thought he'd buried it over the years, especially since leaving for college when he didn't have to take the daily scorn and verbal jabs from his mother.

He didn't know what his father had seen in her, other than a body to be his *beard*—a cover so people wouldn't think he was gay—so he could go behind her back and fuck men on his way home from work or maybe on his many business trips out of town.

"He was flawed," Demetri said at last. "But no one is perfect. I don't doubt that he loved you, though." He held Roman's gaze, an empathetic smile on his face. "That would be the easy part."

"Do you have any idea what it would have meant to me growing up, knowing my father was also gay? That I wouldn't have had to go years thinking I was the only boy who plastered his room with posters of superheroes because they turned me the fuck on? It would have been nice to talk to someone else who was paranoid about looking left or right in the locker room because they didn't want to take a chance that someone would see them pop a boner."

"It was a different time."

"It was *thirteen* fucking years ago. Not so different. He could have been out if wanted to. He could have protected me, but he chose the easy way out."

"I don't think deciding to discontinue the medication that kept him alive was taking the 'easy way out.' I think it was probably the hardest decision of his life."

Roman's voice broke. "Then why the fuck did he do it?"

"I don't know, babe."

Demetri stiffened as the endearment slipped from his lips. "Sorry, I—"

"Forget it."

But Roman didn't want to forget it. He liked the way 'babe' rolled off Demetri's tongue and how it spread warmth throughout Roman's chest. "I know you didn't mean it."

"I didn't say that."

Roman's brow went up, but Demetri didn't elaborate. He

climbed down and sat next to Roman on the guardrail, facing the city instead of the car. They both turned so they could see each other more easily in the moonlight.

Demetri put his hand over Roman's on the guardrail and bowed his head. "I thought... I thought when you ran out after I told you I was poz, that you feared my diagnosis. That you didn't know or have all the facts. That you'd thought I'd put your health in danger."

"We didn't do anything that could have infected me, even if you weren't undetectable."

"I know. It took me a long time to allow myself to start dating again, even after my viral counts dropped below the detectable range. I felt tainted. Embarrassed for letting something like that happen to me. Everyone I asked out, I disclosed my status to. It seemed only fair since I would want someone to tell me."

"How did that work out for you?"

Demetri rubbed his thumb over Roman's knuckles. Roman should take his hand back because Demetri's touch made him forget all the reasons why he'd walked out that door. But he kept his hand in place, Demetri's thumb bumping from knuckle to knuckle.

"Let's say I rarely went out on a second date. A third was unheard of. And more often than not, they flaked before even making it to the first one."

Considering his father's history, Roman had done a ton of personal research into HIV and AIDS, trying to learn as much as he could, hoping it would bring some closure or understanding for how his father had treated him. And while it hadn't brought the closure, it had given him the knowledge that perhaps other people hadn't sought. Unlike some of the other men Demetri had tried to date, knowing Demetri had HIV wasn't a deal-breaker for Roman.

"Then what made me different? Why didn't you tell me from the start?"

———

Demetri didn't answer Roman right away, trying to find the best way to answer the question and not sound like he was trying to shift the blame away from himself.

"I listened to some bad advice. That's not an excuse. More of an explanation. The theory was that if someone got to know me —the real me and not some statistic on the CDC's website—that the person might think twice about giving me a chance."

Demetri held his hands out to the side. "I didn't think it through. I didn't weigh the damage I might do. All I knew was that you intrigued me in a way a man hadn't for an awfully long time. The connection I felt with you was immediate. But I also never thought I'd see you again after that first night."

"But you did see me again. And yet you said nothing."

"I was waiting for a good time to tell you, and—"

Roman stood abruptly and paced a few strides away before coming back. "A good time to tell me would have been the first time I wanted to blow you. Or maybe the first time I asked if I could fuck you. Or when I started questioning what was wrong with me that you didn't want to fuck me. Or maybe when I fucking asked you what was wrong."

Although it would be easier, Demetri wouldn't allow himself to look away. "Any one of those times would have been good. I see that now. And I wanted to. It ate me up inside that I was falling for you but knew whatever you felt for me couldn't be real, not without you knowing the truth."

"And still, you said nothing."

Demetri went all in. If he and Roman had a chance of working through this, he had to be honest and vulnerable and not hold back no matter how hard it would be to find the words. "I was afraid of losing you. Of getting hurt. Of being rejected *again.*"

"It's not all about you. What about my feelings? My hurt? Knowing that, like with my father, I can't be trusted with your truth? That I'm unworthy of it."

Demetri reached out and took hold of Roman's arm as he stalked by. Roman stopped but kept his focus straight ahead, his body stiff, his chin high.

"I'm sorry." As Demetri's words came out, he knew they were the truest words he'd ever spoken. Even though he knew they weren't enough. "How do I make this better?"

Roman took a step back and leaned against the car. "I don't know." They sat in silence, staring out at the sky, at the blinking lights of the planes as they lined up on the runway in the distance. "How did you get it?"

Demetri glanced over at Roman, watching him in profile. "Does it matter?"

Roman shrugged. "I guess not."

"Do you think I was promiscuous? That I went from hookup to hookup and—"

"Stop." Roman looked at him then, his gaze fierce, protective, and wholly unexpected. "It doesn't matter how you got it. Whether you fucked five hundred or one. HIV is not a judgment on your character or a punishment for perceived wrongs. It's not the morality police. It's a vicious disease that doesn't care who it infects or fucks over."

A corner of Demetri's mouth tilted up into a smile, and he didn't fight it. "Careful there. You almost sound like you're on my side."

"I *am* on your side. Just because I hate the way this all rolled out, don't for one minute think I'm against you, because I'm not."

Demetri held Roman's gaze but could only nod with the lump in his throat pressing so hard it made breathing a chore.

Roman lay back on the hood, scrubbing his hands down his face as he stared up at the sky. A car pulled in at the other end of the parking lot, but the interior lights didn't come on, and no one got out.

Demetri stretched out beside Roman, not touching, but close enough to feel Roman's body heat. A satellite passed by overhead before Demetri said, "It was my previous boyfriend who gave it to me. Kind of a parting gift as our relationship crumbled."

"For fuck's sake," Roman muttered.

Demetri took that as a cue to continue. "We'd been monogamous. On his insistence. We'd both been on PrEP, but it messed with his liver, so we agreed he should stop taking it. We'd both tested negative multiple times on full STI screens. Eventually, I stopped taking mine, too. We'd made a pact from the start, that if either one of us slipped, if we had unprotected sex with someone else, we would disclose and go back to using condoms until we could both go through testing again.

"Then, near the end, as our relationship coming to an end, I found out he'd been cheating on me for months."

"Where is he now?"

"Around. I've bumped into him a time or two."

"And you didn't deck him?"

Demetri laughed. "I wanted to. But that wouldn't have changed anything, and it wouldn't have done me any good to break my hand on his face and not be able to paint or draw."

"Lucky bastard. I think I would have taken that chance. Who is he?"

It was what it was. Giving Roman the name of his ex to focus on wouldn't change anything. Not Demetri's HIV status. Not how royally Demetri had fucked up his and Roman's relationship.

Shaking his head, Demetri said, "Not anyone who matters anymore."

They let the conversation trail off into a comfortable silence. The car parked at the end of the lot started its engine and drove away. Demetri had no idea what time it was, but they both had to be back at the community lot early in the morning. His eyes wanted to drift closed. If he didn't leave soon, he'd be falling asleep at the wheel.

"We should head back, huh?" Demetri asked.

Roman startled as if he'd fallen asleep. "Yeah. I'm fried."

That late at night, traffic going into the valley was relatively light even for a Saturday night.

Demetri pulled up beside Roman's car and turned toward him, the parking lot lights illuminating the interior. "Thanks for agreeing to talk with me."

"Where do we go from here?"

"I'm leaving that up to you."

Roman stared down at his lap and nodded. Demetri took a chance and took Roman's chin in his hand until their eyes met. "If I could take it all back, I would."

"All of it?"

"No. Even if this doesn't work out, I'm fortunate to have gotten a chance to know you."

Demetri leaned in, and when Roman didn't move away, he pressed his lips to Roman's. It was meant to be chaste and sweet. But Roman groaned and opened his mouth, inviting Demetri in.

Demetri's heart raced like it was the last lap of the Indy 500, and the checkered flag lay in his sights. Roman reached for him, cupping a fierce hand behind Demetri's neck and deepening the kiss.

Demetri's lungs screamed for air, but he didn't want to break the kiss and lose their precious, tenuous connection.

Oxygen deprived and breathing hard, Roman pulled away, resting his forehead on Demetri's. "You've gotta stop doing that. It messes with my head."

"I should apologize for that too, but I'm not sorry."

Though all Demetri wanted to do was drag Roman across the center console and into his lap, he sat back. "Come find me when you've made your decision. Yeah?"

18

It was Sunday night, and between working at the community lot all day and the few precious hours of sleep he'd managed the night before, Demetri rolled up into his driveway, stifling a yawn and looking forward to a nice shower.

He tried to ignore the fact that he hadn't heard from Roman. Of course, he'd seen him all day long as they worked with the kids and painted the fence. And they'd talked. But nothing consequential.

You can't push him. You have to give him the space to come back to you or decide the damage is too great to repair.

But how long would that take? Each minute seemed like an hour. Each day a week. His concentration hadn't been that low since he'd received his diagnosis. At least back then, it had been in the summer, and he hadn't had to worry about being prepared for another week of classes.

Maybe he'd extend the project deadline, give everyone more time to work in class, and him a chance to veg.

And feel sorry for yourself.

That too.

He climbed out of his car, surprised to see Joss's Jeep still in his driveway. The front door to his house was unlocked, and Demetri walked in and called out. "It's me. I'm home."

Making his way into the kitchen for a beer, Joss popped out of the hall bathroom, wiping his hands on a rag. "Long day?"

Demetri pulled out a beer for Joss. "I could say the same to you. I thought you were only working a half-day today."

"So did I." Joss twisted off the top, and they both pulled out a chair at the kitchen table to take the weight off their feet. "The wind looks like it's going to cooperate next week, and I made plans to take some people up. I'm so backed up on my schedule. It could be weeks before I have a chance to come back and finish the bathroom, so I wanted to make sure the bathroom was at least functional before I left."

"How much more before you're finished?"

"Come look." Joss stood, and Demetri followed him to the bathroom. "I've got touch-up painting to do, the new mirror to hand, and the toilet paper holder and the towel bar to install. But I finished the caulking in the shower and around the base of the toilet. Plumbing under the sink is finished. I even got the shower rod installed so you can hang a curtain and use the shower."

"It looks amazing. You do good work."

Joss took a long pull on his beer. "Thanks... but?"

"No 'but.' It's great."

Pushing away from the door jamb, Joss headed to the kitchen. Over his shoulder, he said, "You say that with the enthusiasm of someone going in for a kidney stone removal."

Demetri chuckled. "Sorry. Just tired."

"Not sleeping?"

He shrugged, not wanting to get into it.

Joss sucked down the rest of his beer. For a big man, that didn't take much effort. He started packing up his tools. "This wouldn't have something to do with what's his name, would it?"

"Roman?"

"Unless you're having problems with more than one man."

Demetri chuckled. "I'm not like my cousin Sebastian and his fiancé. One man at a time is all I can handle. And I don't even do that well."

Joss zipped up his tool bag and glanced up at him. "You didn't tell him?"

"I did. Not the way I wanted. Spectacular fail, by the way. We're trying to pick up the pieces, but I think I did irreparable damage."

Handing Demetri his empty bottle, Joss said, "All I know is that if I felt about someone the way you feel about him, I'd do everything in my power to find a way to make it better."

"I wish I knew how."

Joss clapped him on the shoulder. "You're a smart guy. I'm sure you'll figure it out."

Demetri drained his beer and followed Joss to the front door, locking it behind him. He cut all the house lights in the house and—against his better judgment—packed his small cooler with beer and headed out to sit by his pool. The underwater lights drowned out the stars, and the ripples in the water from the skimmer cast reflections inside his house.

He stared at the ever-changing patterns, and his thoughts turned inward as he drank beer after beer. Morning Demetri would hate himself, but late-night Demetri didn't care.

Sometime in the middle of the night—or was it early morning?—drunk Demetri pulled out his phone, brought up his video app, and started talking. About his diagnosis and his battered self-esteem and self-recrimination. The shame. The guilt. The feeling sorry for himself. He rambled on and on. Beer was good at helping him do that, especially after the sixth or seventh—or was that the eighth?—one.

He didn't leave any of it out. His mistakes. His failings—his many, many failings. Pouring his heart out if only for the universe to hear. At some point, he stopped recording and set his empty beer bottle down. It fell over and rolled to the lip of the pool.

Then, even drunker Demetri did something foolish. He added a title. A few pertinent hashtags and uploaded his ramblings to his Twitter feed. He had few followers, so it was akin to shouting into the void.

He leaned back against the lounger, his eyes falling closed and his phone slipping out of his hand. It clattered onto the pool deck, but Demetri couldn't be bothered to retrieve it.

Maybe in the morning, the universe would have an answer to his big, sexy problem.

MONDAY MORNING CAME, AND ROMAN HIT SNOOZE FOR THE THIRD time. When his alarm went off again, he shut it off for good and tossed his phone onto the nightstand.

He groaned as he shifted, every muscle hurting from all the hard work over the weekend. But as sore as he was, his heart had taken the brunt of the abuse.

Ever since Saturday night, when he and Demetri had driven to the overlook and tried to talk things out, he couldn't get their conversation out of his head. He'd turned it over and over in his mind, coming at it from every angle. And damn if maybe he could understand where Demetri had come from. Why he had done what he had.

But that didn't make it hurt any less.

Moses pounded on his door so loud it hurt his head even though he hadn't been drinking.

"You're going to miss class."

"Go away."

Moses opened the door, surprisingly alert for him on a Monday morning. "Dude. I'm the fuckup, not you. You're the one who goes to class even when you went on a bender the night before and puked your guts out."

"Okay, okay." Roman pushed himself up and sat. "I get the point."

"You know he's trying, right?"

What the hell did Moses know about Demetri anyway? He and Moses had hardly seen each other all week. And while Roman had mentioned that he'd helped the pastor at the church, he'd never told him about the talk he and Demetri had that same night. Roman squinted up at his friend, the light from the hallway bright enough to blind. "What are you even talking about?"

"The video." Moses had one of those 'duh' expressions on his face.

If Moses thought that explained everything, it didn't. Roman was still lost. "What video?"

"Holy fuck." Moses laughed. "You haven't seen it, have you?"

He wasn't in the mood to stretch twenty questions into forty. "*Moses.*"

"Okay, okay."

Roman recoiled against the overhead light Moses switched on and rubbed the sleep out of his eyes. His mattress dipped, and when he could focus again, Moses sat cross-legged beside him on the bed, his phone in his hand as he brought up his Twitter feed.

"Your boyfriend has gone viral."

"Since when? And he's not my boyfriend."

"Since I don't know. Sometime this morning maybe. Gay Twitter is all atwitter." Moses laughed at his pathetic joke. Roman didn't. "Aw c'mon, man. That was hilarious."

"Just show me the video."

Moses pressed play and handed over his phone. Instead of watching it over Roman's shoulder the way he expected Moses would, Moses bounced off the bed and at the threshold said, "I'll be in the kitchen if you wanna talk after."

He didn't watch his roommate leave because Demetri's voice came through the speaker. Demetri's slightly slurred, still sexy as hell, voice.

"Being poz isn't the end of the world," Demetri said. "But when you first get that call, you're going to think it is..."

Demetri's video came straight from his heart. He talked about being gay, about how not being out about his diagnosis had forced him back into the closet in a way. About how important he realized it was to be honest because that's how you fought and broke stigmas. He went on to talk about his struggles with relationships, in far greater, drunken detail than he had a couple of nights before.

"You know," Demetri said as if he was winding down. "A very wise man once told me that 'HIV is not a judgment on your character or a punishment for perceived wrongs. It's not the morality police. It's a vicious disease that doesn't care who it infects or fucks over.'

"So, if you are watching this, don't be an idiot like me. Learn from my mistakes. Don't hide in shame because you have nothing to be ashamed of. Be kind. Be truthful. But most of all, don't be afraid to be the real you."

A finger went toward the phone as if Demetri were about to turn off the video, then backed off. "Oh, and wear a condom. Take your PrEP. And, babe, if you're watching... I truly am sorry. And I love you."

Demetri kissed two fingers and made a peace sign at the camera. "Peace out."

That showed how drunk Demetri was. He probably hadn't said 'peace out' since high school. But that lump in Roman's throat refused to dislodge no matter how many times he tried to swallow.

And, babe, if you're watching... I truly am sorry. And I love you.

Did Demetri mean that? Or did those words only come out because he was too drunk to know what he was saying?

And I love you.

Roman stumbled out of his bedroom in only his boxers and dropped down onto one of the kitchen chairs. Moses grinned over at him and poured Roman a bowl of Lucky Charms. He wrinkled his nose at the sour milk he pulled from the fridge and slid the bowl of dry cereal in front of Roman.

"Well?" Moses raised an impatient, expectant brow.

Around a handful of cereal shoved into his mouth, Roman said, "Well, what?" It came out sounding like "'ell ut.'

"*Gurl.* You can't be serious."

Roman didn't answer. He was too busy trying to chew and swallow, but that didn't stop Moses from going off on him.

"I can't believe you. You can forgive a homophobic pastor, but you can't forgive the man who told the whole world in a viral video that he loves you?"

Roman blinked at Moses, at a loss for what to say.

"*Dude.* That's seriously messed up."

No. What was *messed up* was Moses, of all people, being the voice of reason.

Roman kept chewing. Moses stared at him, that *I know you* expression on his face with perhaps a little bit of *who are you and what have you done with my friend* thrown in.

With both hands, Moses gripped the back of a chair and leaned across the table, his gaze unwavering. "What are you really afraid of?"

What the actual fuck?

"That he's going to stop taking his meds? That he's going to die and leave you the way your father did?" Moses paced to the sink and back, scrubbing a hand through his bed-tousled hair. "News flash. The professor's not your father."

"I know that."

"*Do you?*"

Roman stood and grabbed his keys off the counter. "I've got class."

He made it to the door before Moses called out, "Yeah, but you don't have any clothes on."

He glanced down at his bare chest, legs, and feet.

Fuck me.

He got dressed and drove to campus. Classes passed by in a haze of lectures that Roman didn't take notes on. All he could think about was the video. With Demetri being one of the professors at the college, he overheard bits and pieces of conversation about it. The post probably wouldn't have gone beyond the gay community on Twitter if Demetri hadn't been associated with the school.

Roman didn't get any side-eye from the other students because no one knew Demetri had been talking about him. Except maybe Emily, and he'd managed to avoid her.

And when he'd gotten to the Center to work that night, Grant had been holed up in his office planning out the last weekends of work for the community lot while Roman wrangled the kids. Luckily, the kids were mostly too young for social media. And those who had it weren't on Twitter.

After the last kid left, he went back into the gym to put away the sports equipment. He picked up a basketball and started making free throws. He fell into the mindless physicality of it, the hollow bounce of the ball, the soft swoosh of the net, the squeak of his shoes on the wood floor.

A ball bounced him, and he turned to find Grant. Grant made a shot from across the court. It bounced off the edge of the backboard and skittered into the corner.

"You okay?" Grant asked.

Roman passed his ball to Grant. "Why wouldn't I be?"

Grant moved to half court, bouncing the ball between his legs, acting like he was going to make a run for the net. Roman moved to block him. Grant faked to the left, but he telegraphed the move, and Roman hung with him to the foul line behind the net, his arms in the air, blocking Grant's shot.

When Roman came up with the ball, Grant said, "I've been busy. But not that busy. Especially when Sebastian DMed me the video."

Roman made an easy shot look difficult. It hit the backboard, nowhere close to the rim, and it fell into Grant's hands on the far side of the basket. He jumped and made a three-point shot with nothing but net.

Roman was in over his head.

And he wasn't just talking about the impromptu one-on-one game.

"We're trying to figure things out."

"Demetri took a huge risk, saying what he said in that video. I know it wasn't all about you, but it was *because* of you."

Grant held his hands out, and Roman passed him the ball even though it wasn't his possession. He didn't shoot. Grant tucked the ball under his arm and closed the distance between them. "Demetri's a good man. I'm not saying I know what happened between you two. All I'm saying is he's not the type of guy who deliberately sets out to hurt someone. But take what I have to say with a grain of salt. I'm on the outside looking in. Whatever you're feeling is valid."

"Thanks." Roman held out his hand, and Grant shook it.

"Now get out of here."

"I still need to finish cleaning up here and in the art room."

"I'll get it. You go home and get some rest. It looks like you could use it before the zombies come and claim you as one of their own."

He probably wasn't far from wrong. The exhaustion settled into Roman's bones as he got into his car to drive home.

Unfortunately, he wasn't any closer to solving his Demetri problem than he'd been when he'd woken up that morning.

***

Joss's drill whirred in the bathroom. He'd found some time to finish up the last few checklist items and was trying to get everything finished. Demetri sat at his kitchen table, staring out the front windows, his microwaved pizza untouched, and growing cold. But all he saw against the darkened window was his pathetic reflection.

He glanced down at his phone, checking his DMs. He didn't expect to hear from Roman but had hoped that he would. In his long string of notifications, it would be easy to miss it if Roman responded.

At least that's what he kept telling himself.

"That's me done then," Joss said as he walked into the kitchen, his tool bag slung over one shoulder.

"Let me get my checkbook."

Joss waved him off. "PayPal it to me. It's fine. I trust you."

At least somebody trusted him.

Joss tapped a finger on the table as if he had something else to say but didn't know how to say it. "For what it's worth, what you said in that video... It was beautiful. And brave. And from what I read in the comments, much needed."

"I was drunk."

Joss shook his head. "Not that drunk. But hey, if that excuse helps, I'm not going to judge."

Headlights flashed as a car pulled up to the curb. Joss watched until someone climbed out. "You've got company."

His empty stomach rolled. Demetri shoved his plate away. He didn't need the cheap pizza to add insult. Besides, Demetri wouldn't be able to swallow with the way his saliva had dried up, and his mouth had gone dry.

His palms sweated. Bracing a hand on the table, he stood, leaving a damp handprint behind.

This was it. Either Roman had come to dump him face to face, or...

It was the 'or' that kept Demetri's heart beating with the dregs of hope.

"I'm gonna get," Joss said as Roman strode up the sidewalk. "I still have two chutes to pack before my hop tomorrow." Then he turned back at the front door. "Good luck. I mean it."

"Thanks." Demetri's voice croaked, but there wasn't anything he could do about that.

Joss opened the door before Roman had a chance to knock. He clamped one hand on Roman's shoulder as he left. "Don't fuck it up."

Joss had one of those voices that carried, even when he tried to keep it down.

Roman said something back, but the pounding behind Demetri's ears blocked the sound. He wished he'd heard, then maybe he would have a few precious seconds to prepare himself before Roman made it into the kitchen and said whatever he'd come to say.

Now... he could only watch Roman approach as Joss closed the door behind him.

"Hey." Roman stepped into the kitchen, a self-conscious, shy smile on his face that melted Demetri from the inside out.

"H-hey, yourself."

"Can we talk?"

"I'd like that," Demetri said, even though that conversation could be the beginning of the end. At least when the talking was done, he'd have his answer. The waiting and not knowing and the uncertainly were killing him. "Here, okay?"

The way Roman grinned, Demetri couldn't imagine this conversation going bad, then that smile slipped off Roman's face. "I think that would be safest. Out here in a fishbowl with the shades up and the lights on. It'll keep us from getting ourselves into trouble before we hash things out."

Demetri held his hand out in invitation and retook his seat. Roman sat across from him. He had on a pair of jeans so soft it wore like a second skin. His tank top showed off the balls of his shoulders and the bulge of his biceps. He had scruff on his jaw that looked like it had been there since Friday and bags under his eyes that Demetri felt responsible for putting there.

Still, Demetri wanted to say fuck the talk and just get his hands on Roman. So yeah, the fishbowl was the safest place for them. Good call.

"First off," Roman said, "I'm pissed that the only art class that fulfilled my graduation requirement was landscape drawing. If I have to draw one more leaf, I'm going to go insane. I'm not sure I can ever forgive you for that."

Roman didn't smile, but his eyes lit with a spark.

Demetri held back his return smile as best he could, but he wasn't nearly as successful as Roman had been.

The fact that Roman cracked a joke had to be a good sign. Right?

"Duly noted." Demetri injected as much solemnity as he could muster. "You said 'first off.' Is that the start of a list of demands? Should I get a pen and paper to take notes?"

"It's not that long of a list. Second..." Roman's gaze went around the room but didn't stop and focus on anything particular. Demetri waited Roman out, while Demetri's brainstem forgot to tell him to breathe. "You said you loved me. I heard it. So did—" he checked something on his phone. "One point five million others at last count."

Demetri blew out a breath. Besides scrolling through his DMs, he'd stayed off the platform, knowing you should never read the comments. Still, those kinds of numbers were staggering. "You can't be serious?"

Roman held the phone up for Demetri to see. He'd rounded the numbers down by about fifty thousand.

"About that."

"You don't... love me?"

"I do." Demetri held Roman's assessing gaze, never wavering. "But I know it's early, and I don't want you freaking out and feeling any pressure if it takes longer for you to get there."

"What if I never do?" The shift in Roman's expression made the words come out more like a teasing jab.

"That wouldn't be as ideal."

Roman leaned those beefy arms on the table. "Why not?"

"Because I think if I have to leave you tied to my bed day in and day out, the neighbors are close enough to hear you scream for help. Maybe a house with a basement is a better option."

"What if I don't need rescuing?"

And fuck if those six little words didn't make the back of Demetri's eyes sting. "What are you trying to say?" With his chest tight with emotion, he sounded winded when he spoke.

"That maybe all this isn't your fault." Roman's eyes reddened. "I have a lot more baggage than I thought. This ride we're on... it's made me realize how much it weighs me down."

"I'm sorry for what your father did. Not telling you he had AIDS, it wasn't right. But I don't think he did it to hurt you. I think he did it to protect himself."

"The way you did?"

That previous ray of hope Roman's teasing had brought him snuffed out.

Demetri nodded. "I'll understand if what I did is too much to forgive." He reached across the table and squeezed Roman's hand. "But I appreciate you coming here and telling me in person and not doing it over text, or completely ghosting me. I know this couldn't have been easy."

Somehow Demetri got all the words out without his voice failing him. And if he blinked fast enough, stray tears wouldn't fall either.

"I've been thinking. About my dad. He must have had the same fear of rejection. And while I'll never understand why he stopped taking his meds, I don't believe he did it with malice. I had to dig deep, but I found forgiveness for him. Something I was never allowed to give him while he was alive. But you're still here and deserving of the same grace, I think.

"What I'm trying to say and failing spectacularly is..." Roman flipped his hand over and held onto Demetri's before he could take it away. "...is that I'm not breaking up with you. Or at least I wouldn't be if we hadn't split already. I mean... I'd like to see where this might go. If you still want me."

"More than anything." His grip tightened on Roman's hand. "I'm sorry I lied. Even more, I'm sorry you have to sit through a landscape drawing class for the rest of the semester."

Roman laughed and leaned across the table. He kissed Demetri, a strong hand around his neck to keep him in place. Their tongues teased and tasted when all Demetri wanted to do was devour him. When Roman finally let go, Demetri's hard-on pressed against the soft fabric of his athletic shorts, begging to come out and play.

But he wasn't going to make the first move. That Roman had come to his house ready to give them another try was more than enough.

Roman gestured at the pizza on the plate. "You going to eat that?"

"Go ahead."

After Roman took a slice, Demetri took one as well. It tasted like ketchup spread on cardboard with a layer of plastic cheese melted on top. But damn if it wasn't also the best pizza Demetri had ever sunk his teeth into.

They swallowed down the last of it, and Demetri asked, "What changed your mind?"

"It wasn't one thing. It was a bunch of little things. The way you made me feel when I was around you, like you'd won both the jackpot and the lottery. It was also your smile. The way you held me in your arms. The way you had so many people on your side."

"There are no sides. No one is against you. Especially me."

"I know that. But having everyone advocate for you high-lighted the fact that you wouldn't have so many people in the world who love you if your heart weren't in the right place."

Roman fell silent, but Demetri waited him out. "And then Moses... fucking Moses of all people," Roman said with a laugh, "challenged me. He said something to the effect of how it had been so easy for me to forgive the pastor, but that I couldn't find it in me to forgive you."

Meeting Demetri's eyes again, Roman's jaw worked side to side. "It hit *hard*. And he was so right."

Roman continued. "It's the people I care about the most who deserve grace and forgiveness. And it took my dope-head friend to help me see that. And for that, I'm sorry."

"Roman?"

"Yeah?"

"Stop talking and get your ass over here."

19

DEMETRI STOOD, AND ROMAN HURRIED AROUND THE TABLE AND walked into Demetri's waiting arms. Roman couldn't think of any other place he'd rather be. As the tightness in his chest eased and his eyes started to dry, he knew he had to get one more thing out before they could move forward.

Demetri might think it was stupid, but it was crucial to that part of Roman who feared getting left behind. Roman pulled back, and Demetri rubbed his cheeks dry.

"I need one promise," Roman said.

"Anything."

"You can't ever stop taking your meds. You can't let me fall in love with you and do something stupid like that down the road."

Demetri sobered. "That's one promise that will be easy for me to keep. I want to live, especially with you in my life. But even if you aren't, if we don't work out, life's too beautiful, and too many people have already died from this disease for me to throw what I have away."

"You swear?" Roman held up his hand, his pinky finger extended toward Demetri.

"A pinkie promise?"

"Hey, they're unbreakable." He held his hands up as if the rules were out of his control. "I don't make the rules."

Demetri locked fingers with him. "Promise."

Roman pulled him in for a simple kiss when he wanted so much more. Demetri tasted of crappy college dorm pizza and a wish come true. God, he wanted him.

He backed Demetri to the wall, his hard-on pressed against Demetri's lower abdomen. He'd been dreaming of sucking Demetri off since that night in the alley, and Demetri had no reason to refuse him now.

Roman palmed Demetri through his athletic shorts, his mouth working its way up Demetri's jawline to his ear. "I want this. What do you think?"

Demetri chuckled. "I think we're about to give the Reynoldses across the street a gay education."

Roman nipped at Demetri's earlobe and broke away. "Hold that thought."

He ran over to the front windows and lowered the blinds. Though unnecessary, did the same to the blinds on the sliding glass doors overlooking the pool. Once he and Demetri got started, he didn't plan on stopping until they were nothing but a puddle of sweat and sated bodies.

They'd have plenty of time for the bedroom later, but Roman couldn't wait the seconds it would take for them to walk the forty or so extra feet.

He hooked his fingers in Demetri's elastic waistband and slowly drew the shorts down. A line of exposed skin appeared first, that sexy trail of hair arrowing down, pointing to where Roman wanted to be most.

Demetri's hand gently held the back of Roman's head in anticipation. Roman tugged on the fabric some more. Demetri must have adjusted himself while Roman dealt with the shades because the slick tip of Demetri's hard cock greeted him first.

He slid the shorts to the tops of Demetri's thighs, fully exposing Demetri's goods. And what goods they were. He skimmed a finger along the underside of Demetri's dick.

Demetri sucked in a breath. "Don't be shy."

Roman had always found Demetri's low, thick voice so damn sexy, and he wanted to kiss that half-grin off Demetri's face.

"I'm not shy. I'm building the sexual tension."

"The anticipation is already there. I've been jacking off almost every night to the thought of those lips working their magic on my dick. In fact, I've jacked off so much, I considered buying stock in lube."

Roman feigned like he was about to get up. "Well, I wouldn't want to ruin the lube sales projections for the next quarter."

Demetri put a firm, staying hand on Roman's shoulder. "Your mouth. My dick. Now."

Chuckling, Roman did as Demetri demanded. Not that it was any hardship on his part. He traced the same trail up the underside of Demetri's cock with his tongue, loving Demetri's musky smell. He buried his nose in his short, cropped pubes and breathed him in, Roman's hard-on crying for relief.

But this was about pleasuring Demetri. Up to this point, Demetri had showered all the attention on Roman. Now it was Demetri's turn to be on the receiving end of all that delicious pleasure.

He swirled his tongue around Demetri's tip, the salty precum a taste Roman would never tire of. Then he gripped the base and took Demetri to the back of his throat. Demetri grunted, his head thumping back against the wall with a thud. Demetri was the perfect length, stopping short of making Roman gag. And that girth? *Jesus.* Utter perfection.

The Goldilocks of dicks.

Not so big that Roman would have to psyche himself up

before he jumped on it. But big enough—and with the slight upward curve—to reach the best spots and fill him fully.

He bobbed up and down on Demetri's dick, driving Demetri ever closer to that edge. Roman's felt the faintest contractions along Demetri's taint. He stopped and ran his hands down Demetri's thighs and a finger along the crack of Demetri's ass.

When Roman decided he'd let Demetri come, Demetri stepped away and pulled Roman to his feet. "As much as I love that sexy mouth of yours on me, I really want to fuck you."

Though Roman liked to top, bottoming was where it was at for him. So much so that he'd prepped himself before going over. You know... just in case.

"Oh, hell yeah."

Demetri grinned. Roman would willingly say yes for the rest of his life to see Demetri's face light up like that. It was like the sun shined brighter, the moon rose higher, the stars got *starrier*. If that were even a word. But Roman had better things to contemplate than word choice.

Shucking his shorts and underwear, Demetri took Roman's hand and led him to the bedroom. The underwater lights from the pool shined through Demetri's sliding glass door. The reflection of water on the wall made it feel like an underwater paradise.

Roman didn't waste time on a slow tease taking off his clothes. Demetri had already seen him naked. Demetri's shirt quickly joined Roman's clothes on the floor in a messy pile. Turning to the bedside table, Demetri found a strip of condoms and a rather large bottle of lube.

Roman's eyes went wide, and he grinned. That's what he was talking about. "Where do you want me?"

"On your back," Demetri said, "I want to see your face when I sink into you."

ROMAN NAKED ON HIS BACK IN THE MIDDLE OF DEMETRI'S BED WAS a sight to behold. The way the pool light reflected off his body, highlighting dips and valleys and the bulge of muscle and brawn, would have made Demetri want to reach for his sketch pad if he didn't have more immediate plans for Roman.

He climbed onto the bed in between Roman's legs, bracing himself above him, unable to believe Roman hadn't rejected him out of hand. Sure, they had a connection and attraction. But for Roman to be able to get past Demetri's omission, to forgive him and accept him and his diagnosis, spoke to the incredible kind of man Roman was.

"Demetri?"

He shook those thoughts away and focused on the man beneath him. "Yeah?"

"I can see those wheels churning. Stop it. It's just you and me. Forget all the other bullshit. Think you can do that?" Roman licked his hand and took hold of Demetri's dick. His grip warm and firm as he started to stoke. "Or do you need me to show you how to forget?"

Demetri's eyes drifted closed. He thrust into Roman's hand. Within seconds, the rest of the world disappeared.

When he opened his eyes, Roman grinned up at him. "I love that my touch can make you forget to breathe."

Demetri chuckled and let out the breath he held. "You took my brain offline."

"That's the whole idea."

Roman pulled Demetri in for a kiss, his hand holding Demetri's hip until Roman took all his weight. Their cocks aligned, and they ground against each other, the friction shooting sparks straight to Demetri's balls. Roman's strong hands kneaded Demetri's ass. Then Roman lightly dragged his fingers up Demetri's spine, sending out shock waves of goosebumps all over Demetri's skin.

He needed to be inside Roman. The drive almost unbearable. He kissed across the stubble on Roman's jaw and worked his way down, paying extra close attention to Roman's nipples. One lick across the stiff peaks had Roman's back arching, his grunt and low growl one of the sexiest sounds Demetri had ever heard.

"Are you going to fuck me or not?" Roman grumbled, his feigned petulance fucking adorable.

"I'll get there," Demetri said, loving the way Roman's precum smeared across Demetri's chest as Roman fought to find the friction he needed to get off.

But Demetri was determined to make Roman wait, wanting to drive him to the brink of reason. He scooted farther down Roman's body, licking a trail down his centerline, making Roman's cock bob in anticipation.

Demetri went around Roman's dick, nipping at his hip bones instead.

"Motherfucker," Roman complained. "Just—" Demetri sucked one of Roman's balls into his mouth. "Fuck, yeah. That's what I'm talking about."

Roman started stroking himself. Demetri came up for air and said, "Did I say you could do that? Hands behind your head."

"That's cruel," Roman said, though he complied, his dick standing straight out from his body.

"We're both gonna get off soon enough." Demetri settled on his haunches, throwing Roman's legs over his shoulders and diving in to get another taste of him.

Demetri loved eating ass.

And he loved eating Roman's ass the most.

Roman's hands went to the back of Demetri's head, holding

him in place as Demetri licked and sucked his way down Roman's taint to that delicious hole waiting for his attention.

His tongue teased the tight rim of muscle. Roman thrust against Demetri's face until his tongue breached his hole. Roman gasped, and a growly, sexy chuckle escaped. "Oh, fuck yeah."

He worked Roman's hole harder. The scent of musk thick in the air only made him hungrier for more.

Demetri stroked his already supercharged dick. Roman's breaths came quick, his chest billowing. Demetri pulled away with a grunt of disapproval from Roman. As great as it was eating him out, Demetri wanted to bury himself inside him even more.

He reached for the strip of condoms, pulled one free, and quickly sheathed himself. He flipped the top on the bottle of lube and poured it into his hand, slicking himself up generously before doing the same to Roman's hole.

Roman reached for him, and he braced himself on one arm, devouring Roman in a kiss. Their tongues dueling. Mating.

More.

He needed more.

Roman pushed back on the finger Demetri used to lube him up, and his finger slid in with ease. Roman's head fell back, breaking the kiss, his breath hitching on a long, throaty groan.

"Fuck that feels good."

"Ready for more?"

Roman nodded. "Always."

Demetri chuckled and scraped his teeth over one of Roman's nipples. "I love a hungry bottom."

He sunk a second finger inside Roman. "Jesus Christ," Roman muttered as he fucked himself on Demetri's fingers. Then Demetri rubbed against Roman's prostate, Roman's head slinging side to side as his legs began to quake.

"Right... fuck...uh... there." Roman's words little more than guttural grunts and groans.

When his two fingers easily slid in and out of Roman, Demetri shifted and laid Roman's thighs laid over his own. He placed the tip of his cock against Roman's hole, waiting for Roman to meet his eyes before continuing. "You sure this is what you want?"

Roman put a hand over the one Demetri had resting on Roman's thigh. "I want you, professor. That's what I want."

The way the word 'professor' rolled off Roman's tongue like an endearment made Demetri's chest tight. And the sincerity in those words made it sound as if Roman wanted more than his dick. That maybe they'd find their way through the mess Demetri had made of everything.

"You're thinking again. Stop."

"I'm stopping."

He wrapped his hands around Roman's thighs and eased inside, the tight ring of muscle gripping his cock until he'd sunk to his balls. He stilled. Caught his breath—only seconds away from it ending all too soon.

Those beautiful green eyes of Roman's that had intrigued him from the start drifted closed, Roman's his jaw slack and hanging open. He rolled his pelvis, taking Demetri even deeper.

Demetri watched as Roman's balls drew up tight, much like his own, and gripped Roman's hips to hold him still. "You gotta give me a minute."

"Nope." Roman hooked his hands behind Demetri's thighs, urging him to move.

Demetri gave up. The need to pound into Roman nearly overwhelming, he braced his hands on either side of Roman's chest and gave Roman what he needed.

He nearly pulled out before sliding back in again. Long, smooth strokes. Then he shifted, aiming for Roman's prostate.

Roman shook with pleasure. "Harder. Faster," Roman grunted. "Show me what you've got, old man."

"Fuck you." Demetri's laugh turned into a grunt when Roman gripped Demetri's hips and took over, fucking himself on Demetri's dick.

"*Exactly.*"

Demetri couldn't hold out any longer, the exquisite torture rocketing him to the brink. He drove into Roman, giving him the pounding he'd been craving. *Demanding.*

Sweat slicked Demetri's body, and he had a hard time drawing enough oxygen, his lungs working double time. Roman was so tight, so...

The tingling at the base of Demetri's spine exploded, sending pulses of lightning shooting down his nerves. Roman gripped his dick and started jacking himself. If Demetri hadn't already been on the edge, watching Roman would have been enough to make him come.

Demetri stiffened above Roman as his climax hit, his body shaking from the effects and the effort. Roman didn't slow, ramming himself down on Demetri dick over and over, his hand a blur on his cock. Then he shouted out. Thick ropes of cum shot across his abdomen.

The expression on Roman's face was one Demetri never wanted to forget. The throes of lust and passion etched deeply in his features. Roman's hand finally fell away, his cock gradually softened and fell off to the side. Demetri gently pulled out and stretched out beside Roman while they both caught their breath.

He rested his head on Roman's shoulder, drawing a lazy finger through the jizz on Roman's chest. He brought the finger to his lips and licked it clean. "Mmm. I love how you taste."

Roman chuckled and pulled Demetri in for a kiss. "And I love the way I taste on you. So. Fucking. Sexy."

Demetri rolled onto his back. "My vote is we stay here forever. Fuck and have food delivered until we run out of funds."

If only he could be so lucky. "Works for me. But maybe we should wait until you get tenure. Then they'd have a much harder time firing your ass when you stop showing up for classes."

Demetri braced himself on an elbow. "I could always put in for a sabbatical. Tell them it's for research into the male form." He dragged a finger up the inside of Roman's thigh, and though spent, Roman's blood flow started to return. It wouldn't take much for him to get totally hard again.

"Are we talking any male form, or do you have a particular one in mind?"

"There's this fitness model who DMed me. He might be interested." Demetri couldn't keep his face straight, the grin breaking out.

Roman loved Demetri's teasing side. "Maybe we'll need that basement after all. I could keep you chained down there so you could service me."

Demetri groaned and sat up. "How the hell do you make that sound so enticing?"

"Where you going?"

"Getting rid of the condom. Trust me. I'm not going anywhere."

Why those words made Roman's chest tight, he didn't know. But it didn't sound like Demetri meant he wasn't going anywhere right then, it sounded like he meant *ever*.

It was too early to talk seriously about their future, but even though their relationship wasn't in the clear, it didn't seem on the skids anymore.

He watched Demetri walk away, unable to keep his eyes off

that ass and the play of muscle across his back. Demetri had the strong, trim physique of an X-Game-level skateboarder. A lot of raw power in a slim package. It fascinated Roman.

Demetri returned with a warm, wet washcloth. He knelt on the bed and cleaned Roman up with a care and reverence Roman found endearing. Demetri's thoughts had gone inward again, a kind of melancholy coming over him.

Roman caught his wrist. "What is it?"

"Fuck, babe. I keep thinking how stupid I was. How I almost ruined everything."

The term of endearment raised a lump in Roman's throat. He loved the sound of it. Loved that Demetri had used it. "You can't take all of the blame. My past didn't help. It took me some time to see that. And a nudge from Moses to look at it from another perspective. I understand your need to protect yourself because that's what I'd been trying to do myself."

Demetri tossed the wet rag into the bathroom. It sailed through the open door of the shower and landed with a slap.

"Nice shot."

Demetri grinned. Part devilment and all sexy. "What's my reward?"

Roman sprung up and rolled on top of him, penning Demetri's arms above his head. He was already getting hard again. So was Demetri. "I think that's something better shown than told."

Roman took Demetri in his hand. He wanted—needed—to taste him. And this time he'd wouldn't let Demetri distract him before he reached his goal.

By the time he'd finished with Demetri, his jaws ached, and his biceps were fatigued, but fuck if it hadn't been worth it to finally taste Demetri on his tongue.

They lay on the bed in sticky, sweaty bliss. A pile of limp arms and legs and dicks.

Overhead, the ceiling fan turned lazily, the light breeze cooling their over-heated skin. He had no idea what time it was and decided he'd be better off not knowing in the morning how little sleep he got.

They showered off—too exhausted to do more than a perfunctory wash—and changed the damp, cum-stained sheets before falling into bed naked. He curled up behind Demetri and pulled him into his chest, his cock lining up with Demetri's sexy ass, too worn out to do anything about it.

But with the way things were going, he felt confident there would be a next time to explore that option.

Then he realized that Demetri hadn't asked him to stay. Was Demetri laying there wondering how to ask him to leave? Demetri had joked about wanting to stay in bed together forever, but that could have been the afterglow of sex talking.

"Hey," Roman said. Demetri jerked as if Roman had woken him. "I can go if—"

Demetri made a sound in the back of his throat. The kind of sound you'd make if your dog were getting into the garbage. Then he reached back and cupped Roman's head. "Babe, I want you to stay."

He kissed that tender spot where Demetri's neck met his shoulder. "Okay."

Roman woke sometime later, the light shades of a pink sun peeking over the back fence. He lay on his stomach on the bed on a diagonal, one arm flopped over one side, one foot hanging off the other, his morning wood trapped beneath him. That slow turning fan emitting the faintest squeak with every turn.

He heard a noise behind him and braced himself on his arms and glanced over his shoulder. Demetri was sitting naked in a folding chair he'd brought into the room, his heel tucked up on the edge of the seat, with a sketchpad on his upturned knee.

"What are you doing?"

"Don't move," Demetri said. Roman resettled into the position he'd woken in. "And I'm drawing you. What's it look like I'm doing?"

Roman wiggled his ass, and he heard Demetri's short intake of breath. "Don't do that or I'll never get this done."

"I'm okay with that." Roman started to move.

"Hold still."

"I've gotta piss."

The warm, soft notes of Demetri laugh touched him like a caress. "Tough. All I need is five more minutes."

Five minutes remaining in one of Roman's exams flew by in seconds. This five minutes, with his over-full bladder pressed against the mattress, would feel like an hour.

"Ten minutes tops."

Roman groaned. "Fuck me."

"When I'm finished."

It was Roman's turn to laugh. He could still feel the aftereffects of being fucked the night before, but if Demetri wanted to fuck him again, he was a go.

As Roman lay there, the only sound came from the ceiling fan and the light scratching of Demetri's pencils on the sketchpad. When he didn't think he could wait any longer to pee, Demetri said, "Done. You can get up now."

Roman sprinted for the bathroom and hung his head in relief as he emptied his bladder. He flushed and washed his hands before returning to the bedroom.

Demetri was still where he'd left him, working on some aspect of the drawing. How Demetri had managed to see well enough to put pencil to paper in the dim morning light, Roman would never know. "Can I see?"

Demetri held the pad to his chest and glanced up. "Not yet."

"Fair enough." Roman dropped down onto the bed again.

Judging from the morning light, he probably had another

hour before he had to get up, grab a change of clothes from his apartment, and go to class. He fluffed up a pillow and rolled on his side, his legs slightly splayed and his semi-hard dick resting on his thigh as he watched Demetri work.

He couldn't help the hard-on. Just looking at Demetri did that to him, especially when he had the memories of the night before playing in his mind like his own erotic OnlyFans page.

He didn't have a fraction of the drawing talent that Demetri had, so he appreciated watching him work, even if it was from the wrong side of the sketchpad.

"Right there. Don't move."

Demetri's brows knit together as he concentrated on his drawing, and fuck if he wasn't sexy as hell when he settled deep into artist mode. It almost made Roman want to grab a pad of paper himself, but he knew he could never do Demetri justice. He wouldn't be able to capture his warmth, his kindness, his vulnerability.

Demetri glanced up, his concentration shifting. "What are you doing?"

Roman glanced down at the hand that had drifted to his dick without conscious thought. A pool of precum collected on his thigh, a drop or two spilling over the side. "Come over here, and I'll explain it to you."

Demetri's eyes turned dark and smoldering. "Don't tempt me."

It was hard to tempt someone so intent on their work. Roman could almost feel every line of his body that Demetri traced with his pencils, could feel the shading on his inner thigh, the light strokes as Demetri fleshed out his dick.

His skin pricked, and his balls drew up. He was going to blow a load, Demetri's drawing be damned. Half expecting a verbal reprimand, Roman glanced up to find that Demetri had set his sketchpad aside and had his dick in his hand, his eyes locked on Roman as he matched him stroke for stroke.

Watching Demetri jack off while watching him do the same immediately threw Roman over the edge. "Fuck," Roman gritted out as his orgasm crashed through his system, his heart racing laps in his chest.

"*Jesus.*" The word coming out strangled, as Demetri threw back his head and came all over his bare chest. When he finished, he laughed as he came back to himself.

Roman smiled. "I've never had that much fun jacking off before. I highly recommend. Five stars."

Demetri grabbed his T-shirt off the floor and mopped up the mess on his torso before crawling across the bed and cleaning up Roman, too.

"Do me favor." Demetri leaned over and pressed a kiss to Roman's lips.

"What's that?"

"Stay here with me today. I already emailed my students and canceled my classes."

"You can do that?"

Demetri shrugged and sat back on his haunches. "I just did."

It was afternoon, and Demetri still had his blinds drawn because he and Roman hadn't bothered getting dressed. Usually, he loved the way the afternoon light came into his den. He had his easel set up there in the extra space behind the couch.

It surprised him to find that the filtered light coming through the shades was equally as interesting. Earlier, he'd turned the couch around to catch the best of the light and picked up his sketchpad after Roman had fallen asleep on the couch. The lazy morning had given them both the time to relax and recharge.

At least on Demetri's end. The stress of being apart and the worry about when he should disclose, as well as the total mind-fuck of knowing how much he'd hurt Roman, had left him emotionally battered. Having a few precious hours to reconnect and *breathe* while cocooned in his house was a gift.

And being able to tap back into his creative energy now that things had settled somewhat gave him the charge that he needed. As he sketched the outline of Roman's prone form, his mind wandered back to the drunk video he'd posted. He hadn't expected it to resonate with so many people. He'd only hoped to reach one man.

In the back of his head, he had a niggling thought. Roman hadn't told him he loved him. Demetri hadn't expected him to say that right away. Demetri knew despite Roman's forgiveness, he still had a lot to make up for.

But some kind of affirmation that Roman had strong feelings for him would go a long way to setting his mind at ease.

Don't push. Don't cling. Give him the space to come to you when and if his feelings match yours. You've got all the time in the world.

Or until Roman graduates at the end of the fall semester.

What if he got a job offer out of the valley?

What if all the time they had left was a couple of months?

Stop. Breathe. Paint.

His phone dinged, and he glanced at the notification. Overall, the DMs he'd received about the video had been amazing and uplifting. There were always a few trolls, but he blocked them and moved on with his life. He didn't need that kind of negativity swirling around him.

But *this* DM was different. He clicked to expand it. And holy cow... It was from the producers at TBSX. They wanted him to be part of a documentary they were doing about living with HIV.

"Why are you grinning?" Roman's voice rolled out of him, the edges rough with sleep.

He told Roman about the documentary.

Roman hugged the pillow he'd had behind his head to his chest. "You going to do it?"

"I don't know yet. I think I'm interested, though. The more we can break down stereotypes and stigmas, the better off everyone will be. And maybe if I'm not hammered, my thoughts will be a little more coherent."

"You think?" Roman stood and stretched. He went over and gave Demetri a quick kiss. "The rawness helped get your point across, and your vulnerability and sweet nature shined through. I think that's what people are connecting with. A real person who made real mistakes. Not some buffed and polished Hollywood version of yourself."

Demetri took Roman's hand, guided him onto his lap, and wrapped his arm around Roman's waist. "I'm glad the video's helping people. I'm glad it's opening up the conversation about HIV, but most of all, I'm glad it brought you back to me."

"Me, too."

Roman's stomach growled. Demetri's pantry was empty of anything that resembled real food. They'd been lucky he'd had enough mold-less bread to make toast that morning when they'd finally come up for air and climbed out of bed.

"I've been a bad boyfriend," Demetri said. "Demanding all the sex but not feeding you properly. Get dressed, and I'll take you to a very late lunch or an early dinner." The way he'd wanted to from the start but concerns about his job prevented him from doing so.

"*Boyfriend*." Roman grinned. He had the warmest smile. "I like the sound of that."

"It's got a good ring to it."

"But if we go out, I'll have to get dressed. And you would have to get dressed. And I wouldn't be able to sit on your lap naked and do this." Roman grazed his thumb across the tip of Demetri dick. His thumb came away slick, and he brought it to his mouth and sucked it dry.

As much as it pained him, when Roman went back for more, Demetri laid his hand over Roman's and stopped him. "You keep doing that, and we're both likely to die of starvation."

Roman cut him a smile as he stood. "But what a way to go, right?"

Demetri laughed and swatted his ass. "I can order in Chinese. There's this great place up the road that delivers."

"Chinese sounds amazing." Roman picked up the sketchpad. "May I?"

Demetri found his phone. He didn't know why he hadn't wanted Roman to see his drawing earlier. Maybe it had felt too vulnerable for Roman to see the way that Demetri saw him, but the drawings also spoke in a way his words never could.

"Sure, go ahead. I'll call in the order. What do you want?"

"I'll eat anything."

"A little bit of everything it is."

Demetri pulled out the menu from his menu drawer and dialed the restaurant. As hungry as he was, there wasn't a single item on the menu that didn't make his mouth water. When he finished, he hung up and glanced over at Roman, who'd confiscated the chair Demetri had abandoned.

He watched the play of emotions run across Roman's face as he flipped from page to page, turning the pad this way and that. Roman must have felt Demetri's eyes on him because he glanced up.

"What do you think?" Demetri asked.

"That your talents are wasted teaching at the college. These should be hanging in a gallery somewhere or auctioned off to the highest bidder."

"They're quick sketches. A moment in time. Nothing more."

Roman walked over, sketchpad in hand, and Demetri couldn't take his eyes off him or the way the light splashed and highlighted all the most interesting parts.

He laid the drawings on the table in front of Demetri. "I love this page the best."

On the paper was a compilation of drawings. Closeups of Roman's body. His feet. The curve of his calf. His ribcage with his arm thrown over his head. The muscularity of his ass. His soft junk.

"You wouldn't think that you could feel the emotion in such

a small study of the body, but I can see the way you look at me, almost with reverence and..."

"Love," Demetri filled in for him.

"Is that what that is?"

Demetri put a hand around Roman's neck and pulled him in for a kiss. He wanted more. To take it deeper.

Their food would be there soon, and he still didn't have any clothes on. And another shower was probably in order. "Why do I get the impression that makes you uncomfortable?"

A DECLARATION OF LOVE SHOULDN'T FREAK SOMEONE OUT, BUT Roman would be lying if he said he wasn't low-key freaking.

"I don't know," Roman said.

"Is it unwelcome?" Demetri's smile slipped, and Roman hated to see the wattage of his smile dimmed.

"No. It's not that. It feels..." Roman sifted through adjectives in his mind until he found the closest one that fit. "...undeserving."

Demetri opened his mouth to say something, but his phone chimed. He held up a finger and checked it. "That's the restaurant. The food is out for delivery. Hold that thought. I need to pop into the shower and throw on some shorts. Then I want to unpack that. Yeah?"

"Yeah. No. Shower. And forget it, I—" Roman cut himself off. He couldn't even get a thought straight in his head, so he had little way of effectively communicating what he was trying to say. "Forget it."

Demetri kissed him on the cheek as he hurried on his way to the shower. "I'm not forgetting it."

Roman threw on his shorts, and not long after, Demetri emerged from the shower dressed in a pair of navy athletic shorts that hugged his ass and almost made Roman strip him bare again. But the doorbell rang, and Roman's stomach grumbled again. He needed food if he wanted to have the energy to do all the things to Demetri that he still wanted to do.

You know you don't have *to do everything today, right? It's not like you're never going to see him again.*

As much as his head agreed, the feeling that they were on borrowed time sat heavy in his gut and refused to leave.

They sat down to eat, too hungry to talk. The quiet gave Roman time to get his mind straight. He knew what his father had done had left him with scars and insecurities. He'd have to learn to deal with them if he had any hopes of making his relationship with Demetri work.

Roman ate until his stomach hurt, and he couldn't eat another bite. Demetri pushed his plate away around the same time. They probably hadn't eaten half of what Demetri had ordered, but at least they had plenty of leftovers for later.

Demetri went to the fridge. "Want another beer?"

"Are we still going to talk, or are you going to let it drop?"

"I'm not letting it drop."

"Then, yeah, I'll need another beer."

Demetri chuckled. "Understood."

He popped the tops on the beer and handed one to Roman as he reclaimed his seat across from him. Roman couldn't keep his eyes off the play of Demetri's throat as he swallowed or the short-cropped hair on his chest. Maybe he should make Demetri put a shirt on before they started.

"You gotta stop looking at me like that," Demetri said as he set his beer down. "I don't have that kind of willpower."

"Hang on a minute." Roman disappeared into Demetri's bedroom, the faint smell of musk and sex still hung in the air, and it took everything in him not to strip and walk out of the room naked. But while the sex had been mind-blowing, he knew there was more to relationships than that.

He returned to the kitchen and tossed Demetri a shirt. "Put that on."

Demetri slipped the shirt over his head, then took Roman's hand and led him to the couch, taking the corner seat and settling Roman against his side. Demetri's put his arm around Roman's shoulders, drawing him even closer.

"I know this issue is on me," Roman said, "I just need to get over my shit and—"

"You can't help the way you feel. And if you don't want me to say I love you, I can stop. For now. Or keep saying it until you believe it. What your father did, what *I* did, was shitty. And I'm sorry. But I didn't set out to hurt you. In a warped way, it was because I cared so much that I couldn't bring myself to be honest. Fucked up. I know. That's on me. It's not because you are undeserving of the truth or love. You get me?"

Roman nodded. Demetri's words weren't new. He'd said them before, but in the repeating, they hit home in a way they hadn't hit before. Maybe there was something to the repetition that made Demetri's words more believable.

Roman blew out a shaky breath, his voice cracking. "Don't stop."

"What don't you want me to stop, Roman?"

Roman shook his head, a soft chuff of a laugh escaping. "You're going to make me say it aren't you?"

"Yeah. I am."

Roman shifted so he could see Demetri's face. "Don't stop telling me you love me. I think it's something I need to hear."

"Then I won't stop."

Roman leaned in and kissed him, and because he couldn't say those words back to Demetri, he poured his heart into the tenderest of kisses, hoping Demetri could feel the love blooming in his heart.

At least that's what he thought that weird fluttery feeling in his chest was. He'd never been in love before. Never felt for another man what he felt for Demetri. But did that automatically make it love?

When he finally broke the kiss, he said, "Thank you for loving me the way you do. I wish I could—" *It's three fucking words. What is wrong with you? Why can't you say them?* "I wish—"

Demetri squeezed his hand. "Take your time. I'm not leaving. And I'm not falling out of love with you. One of these days, you'll realize that's true."

Roman's phone buzzed in his pocket, but he ignored it and laid himself out on the couch, his head in Demetri's lap. Demetri's hand went to Roman's side and traced lazy circles on Roman's ribs. When the reminder buzz went off, he remembered he had an important document he'd been waiting on. He pulled his phone out of his pocket.

Roman rolled onto his back and read the email from Student Health on campus. His STI screening results were in.

"What is it?" Demetri asked.

Roman held up his phone. It took Demetri a second before he realized what he was looking at. "You're negative across the board. That's good news."

"Do you know what this means?"

"That you don't have any STIs?" By the tone of Demetri's voice, it was clear he thought he was missing a vital detail.

"It means I can get on PrEP. I know you're untransmittable and studies show that—"

"That couples in serodiscordant relationships can have sex without condoms without any issues as long as the positive partner's viral loads remain undetectable. I've read all the studies."

"I've always used condoms before. But I don't want to use condoms with you. But even knowing what I know and what the studies show, I'd rather be on PrEP before we do."

"Babe, I'll take you any way I can have you. With condoms, without condoms. With PrEP or without. I want you safe, and any steps we can take to make sure what happened to me never happens to you, I'm all for it."

They lapsed into silence for a while. He hadn't expected Demetri's reaction to be anything other than positive, but it was still good to hear it.

"Wait," Demetri said.

"What?"

"If you got the results today, that means you got tested yesterday. Before you came over and we got back together."

Roman grinned. "You should have seen the line. I've never seen it so crazy at the student health clinic, but I waited. And I may have been overly optimistic about how our talk would go, but the reality was, I wanted you back, and you saying no hadn't been an option."

DEMETRI SHUT DOWN THE COMPUTER AT FIVE O'CLOCK ON Friday afternoon. His official office hours had ended, and he had plans with Roman as soon as Roman finished his test.

A knock came at Demetri's door. It was closed, so he considered not answering and pretending he'd already left, but he didn't want to leave a student hanging if they needed something before the weekend hit.

He came around his desk and opened the door. "Oh, hey, Dean Pittman." Demetri held open the door and stepped back. "What can I do for you?"

Pittman motioned to the chair behind the desk. "Why don't you have a seat?"

Fuckity-fuck-fuck.

Having the dean of the department come knocking on your office on a Friday afternoon with an enigmatic expression on their face didn't bode well. Or maybe it did. Pittman had never been an easy man to read.

Demetri reclaimed his seat, an open, inquisitive smile stitched into place. He waited while Pittman took the chair opposite him while stinging hornets performed Cirque du Soleil quality backflips in his belly. Is this how Chadwick had felt before Pittman had run his ass off campus for having an affair?

Was Demetri in trouble? Technically, Roman wasn't his student anymore, but...

"I saw the video."

Demetri nodded. There could only be one video important to their conversation. "If I could explain—"

"It's self-explanatory, don't you think?" Pittman raised one of his bushy brows.

"I suppose."

"First, I want to apologize," Pittman said, "that you didn't feel you could trust that the department would have your back concerning your diagnosis. As dean, I want to address any issues that make my professors uneasy."

Demetri blinked dumbly. He heard Pittman's words, but they were not words he'd ever expected to hear coming out of the man's mouth. He was still positive the dean didn't like him.

"My status is personal. It's not something I tell everyone."

Pittman gave him a look. "It's not so private now."

Demetri laughed, and those hornets settled into an agitated buzz in his belly. Maybe he wasn't getting fired after all. "No, sir. I guess it isn't."

"I spoke with President Arcevedo. Your video has given the

college good press, and by what the director of Student Health has told him, the numbers of students, gay and straight, getting STI screening is way up. That's a good thing you did, even if you were drunk videoing."

"I'm glad some good came of it. And I appreciate your support."

Pittman stood to leave. Was that it? Demetri stood as well, walking him to the door on wobbly knees. At the door, Pittman turned back and said. "I heard a rumor that the man you were talking about in the video is a student?"

Demetri had to fight the audible gulp. "Not since add/drop and—"

He was about to go into how they weren't exactly seeing each other back then, or were actively trying not to, but he didn't quite know how to word it without getting himself into any more trouble. Pittman raised his hand to stop him from speaking.

"That's a very distorted fine line. Nothing like this better happen again."

"No worries, sir. It won't. I'm with the only man I want."

21

DEMETRI AND ROMAN DROVE TO THE COMMUNITY LOT TOGETHER. Roman hadn't been to his apartment except to get changes of clothes since he'd arrived on Demetri's doorstep late that Monday evening a few weeks before.

He hadn't moved in. But he hadn't *not* moved in either.

And as much as Demetri wanted Roman to live with him, things were going well the way they were, and he didn't want to do anything that might upset that. And while Roman still hadn't uttered those three little words, his smiles got all shy, and he snuggled in deeper whenever Demetri told Roman he loved him.

Progress. He'd take it.

"It's looking good," Roman said as they walked up to the lot, their fingers linked together.

Demetri kissed him on the cheek. Glad that he didn't have to worry anymore who saw him with Roman. "We do good work."

They were a couple of weeks behind on completing the lot due to an issue with the concrete company pouring the last pad, and then there had been some rain—in southern California. Go figure—that hadn't helped with the schedule either.

If they pushed hard over the next two days, they might be able to get it all finished.

The painted walls were nearly done. They needed touch-ups and a clear coat on all of it. The planters needed paint. And the remainder of the game patterns placed on the concrete pads. Then all they needed was a thorough general cleanup, and they'd be finished.

Tavi, Remy, and Grant were already there when they arrived. Grant came over and shook their hands, and Tavi and Remy waved from the far corner where it looked like they were laying out stencils to paint on the concrete to paint.

"You boys look happy," Grant said.

As much as Demetri liked Grant, he didn't want to get into the details of his relationship with Roman. Too much of their relationship was already public fodder. "We worked out a lot of the kinks."

Grant grinned. "Is that so? Sebastian and I usually like it when we can work the kinks *in*. But hey, I'm not judging."

Roman laughed. Demetri did *not* need to know about his cousin Sebastian's sex life. But he loved that Grant didn't give two fucks what anyone thought. For a guy so recently out of the closet, that was refreshing.

"You boys ready to get to work?"

Roman glanced around. "Is it just us today?"

"Afraid so. Niko wrangled Sebastian into helping with some big project at the studio, and we figured we're at the point where the younger kids would be more in the way than a help."

Demetri groaned. It was going to be a long day. "Let's get to it then."

A construction crew worked next door at the church. Apparently, after the fire, they decided to do some much-needed remodeling, so the normal Saturday activities were non-existent. As Demetri rolled the protective clear coat onto the wall near the churchyard, he missed the shouts and shrieks and laughter of the kids that normally played on the church playground beyond where he stood.

He caught movement in his peripheral vision and set his roller down. The pastor approached, not in his usual church clothes, but in ratty shorts and a T-shirt.

"You need help?" Demetri asked. They hadn't heard much from the man since he and Roman had helped him move stuff out of his flooded basement. Demetri called that a win.

"What? No. I..." The pastor glanced around, then met Demetri's eyes. "I came to see if I could help you."

Demetri sputtered. He wasn't proud of that, but that had been the absolute last thing he expected the pastor to say. "Excuse me?"

Demetri felt a familiar hand on his shoulder. "Is there a problem here?"

Roman's protective streak was something else about Roman that Demetri had come to appreciate and love. He was always the first person to stick up for someone if he perceived a threat.

"No. The pastor here was offering to help."

"Call me, Tom." He held out his hand, and Demetri and Roman shook it in turn.

Roman didn't question Tom's motivation. He clapped him on the back and said, "Come with me. I've got the perfect project for you."

At the end of the long day, Demetri put a lid on the last of the cans of clear coat and walked across the lot to where everyone else looked like they were finishing up, too.

"Hey, babe." Though they were both hot and sweaty, Demetri threw his arm around Roman's shoulders and kissed him on the cheek then addressed the rest of them. "You guys about done?"

"Just about." Grant stuck out his hand. "Thanks, Tom. We

appreciate the help. Especially when we were so shorthanded today. And if I ever need someone to paint planters for me, I know who to ask."

Tavi and Remy walked up holding hands but dropped them when Grant shifted, and they saw Tom. Tavi hitched his thumb over his shoulder toward the truck. "Yeah, so...We're going to wait over there."

"Hold on a minute, son," Tom said. He had a presence to his voice, probably from all those sermons he gave.

Tavi stopped, but Grant and Roman both stiffened, ready to jump in if Tavi needed protection.

Grant folded his arms over his chest. "What is it?"

"I owe you all an apology. I'm not saying I agree with your lifestyle. I'm not saying I'll ever understand. But you've all done good work here for the kids, and our city. I can respect and appreciate that."

"We're trying to help the community the best way we can," Grant said. "Just like you."

Tom glanced at the bright reds, blues, and yellows painted on the fence. "You might do it with a little more color than I do," Tom said as he looked around the lot. "But yes, I get that now."

They shook hands all around. Even Tavi and Remy. It wasn't like Tom had given them his blessing—not that they needed it—but seeing him move on his position, for him to see their humanity, it meant something.

After saying their goodbyes, Demetri and Roman walked back to his car and pulled out into the Saturday traffic.

At a stoplight, Demetri turned right instead of left.

"Where are we going?"

"Sneaky Pete's. I think we need to celebrate the near completion of the lot."

"I'm kind of sweaty and stinky."

Demetri gave him the side-eye but served it with a smile. "You wanting to pick someone up?"

"Nope." Roman linked fingers with Demetri over the center console. It was a simple gesture, but damn if it still didn't send a shock of awareness through his body. Maybe home was a better option.

The tinted door for Sneaky Pete's came into view, and before Demetri could pull into the parking lot behind it, Roman said, "Or we could go home, skinny dip in the pool. We have plenty of beer in the fridge."

Home. He loved the sound of that word falling from Roman's lips. Demetri pulled a U-ey in the middle of the street, his tires barking as he accelerated toward home.

Roman laughed. "That's what I thought."

"You should know by now that I'll never pass up an opportunity to get you naked."

ROMAN CANNONBALLED INTO THE POOL. BENEATH THE WATER, HE heard Demetri's shout as the wall of water he sent up engulfed Demetri on the side of the pool.

He came up for air to find Demetri's powerful strokes, propelling him through the water, aiming for Roman. By the look on Demetri's face when he came up for air, Roman was dead meat.

But in the best way.

Demetri dunked him, and they wrestled underwater until their lungs burned. Roman spit out water, panting as he caught his breath. He groaned as he wiped the water off his face. "This water feels so damn good."

Demetri pulled him close, wrapping his legs around

Roman's waist and his arms around his neck. "I know something else that will feel good about now."

"You're incorrigible."

Demetri grinned and whispered in his ear. "Is that a complaint?"

Roman palmed Demetri's ass and rubbed him up against him. "What do you think?"

Leaning back so he could see Roman's face, Demetri said, "I think you're sexy as hell. Your eyes are bewitching, and I'm never going to get enough of you. If Ming doesn't hurry with our takeout delivery, he's going to get an eyeful."

"I'm good with that."

Headlights flashed through Demetri's windows. "Food's here."

They probably ordered from the Chinese restaurant up the street a couple of times a week and had become friends with the delivery driver. They'd even gotten to the point where they left the key under the front doormat, and Ming let himself in.

They waved as Ming opened the sliding glass door, a bag full of food in his right hand. He set the food in a dry spot by the edge of the pool and squatted down. "You boys want company?"

"Any time you and your boyfriend want to come over and swim, you're welcome."

"Maybe once the semester is over, we'll take you up on it. He's either working or has his nose in a textbook."

"Thanks for the special delivery," Roman said. "I'm sure the neighbors appreciate us not getting out of the pool naked to answer the door."

Ming smiled. "If you two were my neighbors, I'd be fine with it." He stood to leave. "You two have a nice night."

"You, too," they said in unison.

Demetri reached for his phone and quickly added his usual overly generous tip. Then they laid the cartons of food on the pool deck, grabbed a beer out of the little cooler Demetri had packed, and dug into the food.

All conversation stopped except for the occasional 'can you pass the soy sauce' while they filled their bellies.

Roman thought back to earlier in the day with the pastor. When Roman started getting full, he dropped his chopsticks and washed his food down with his beer. "What did you make of Tom? I never expected him to come around."

Demetri huffed out a rueful laugh. "Tell me about it. I don't think Tom will ever wave a rainbow flag in the pride parade, but maybe there'll be a little less fire and brimstone and hate in his sermons and a little more acceptance and love."

Roman closed the small gap between them, bracing his hands on the pool deck on either side Demetri. He leaned in for a kiss, tasting the hops and the Kung Pao chicken on Demetri's tongue. "I love your optimism."

"Oh yeah?" Demetri wrapped his arms around Roman's waist and pulled him in tighter, his dick already getting hard and pressing against Roman's hip. He nibbled on Roman's ear and ground against him. "What else do you love about me?"

Roman knew Demetri expected something crude to come out of his mouth. This wasn't the first time Demetri had asked that question in a similar manner, and it usually ended up with someone getting fucked and them both getting off.

But after all the time they'd spent together, practically living under the same roof, Roman had a different answer this time. "I love your generosity, I love the way you'll drop whatever you're doing to help one of your students, I love your talent, and the way you always remember to buy beer and condoms but can never remember to buy groceries."

Demetri grinned. "Priorities."

Demetri went to kiss him, but Roman knew that if he didn't finish his thought, it might be another month before he got the courage up to tell Demetri what was in his heart. He placed a staying finger on Demetri's lips. Demetri nipped the tip and licked away the sting with his tongue.

If Demetri kept that up, Roman would never get the words out.

"Most of all, I love how you love me."

Demetri blew out a puff of breath as if he'd taken a soft blow to the heart. Were those tears glistening in his eyes?

"There isn't a day that goes by that I question how you feel about me because you show me in all the little and big ways."

"What—"

One shake of his head shut Demetri up. "What I'm trying to say, *professor*, is that I love you."

"You're—" Demetri cleared his throat when it cracked. "You're going to have to say that again. You know, to make sure I heard you right."

Roman took Demetri's face in his hands. "I love you. Thank you for giving me the compassion, understanding, the *space* I needed to figure this out for myself."

"You're a smart man," Demetri said. "I knew it was only a matter of time before you realized what I already knew."

"And what did you already know?"

"That I'm yours. And you're mine."

Roman lifted Demetri, wrapped his legs around his waist, and squeezed Demetri's ass. "Then I guess that makes this mine as well."

"Definitely."

"Hold on." Demetri held on tight as Roman carried him up the pool steps and opened the sliding glass door. "Cut the lights."

Demetri reached in and cut the lights in the den. The blinds were open, but at least they'd be harder to see. Not that Roman cared. Water drained off them, dripping at his feet as he hurried, careful not to slip on the tile and bust his ass.

He dropped Demetri on his back in the middle of the bed, the sheets and bed soaking up the water. They'd have to sleep in the guest room until the mattress dried out, but Roman was good with that.

Demetri rolled to his stomach and shook his delectable ass. Roman palmed it, crawling on the bed between Demetri's legs and biting one of his ass cheeks. "God, I love your ass."

Demetri glanced at him over his shoulder with that mischievous, sexy smile on his face. "Shut up and fuck me."

22

Demetri came out of the bedroom dressed in his tux. "Aren't you going to take a shower? We've got to leave in about twenty-five minutes."

Roman glanced up from his laptop. "I was—"

"Trying to decide between the jobs?" He handed Roman his cuff links, and Roman put them on for him.

Roman scrubbed a hand over his head. Demetri could feel the stress rolling off him. In the month since his December graduation, Roman had had two job offers, and he hadn't accepted one yet.

"Can't this wait? Don't you have another week to decide?"

Roman stood and started stripping off his clothes on his way down the hall to the shower. Demetri followed not only to continue the conversation but also because even after months of being together, he rarely missed an opportunity to see Roman naked.

"I do. With the holidays, it was generous of them to give me that much time to accept the offer."

"Well, it's a big step. Moving to New York. Working for one of the biggest LGBTQ non-profits in the nation. It's a lot to consider. Plus, for a non-profit, the money's very enticing."

"No kidding." Naked, Roman stepped into the shower, his voice muffled under the spray of the water behind the glass door. "I'd be lying if I said that wasn't an incentive."

"As it should be."

Roman sudsed up, and Demetri enjoyed the play of water and bubbles running down Roman's back and down the crack of his ass. Demetri was already getting hard, and as expensive as his tux had been, it didn't exactly provide a lot of room in the crotch area for that sort of thing.

The shower door steamed up, and Roman turned, rubbing a circle clear. "But Grant's job offer wasn't bad. And you know, my friends are here. *You're* here."

Roman rinsed and cut the water off. Demetri handed him his towel and leaned against the counter. "We've been through this. The job in New York is an amazing opportunity. If you want it, take it. I'll come as soon as I can find a position up there. It may take a semester or two, but—"

Roman leaned in and kissed him on the lips. "But I don't want to be away from you."

"It won't be for long. There are these cool things called airplanes, and I can visit over spring break, and we can do naughty things over Zoom."

Roman pulled on the pants to his rented tux. "It's not the same as the real thing."

Demetri hadn't ever said this out loud before, because he didn't want to influence Roman's decision, but he couldn't hold it in any longer. He dropped his voice and said, "Stay then."

Roman buttoned up his shirt, and Demetri fixed his cuffs for him. "But, fuck, it's such a great opportunity."

Demetri smiled. It mostly wasn't forced. No matter what

Roman chose, they would figure it out, and it would be okay. "Then go."

"But your tenure."

Demetri cupped the back of Roman's neck and gave it a squeeze. "Tenure isn't everything. Don't forget that."

Roman nodded. "Yeah. Okay."

Demetri patted his shoulder. "Put it to the back of your mind, babe, and let's enjoy tonight."

"You're right. I'm being an asshole. Today is supposed to be all about you and your show. I can't wait for the world to see how talented you are." Roman glanced at his watch and slipped into his shoes. "We need to be going."

You would think for an art professor, Demetri wouldn't be so nervous about his art show at Premier. But he hadn't been able to eat all day or knock that sick feeling in the pit of his stomach.

Or his nausea had more to do with what was going to happen after the show. He shook his head, not able to think about it without almost throwing up.

They both grabbed the hangers with their tux coats and headed for the car. Roman buckled in beside him, but his door still hung open. Demetri started the car. "We ready?"

Roman unbuckled. "Hang on. I need to do one last thing. It will only take a minute."

Demetri tramped down on the bubble of irritation. "Can't it wait?"

"No."

Demetri's fingers tap-tap-tapped on the steering wheel while he waited. True to his word, Roman wasn't gone more than a minute. He re-buckled and leaned over and kissed Demetri on the cheek. "Let's go. I want everyone to know how amazing my boyfriend is."

By the time they made it to Premier, the crowd inside had grown thick. Demetri knew most of his friends and family had come, but with all the people there, he didn't see anyone he knew right away.

"Whoa," Roman said as they came through the entrance. He hadn't seen the work hanging before. It had taken Demetri's breath away to see all his artwork displayed on the crisp, white walls. Roman's hand squeezed his, and he leaned in and whispered. "I'm so fucking proud of you."

"This doesn't bother you? Having all the pieces be you?"

The exhibit was appropriately named *Roman*. After Demetri declined Premier's job offer, Roman convinced him to accept their offer to showcase his work. He'd toiled for weeks and weeks, every spare moment preparing. With the theme of Roman, he'd taken it a step further and more literal. Every drawing and painting and sketch were of erotic poses of Roman set back in the time of Caesar. Roman as the peasant, the gladiator, the statesman, the ruler.

"No. I'm flattered. And seeing all of them together, it's breathtaking."

"There you are." Niko and Vin squeezed through the crowd, and they all shook hands. "The man of the hour."

The door opened behind them, and Joss walked in, tugging on the collar of his suit. Demetri stuck out his hand. "Glad you could make it."

"Yeah. Sure."

Niko sipped on his champagne and pointedly glanced behind Joss. "Where's your plus one?"

Vin elbowed Niko in the ribs. "Stop it."

"I was just—"

"It's fine. He couldn't make it. Probably for the best. If you'll excuse me, I think I'll go find the bar."

Vin turned around and watched his ex disappear into the multitude of people. Then to Niko said, "He's had a hard enough time getting back into dating, he doesn't need—"

Niko raised his hand. "You're right. That was out of line."

Vin turned his attention to Demetri. "Niko said you were good, but wow. I don't have any words." Then he pointed over his shoulder at all the people who had shoehorned themselves into the gallery. They had to be violating a couple of fire codes. "But no one can stop talking about them."

A portion of Demetri's apprehension lifted. "I'm glad you like it."

"Go on," Roman said. "Mingle. Everyone will want to talk your ear off."

Demetri kissed him. "Okay. I'll find you in a bit."

"Don't worry about me."

Two hours later and not only had Demetri not seen Roman, but he'd been so busy talking to the patrons that he hadn't even had a drink. But the show would be over soon, and he was going to get that drink.

The crowd thinned, and Tavi walked over, a soda in his hand. "You hanging in there?"

Demetri laughed at his words Tavi had thrown back at him. It looked like they'd come full circle. "I think."

Tavi smiled, recognizing his reply.

Demetri narrowed his eyes at Tavi. "Aren't you a little young to be coming to an opening like this?"

Holding up his cell phone, Tavi said, "We all have porn production studios in our pockets. This is nothing I haven't seen before. Besides, this is art."

"Where are your dads?"

Tavi glanced around. "They're here somewhere. I know they wanted to talk to you, but Sebastian said he refused to stand in a hella long line to talk to his cousin."

Demetri laughed. "I don't blame him."

Demetri glanced around at all of his work, catching the red color of the 'sold' stickers on quite a few of them, pleased with the warm reception. But then again, with Roman as the subject matter, he couldn't go wrong.

With the line of people wanting to speak to him finally gone, he returned his attention to Tavi. "If you'll excuse me, I think there's a drink somewhere with my name on it."

"I saw Roman over by the bar not too long ago."

It took him twenty minutes to walk the fifty feet to the bar, shaking hands and making small talk along the way. He'd seen friends and family from a distance, but they'd kept their distance so other people interested in his art could meet him.

His feet hurt and his legs felt more tired than the days he'd spent standing in front of his classes lecturing all day, and all he wanted to do was get on with his plans for the evening.

Through the people, he saw Roman leaning against the bar, talking to the bartender as the man started cleaning the station in preparation for closing for the night. The man bobbed his chin toward Demetri, and Roman glanced over his shoulder.

The smile that spread on Roman's face made Demetri forget about the pulse in his feet and the knees that refused to lock anymore.

"Hey stranger," Roman leaned in and kissed him on the lips. "Can I buy you a drink?"

"Please."

Roman introduced the bartender, one of the guys he'd worked with when Roman was still working for the catering company before school had started. Drake, he thought Roman had said, though Demetri had heard so many names that night he couldn't be certain.

"What'll you have?" Drake asked.

"Actually," Roman said, "do you mind if I make it?"

Drake backed away. "Fine with me. I've got glasses in the back I need to load."

Roman stepped behind the bar. "Well, handsome. What will it be?"

Demetri leaned against the bar. "Why don't you surprise me."

The sexy grin that spread across Roman's face stopped Demetri's heart. Fuck, he was a lucky man. Forget waiting for the spring semester to end, or even until he found another job. If Roman took the New York offer, they were moving… together.

Roman handed over the drink, and Demetri couldn't help his grin. "What do you call this?"

"The Spice of Life."

Demetri took a sip. It was as good as he remembered. Maybe better.

Roman leaned against the bar, sneaking a glance behind him where Drake had disappeared and lowered his voice. "You know, I'm off in a few minutes."

All of Demetri's blood ran south, and he got lightheaded. Or maybe that was from the alcohol on an empty stomach. "What did you have in mind?"

Roman flicked a glance at the back hallway. "What do you say?"

"Oh, hell, yeah."

Drake returned, and Demetri took a long sip of his drink and left it on the bar, holding out his hand for Roman to take. They skirted the edges of the thinning crowd, trying not to draw attention to themselves.

By the time they made it to the back hall, Roman was practically dragging Demetri behind him in a rush to get to the exit. He slammed into the exit door's push bar, pulled Demetri through, and closed the door behind him, not even bothering to make sure they had a way back in.

Roman shoved Demetri against the brick wall, straddling one of his legs. He nipped and sucked on the tender flesh of

Demetri's neck and whispered in his ear. "I've wanted to get you out here ever since we arrived."

In the months since they'd been in the alley, not much had changed, except it was January, so it wasn't as hot. But it was southern California, so it wasn't cold either. Roman palmed him through his tux pants and started going down on his knees.

Demetri stopped him. That's not how he wanted this to play out. "That's a rented tux. You can't scuff up the knees."

"Well, fuck."

Demetri reversed their positions, his hand fumbling with the fastener on Roman's pants. Roman covered his hand. "It was my turn to go down on you."

"You forget. I don't keep score. And sucking you off isn't a chore."

Roman chuckled, and it eased the last of the tension in Demetri's belly. He didn't know what would happen next, but there was only one way to find out.

"Make sure no one is coming," Demetri said as he unzipped Roman's pants and went down on one knee.

Roman looked left and right, scanning both ends of the alley. "Looks like the coast is clear."

In his chest, Demetri's heart hammered, a frenetic, almost frantic beat. When Roman glanced down, Demetri held up the velvet box with the platinum band in it.

"What the fuck?"

Demetri chuckled. "I'd planned on doing this later tonight. Not here. But then as you dragged me out, I couldn't think of a better place for a new beginning than where it all started. I love you, babe. Take the New York job and take me with you. I'll resign and—"

Roman shook his head. Even in the dim light, Demetri could see the shine in his eyes. "I can't do that, professor." Roman pulled Demetri to his feet, planting a sweet kiss on his lips as he wrapped his arms around Demetri's neck and pulled him into his chest.

This was it. Roman was saying no.

His legs almost gave out. Luckily Roman held on tight and kept him on his feet. "Why not?"

Roman loosened his grip and held Demetri's face in his hands. "Because I already accepted the job with Grant. I'm now officially an employee of The Corey Center. Or at least I will be once Grant gets home and checks his email."

Demetri narrowed his eyes. "You did that when you went back into the house when we were still in the driveway."

Roman nodded. "I love you. I love our life here. I don't want to change any of that. If that ring is a marriage proposal, I'm saying yes. But we're staying here. Where we belong."

Demetri's breath caught, and his hands shook as he pulled the band out of the box and slipped it over Roman's finger. Then Roman's eyes heated, and he flipped Demetri around, the edges of the brick poking into Demetri's the back.

Roman unfastened Demetri's pants, and Demetri didn't have the will to stop him. Roman pulled Demetri's hard cock free and started going down on his knees.

"Your pants," Demetri said, not that he cared too much, not when Roman's strong hand wrapped around him, his thumb grazing over the sensitive head.

Roman chuckled as he got down on his knees. "Don't worry, professor, I can afford to replace the tux now."

Dear Reader,

Life in the valley is never dull. There's more excitement headed that way.

Do you know how those big guys fall?

Hard and fast.

And when Milo Malone comes knocking on his door, Joss Kincaid is not exception. Milo is the man Joss never knew he needed. But is Joss's broken heart ready for love?

Keep an eye out for Flight of Fancy, the next book in the Valley Boys series out in early fall, 2020.

While you wait, you can catch up on where this world began with One Shot. The first book in the Black Stallion Studios series.

Your next adventure starts here: One Shot

ROMANTIC SUSPENSE

Lazy S Ranch Series
Cowgirl, Unexpectedly (Book 1)
Must Love Horses (Book 2)

Hot on the Trail (Book 3)
Cowboy, Undercover (Book 4)
Cowboy, Unbridled (Book 5)
Cowgirl, Unbroken (Book 6)

Wright's Island Series
Don't Look Back (Book 1)
In Her Defense (Book 2)

Steele-Wolfe Securities
Wyoming Confidential (Book 1)

CONTEMPORARY ROMANCE

Rockin' Rodeo Series
Luck of the Draw (Book 1)
Photo Chute (Book 2)
Reined In (Book 3)
Rockin' Rodeo Series Collection (Books 1-3)

MM ROMANCE

Black Stallion Studios Series
One Shot (Book 1)
Key Grip (Book 2)
Best Boy (Book 3)
Black Stallion Studios Box Set (Books 1-3)

Valley Boys
Art of Love (Book 1)
Flight of Fancy (Book 2 Coming Soon)

ABOUT THE AUTHOR

Vicki Tharp makes her home on small acreage in south Texas with her husband and an embarrassing number of pets. When she isn't writing, you can usually find her on the back of her horse—avoiding anything that remotely resembles housework—smelling like fly spray and horse sweat.

Join my newsletter at: http://bit.ly/V-W-T
Join my street team and receive free Advance Reader Copies of my upcoming books at: http://bit.ly/S-W-S-T
You can find my website at: www.VickiTharp.com
I love to hear from readers. You can email me at vwtharp@VickiTharp.com

Or you can stalk me at:

facebook.com/VickiTharpAuthor
instagram.com/author_Vicki_Tharp
bookbub.com/authors/vicki-tharp
amazon.com/author/vicki_tharp
twitter.com/vwtharp

www.ingramcontent.com/pod-product-compliance
Lightning Source LLC
Chambersburg PA
CBHW032123180726

48284CB00002B/671